ROSEMARY FOR
REMEMBRANCE

A "THYME WILL TELL" MYSTERY

ROSEMARY FOR REMEMBRANCE

AUDREY STALLSMITH

WaterBrook
PRESS
Colorado Springs

ROSEMARY FOR REMEMBRANCE
PUBLISHED BY WATERBROOK PRESS
5446 North Academy Boulevard, Suite 200
Colorado Springs, Colorado 80918
A division of Bantam Doubleday Dell Publishing Group, Inc.

ISBN 1-57856-040-3

Printed in the United States of America

March 1998—First Edition

1 3 5 7 9 10 8 6 4 2

In remembrance of my aunts
Elsie and Marie,
who encouraged my love of plots,
both garden variety and novel.

THE CULVER FAMILY TREE

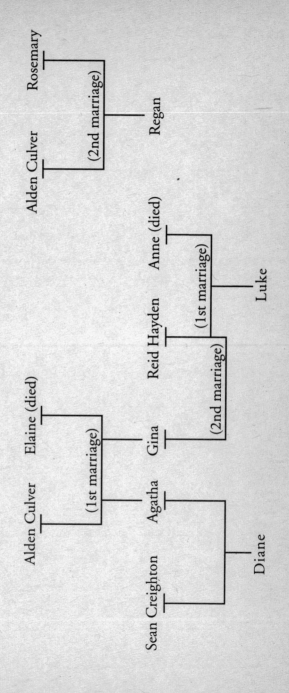

CHAPTER 1

■ ■ ■

There's rosemary, that's for remembrance.

From her seat in the arbor, Regan could look over the downward slope of lawn to the wrought-iron fence. She could see the tree-lined street beyond that fence and the car of the man who was coming to arrest her.

The police cruiser did not appear threatening with the dappled sun and green shade of a June morning washing over the windshield. It glided along the street with dreamlike slowness and silence, like a replay on TV when the sound was cut and the action floated in leisurely but relentless fashion. The car swung into the drive, and the rasp of tires on gravel broke the spell.

Matt got out, hooking his hands awkwardly in his gun belt, the typical picture of a small-town cop from the brawny build and craggy features to the slight thickening about the waist caused by too much diner food. He had tried so hard to fit that image—right down to the dark sunglasses that turned their blank stare in Regan's direction. In elementary school, Matt had been awkward in both speech and action. By high

1

school he had learned to slow down, to choose each word and movement with care. She hadn't heard Matt stutter in years.

A screen of rose and honeysuckle leaves hid her from him. He turned toward the steps leading up to the porch.

The people in the house had seen him arrive too. Regan heard their excited voices, though she was too far away to make out any words. She wondered if they would object to Matt's hauling her off to jail.

At least he had been tactful enough to put off the arrest until after the funeral. Tact must play a large part in small-town law enforcement too.

Regan's mother had waited like this in a garden once. Only her mother's predicament had been poverty and a cancer that would mean imprisonment in a nursing home until death except—except, unexpectedly, someone had come along to rescue her mother. *So that's why I'm out here,* Regan said to God. *Waiting for the miracle.*

She drew her feet up onto the arbor bench, wrapped her arms around her skirt and legs, and turned her head to look at the garden.

She knew that she should be frightened, even angry. But four days ago shock had deadened her reactions. *I want to feel, to cry, to rant, to scream, Daddy. You deserve it. It's like the first minutes after a terrible injury when the victim feels no pain at all. I'm grateful for that numbness on one hand, but . . .*

All of the greenery was lush and fresh looking. Bugs and disease would not arrive in force for another week or so. The clove-scented heads of sweet William stood straight and eyed the sun. The lavender and white Canterbury bells swayed, clapperless, in a desultory breeze. A few beads of dew lingered deep in the pleated leaves of the *alchemilla,* named for the alchemists who had once gathered those silver drops. In the linden's shade reared tall spikes of foxglove, the flowers she had worn like thimbles on all fingers as a child.

A door closed with emphasis, and footsteps clicked decisively across the flagged terrace and down the stone steps. It would be Agatha, of course.

The footsteps died abruptly. Even Agatha couldn't make much noise on a grass path.

Regan beat down a spurt of panic and speeded up her inventory. In the walled garden at the rear were the roses—all her mother's beloved old-fashioned roses. They were all the rage now, but her mother had been in the forefront of that movement when it wasn't yet a movement. The Gallicas, Damasks, rugosas, and ramblers sprawled into the paths, clambered up the stone walls, and tumbled down the outside to tangle with the hollyhocks.

Agatha came into view, stepping along as briskly as high heels on grass could manage. She did not glance at the flower beds. With their borders of thyme and chamomile creeping into the path, they were probably too untidy for her.

Regan tore her gaze away. Over to the right, beyond where the path forked around the walled garden, was the slope going down to the lily pond where all the water-loving types like meadowsweet, marshmallow, and swamp rose would bend to see their reflections in the water—

Agatha planted herself directly in front of her half sister. "Regan. *Regan!* Chief Olin is here and wants to see you." Agatha enunciated slowly and precisely, concentrating on Regan's face to make certain she was getting it.

Regan stood up and shook out her skirt. "Sasha."

The four-year-old, who had been crouched on the ground

at Regan's feet, arranging pebbles and petals in an intricate pattern, looked up. Her short, fawn hair stuck up in wary tufts above a sharp little face.

"I'm going to have to go away for a while," Regan said, her voice catching slightly.

Sasha gathered her stuffed gray rabbit in one thin arm and got up. "Can I come?"

"No, I'm sorry, honey. You can't this time. Diane will take care of you while I'm gone. Okay?"

"Not her!" The child's gaze shot to Agatha. "I won't stay with her!"

"No, no," Regan said quickly. "Not her. Her daughter, Diane. The pretty lady with the blond hair. You like Diane."

Agatha turned with a jerk to stalk back down the path. Regan followed, stopping briefly to snap off a couple of sprigs of rosemary, not looking at the spot by the wall where flourishing monkshood plants had been yanked up by the roots.

She turned to hand one of the sprigs to Sasha, who trailed a couple of paces behind. The little girl accepted the herb without comment, rubbing it first under her nose then under the rabbit's.

Agatha barely paused for them to catch up. "You must understand, Regan," she said, "that under the circumstances we cannot, we really cannot help—" She paused. Agatha at a loss for words was a novelty. "What I mean to say is that we cannot supply you with a lawyer . . . or anything. He was my father too."

"I didn't expect you to," Regan murmured as they ascended the steps to the terrace then walked across to the french doors.

"In fact, under the circumstances, it might look strange for us to allow you to remain in the house."

Since, according to the will, the house now belonged to Regan, that statement was so arrogant as to be almost amusing. Agatha caught Regan's lift of brows and reddened angrily. "Considering what has happened, I think that we have been quite forbearing."

Only Agatha could get away with a word like *forbearing*. Inside the living room, a few people were standing around in awkward attitudes. Diane stepped forward to put a hand on Sasha's shoulder. Sasha stopped and watched Regan and Agatha go on without her.

Matt Olin waited by the front door. Regan noticed that he had left it a little bit open behind him. He again jammed his left thumb under his gun belt and with his right hand plucked a small card from his shirt pocket.

"Regan," he said, "I'm going to have to arrest you." She could not see his eyes at all. Her preoccupation with details—irrelevancies—had begun four days ago too. It was, she supposed, a form of distraction. She had not tried to break through it. The agony would come soon enough. Matt was reading her her rights. She waited with hands pressed together in front of her, rolling the sprig of rosemary back and forth against her palms. The familiar piney scent was reassuring. Her mother had been named Rosemary.

When he finished, the dark glasses turned in her direction again. "Do you understand these rights?"

"Yes," she said.

He waited. She looked back at him patiently.

"Do you want a lawyer?" he said.

"No."

Agatha broke in. "Under the circumstances," she explained to Matt, "we can't, we really can't . . . I mean, considering that it was our father whom she . . ."

It is pretty bad, Regan thought with faint amusement, *when you can't even occupy center stage at your own arrest.*

Officially blank and neutral, Matt was listening to Agatha and saying, "Yes, ma'am."

Another car pulled up, and Regan looked out the open door. A woman with a camera slung around her neck viewed the police car with satisfaction. Jean Francis, owner-editor-reporter for the *Hayden Herald.* She had come from a big-city paper, and tact was not an important ingredient in her style.

Agatha had come to a stop. Matt looked significantly in Regan's direction. She meekly stepped forward. He held the door for her.

There was something close to relief in both their faces: relief that Regan was, as usual, taking her proper place, that there would be no embarrassing scenes. A spark of anger pulsed in the ashes. The piece of rosemary snapped between her fingers.

She stopped in the doorway, hands together and extended toward Matt. "Handcuffs?" she said helpfully.

"Regan!" Agatha said.

Matt jerked the cuffs from his belt and snapped them around Regan's wrists in a movement that was, for him, astonishingly fast and dexterous—but not quite fast enough. Jean sprinted to the edge of the porch just in time to get several shots of the steel bracelets being applied. The camera advanced the film automatically as the shutter clicked voraciously.

"I assume this means that you are arresting her?" Jean inquired. Matt Olin ignored the question, turning his prisoner toward the steps.

"What are you doing?" The child's cry from the hallway brought them up short. Sasha had escaped from Diane and had bolted after Regan, dodging around Agatha's outstretched hand to tear at the cuffs. "Take them off!" she insisted, half-sobbing at Matt in her rage and bewilderment. "Let her go!" Matt, face stiffening, failed to comply, and the child flailed at him with small fists and feet, screaming. He made no attempt to ward her off.

The others who had been waiting in the living room for the arrest to be over now spilled into the hall, looking appalled. Jean Francis gleefully clicked away.

Regan already regretted her brief flare of rebellion.

"Sasha!" she said, reaching with both manacled hands for the child's shoulder.

Sasha stopped and looked up, panting.

"Go with Diane now. Please, Sasha. I'll come back just as soon as I can."

The child's eyes pleaded, but Regan gently pushed her away, nodded at Diane, and turned to Matt. "I'm ready." She had not been fair to him either. The townspeople might see the necessity for arresting Alden Culver's youngest daughter, but they would not appreciate the handcuffs. The chief would get a reputation for being harsh.

When he opened the passenger door of the cruiser for her, she sat and swung her legs in without commenting that she should really be in the back, behind the grille. She extended her manacled hands away from her body to allow him to fasten the seat belt, looking beyond him and the reporter to those who had come out to watch her go. Sasha's head drooped, and Regan could not catch her eye.

"Chief Olin has no comment," Jean drawled aloud, writing briskly.

Matt slammed the passenger door and, stone-faced, veered around the reporter as she tried to intercept him. At the other side of the cruiser, he paused with the driver's door partly open to look up at the group on the porch. He moved his wide shoulders in a shrug and slid onto the seat, closing the door with more than necessary emphasis.

He did not look at Regan or otherwise acknowledge her presence as he started the car and let it roll down the circular drive to the road.

Regan had always been proud of her ability to see the other person's point of view. Matt had come from a welfare family and had spent most of his life being defensive about it. It was to his credit that he was not taking much pleasure in arresting the doctor's daughter.

In school, though, she had been scornful of Matt because he got angry, stammered, and flailed out when taunted. She had been teased too. Because she was withdrawn and acted old for her years, the other kids had thought her stuck-up. But she had known better than to react. "Don't you ever get mad at them?" a teacher had asked.

"No," Regan had replied. "If you let them make you angry, then they have control over you."

Eventually Matt had learned not to react too. And, by high school, he was bigger than most of his tormentors, so they had prudently desisted.

Glancing at his profile, Regan wondered why he had stayed in Hayden.

It had only taken them a few moments to roll through the main part of town to the borough building. For a weekday morning, a lot of people were out on the sidewalks, people who peeked at the car and away again. She saw in the side-view mirror that Jean's car was following.

No sooner had Matt parked at the curb and gone around to open the cruiser's passenger door than Jean was at his shoulder, notebook at the ready. "If the chief has no comment," she was saying as Regan climbed awkwardly out, "how about you, Miss Culver? *Did* you poison your father?"

"No." Regan's answer was faint but definite.

"But you *did* prepare that tea?"

"Yes."

As they entered the building, Matt let the door swing shut in the reporter's face. Undeterred, she surged in after them. They walked down a corridor between offices.

"And the poison was in the tea, wasn't it?"

"Apparently." Regan's tone was breathless because of the pace set by Matt.

They paused before a door marked POLICE while he used a key. "Then how do you explain . . . ," Jean began and then snapped sharply at Matt as he urged Regan through the door. "What time is the hearing?"

"Two o'clock," Matt said. He shut the reporter firmly out of the office.

Matt removed the handcuffs and took Regan's fingerprints in utter silence, then pushed a chair forward for her.

Regan sat down, clasping her hands together in her lap.

The limp piece of rosemary was lying on the desk; she had had to drop it while having her fingertips inked.

Regan's mother, Rosemary, had been a spinster into her late thirties, caring for her own invalid mother. Then, Rosemary's overworked father had suffered a heart attack, and his wife had followed him into the grave only a few months later. For the first time in her life, Rosemary was free to do what she wanted, and that was when she was diagnosed with a virulent cancer that was virtually untreatable. With little money and no close relations, she had no choice but to go into a nursing home at government expense.

But her doctor had confided in one of his colleagues. "It seems so unfair. The woman has had little enough happiness in her life. About the only outlet she's ever had is what little garden she could manage on that scrubby plot of ground, and now she'll be denied even that. But I don't know what else I can do."

The colleague had been Alden Culver, and perhaps the other physician had had a reason for confiding in him. Culver was a wealthy widower who had chosen to retire in his early fifties. And he was known for being, at times, foolishly altruistic.

Rosemary was actually sitting in her garden, a small plot that she had managed to make bloom profusely, waiting for the neighbor who was to drive her to the nursing home, when a Cadillac pulled into the drive. Regan had heard about the scene so often that she could picture it in her mind. Rosemary, thin and dark haired, was huddled on the ground in the midst of the flowers, hugging her knees up against her chest. The sun beat down on her head, but she felt cold. When tires crunched on the gravel, she fully expected it to be the neighbor—and the end of everything. When she saw the Cadillac and the man with rumpled graying hair and a youthful walk striding across to her, she thought that it would only be somebody wanting directions.

Then he said, "You don't know me. My name is Culver, Dr. Alden Culver. And I have a proposition to put to you."

It proved to be a startling proposal. The doctor had retired early to pursue an interest in holistic medicine. He hoped eventually to write a book on alternative treatments for cancer. But he needed, he explained frankly, a guinea pig. Since her case was not treatable by the usual methods, she really had nothing to lose by letting him experiment on her. She had a lot to gain. His big house at the edge of a small town was much preferable to a nursing home. His children were grown, so there was plenty of room. There was also extensive acreage, and she could garden to her heart's content.

It would be a strictly platonic relationship, of course, and she would not be expected to do any cooking or cleaning. He had a housekeeper for that.

Rosemary's acceptance was immediate. One did not, after all, turn down a miracle. She duly made the move to the doctor's home and paid for her keep by bravely downing everything from the Essiac anticancer formula to red clover tea.

His enthusiasm for the project was contagious. Rosemary got interested, came up with some suggestions of her own, and firmly vetoed a few of his.

The doctor was delighted at this mutiny. He had read some of the newer research that linked some cancers to a certain personality type, the type that inevitably submits to the will of others instead of asserting its own individuality.

He had most of the east lawn dug up to make her a garden and a conservatory built on the back of the house. Since she insisted on growing most of her own plants from seed because it was cheaper that way, they spent a happy few months from February to May poring over catalogs, mixing up huge batches of planting medium, and exclaiming happily over their own success as seedlings emerged. Whether it was her new confidence, her belief in the herbs, the herbs themselves, or faith of another kind, nobody was ever quite sure, but by the time her new garden was blooming a year after the doctor had made his strange proposal, the cancer had gone into remission. By October, there was no trace of it in her body.

Rosemary had described to Regan the scene that followed their return from the hospital after viewing the X rays. "I was so happy at first, but then I realized that he had never planned on my being there for always. It was only supposed to be a couple of years. When I tried to say all that, he got more upset than I've ever seen him and blurted, 'Rosemary, this has been the happiest year of my life. You must know by now how I feel about you.'

"Then he got kind of white and went on, 'But I realize that you might want a life of your own now—with somebody younger.'"

Here she had paused with a reminiscent little smile curving her lips, and Regan, leaning forward, had urged. "And then—"

"And then," Rosemary had finished, "I put my arms around him and said, 'Don't be an idiot, darling.'" Winking at her daughter, she added, "And a year after the wedding, you came along."

Rosemary's cancer had never returned. She had become a garden columnist and died in an automobile accident twenty-two years after Regan's birth.

"Rosemary, that's for remembrance." Regan's father had been fond of Shakespeare.

The words of Ophelia's mad little speech about flowers and herbs rambled on at the further reaches of Regan's consciousness. Matt was filling out some sort of form. That was what it was all going to come down to. Black marks on white paper. The state versus Regan Culver. The family versus Regan Culver.

What do I do now? She had carried on silent conversations with God since she was small. Other children had imaginary friends, but Regan, unwilling to settle for second best, had God. Regan's advantage was that her invisible friend was able to answer. The disadvantage was that he did not always say what she wanted to hear.

Should I refuse to have a lawyer? It's the principle of the thing. Why should I have to pay when I haven't done anything wrong?

Okay, that was a bad example to put to you. Because you did. Pay, that is. I can't really refuse anyway. Sasha needs me. I knew that there was a reason you sent her along. So I wouldn't be allowed to crawl off into a corner and block everybody else out like I did after Mother died. Or maybe so I wouldn't be alone, so there would still be one person in that house who loved me after Father died.

■ ■ ■

After Matt took Regan away, Diane urged Sasha toward the stairs. The child moved with dreary resignation.

"I need to change my clothes," Diane said, "and then we'll go for a ride. Okay?" Sasha didn't answer. These strangers could make her stay, her attitude implied, but they couldn't make her like it.

Diane waited until she was sure that the others had returned to the living room before she went back downstairs with the child in tow. She stepped quietly along the hallway, stopping before the mirror for a final critical glance. Usually she did not require much makeup, but lately constant dark circles underscored her eyes, and deep lines curved down to the corners of her mouth. Although she was technically Regan's niece, the two women were both thirty-two. They had even graduated from the same high school class fifteen years before, but they had never been friends.

Luke's face appeared suddenly beside hers in the mirror and only her rigid self-control kept her from starting. "Going somewhere?" he said.

"To find a lawyer for Regan."

He raised his brows. "I thought your mother forbade that."

"Mother isn't thinking clearly right now."

"But you are, of course. And you're right as usual. It's unlikely that Regan will be convicted of anything. Especially with her boyfriend investigating the case. Much better to be on the winning side from the start."

Diane met his eyes in the mirror. "I don't think he *is* her boyfriend. That gushy greeting of hers the other night was merely a hostess talking to a guest she didn't invite—or didn't want. I think Matt came to see Grandfather."

Luke's eyes narrowed. "Why would Alden invite the police chief to his birthday party?"

"I can think of at least one possibility." Diane rested her purse on the table under the mirror as she searched for a tube of lip gloss. She uncapped it and applied it with delicate care.

"We do make a handsome couple, don't we?" Luke commented, viewing their side-by-side reflections and putting a caressing hand on her shoulder, close to the neck. He was blond and good-looking too. They could almost have been brother and sister, but they weren't related at all. They had been teenagers when Luke's father married Diane's aunt, Gina.

Diane ignored the comment and the touch. Recapping the tube, she went on, "He could have, for instance, discovered that a certain member of his family was dealing drugs."

Luke's fingers dug into her shoulder. "Careful, sweetheart."

Suddenly aware of the listening child, Diane turned out from under his hand, tucking her purse under her arm again. *How much could four-year-olds understand?*

Luke spoke to her back. "Your sudden loyalty to Auntie is touching. But watch your step, Diane. I have an idea that Regan isn't quite the innocent she appears. The child was a clever touch and will win Regan some sympathy from the public. Did she tell you to throw that tantrum?" he asked Sasha.

"Don't pay any attention to him, Sasha," Diane said. "Let's go."

Luke's father, Reid, had locked the gates after Matt left with Regan—to keep out reporters. There were already several strange cars parked down on the street. Diane's own little Toyota was behind the garage. She strapped Sasha and her stuffed rabbit into the backseat, drove on out the grassy lane that curved past the empty stable, and jolted down a rough field track to a dirt road. With any luck, the reporters and gawkers would get bored quickly. A money motive wasn't quite enough to sustain interest.

She turned away from town to the country, deliberately blanking out all thought and responding only to the rhythm of the road. She drove down vernal tunnels of arching trees, sweeping around drastic curves where cows peered drowsily down at her from rocky pastures. In the rearview mirror, Diane could see that Sasha had her head back against the seat and turned toward the side window, watching the scenery swim by.

Diane came finally to another large gate and drove through it up a gravel drive to another big house. Sasha had refused to put on any shoes, asserting that Aunt Regan had said she could go barefoot all day. Diane tried to smooth down the child's hair tufts, but they sprang rebelliously up again.

The sprig of rosemary was beginning to wilt, but when Diane reached to take it, Sasha hung on determinedly. Diane shrugged. She rang the bell. A housekeeper showed them out onto a shady side lawn.

A woman sat on a bench, glumly contemplating a patch of spindly *impatiens* and marigolds. She wore a brightly flowered double-knit top and purple stretch pants that emphasized her dumpy figure. She had a book open in her lap. As Diane came up, the woman said accusingly, "It doesn't look at all like this," and thumped a photograph of an English garden in full bloom.

"Those are mostly perennials in that picture," Diane replied, refraining from pointing out that the orange clashed with the pink and that the marigolds, at least, would need much more sun than they were getting.

"But perennials are so expensive!" the other woman moaned.

Diane was not impressed. Mathilda Baker could afford truckloads of perennials if she really wanted them. The lawyer looked for all the world like a slatternly and not very bright fiftyish housewife. Her appearance had fooled many into taking her too lightly—until it was too late. No one could ever be quite sure whether that look was carefully staged, or whether she really did have no sense of taste.

"What's this?" Mathilda Baker caught sight of Sasha, lurking in the background. "An elf? What's that weed you have there?"

Sasha glared. "I'm a little girl. And it *isn't* a weed." She marched several steps away and sat down on the grass with her back to the two women. The rabbit, whose name was Harold, was not a particularly cozy bunny. His features had been sewn on crookedly. He smirked at them over Sasha's shoulder.

"I know somebody who could do that for you," Diane said hastily, inclining her head toward the picture.

Mathilda Baker regarded her elegant visitor with suspicion. Perhaps she was resenting the contrast. "Who?"

"Regan Culver."

"The one who killed her father?"

"She was arrested for his murder this morning. I am sure you would be the first to argue that that doesn't prove her guilt."

Mathilda snorted. "Don't get la-di-da with me, missy. I don't like you cultured types. Never have. Who are you, anyway?"

"My name's Diane Creighton. I am Regan's niece."

"And I'm retired."

Diane persisted. "But you still take cases occasionally. Regan is going to need a lawyer as soon as possible. She's rather naive—"

"So are most of the killers I've known," Mathilda interrupted. "Naive enough to think they could get away with it. Why are you so concerned anyway? Are you fond of your aunt?"

"Somebody has to do something."

"Do you like her?"

"I don't know her that well. We never—"

"Then why bother?"

"We can't abandon her. That would look—" Diane stopped.

"Suspicious?" Mathilda suggested. "Like you all were ganging up on her? Because you all resented Alden Culver's second marriage and his favored youngest child? That's common knowledge hereabouts. And it just might turn the public in her favor." She looked thoughtful.

Diane sat down. "The child needs her."

Mathilda looked startled and shot a dubious glance at the little girl's back. "Hers? First I've heard of it."

"No. Grandfather brought Sasha back from one of those breakaway Russian republics. She had leukemia, and medicine over there is primitive at best. The treatment has been successful. She was supposed to go back to her parents, but then civil war broke out. There are no flights into or out of Chevia now. She is kind of a bristly little thing as you can see. But she took an unexpected shine to Regan.

"Or not so unexpected maybe. Regan seems to attract

strays. That cat of hers, for instance. She found it when it was an infected, half-dead kitten and carried it around inside her shirt for days. Said that was the best way to keep it warm."

"Okay, okay!" Mathilda snapped. "Enough already! But if you're going to have a youngster peering soulfully through the bars at the defendant, one with big doe eyes and ringlets usually works better. We might make Regan herself the underdog in this one, especially since the rest of you are citified outsiders. Devoted younger daughter hated by jealous half sisters. It's been done before, but it's a popular plot. Of course, I'd have to settle on one of you as an alternate suspect. How about you? You got anything to hide?"

Diane's flinch would have been imperceptible to any but a well-trained eye.

"I thought so," Mathilda said. "I'm not quite clear why you're doing this, but I'd advise against it. Despite the buildup, it's obvious you're not too keen on your aunt yourself. Let her find her own lawyer."

Diane swallowed hard. "I tried to talk Regan into getting an attorney on Saturday, the day we found Grandfather dead. It was plain from the first, to me anyway, that she was going to be the chief suspect. The poison was in a cup of tea she made for Grandpa, and she stayed with him while he drank it. She's also the chief heir. She wouldn't listen to me then. She was in a numb state, still is actually. She and her father were close. I don't think any of this is real to her yet. She's careful about money too. It's the way her mother brought her up. Rosemary came from a poor family. Regan would consider it wasteful to retain a lawyer she might not need. But she gave me a nod right before she left, which I took to be a go-ahead. She realizes now that it's the only way she'll get back to Sasha."

As if on cue, Sasha, rubbing the green sprig under her nose, turned to stare at them.

"Regan gave her that," Diane explained. "It's rosemary. We threw some of it on Grandfather's coffin at the cemetery. It's the herb that's supposed to stand for remembrance."

Mathilda stood up. "All right, I'll go change. Just remember, you asked for it."

■ ■ ■

"You need to call a lawyer," Matt Olin told Regan. "Now. If you don't, the court will appoint one for you. And you might not like their choice."

"You can say that again!" a voice interrupted. A dumpy female clad in a cerise pantsuit barged through the door from the borough secretary's office. "You'd get stuck with one of those kids fresh out of law school. All fancy clothes and snooty expressions. 'But, your honor, the facts clearly show . . .' Balderdash! As if a jury was ever interested in facts!"

Looking around for a seat and not finding one, she bounced onto the edge of Matt's desk. "But you're in luck, honey. Your niece has asked me to represent you. Not a very bright move on her part, since she is the type that falls apart the fastest on the witness stand. I think we'd better go for a mostly female jury; they won't like the gorgeous blond. They probably won't like you either. But we can work on that. A few quivering but brave little smiles and a homespun attorney and you've got them eating out of your hand!"

Matt snorted. "When does she get the homespun attorney?"

Mathilda Baker cast him an annoyed glance. "Are you still here? I need to talk to my client."

"Fine by me. I need to get some lunch. When I come back, I want to get her complete story. On tape."

Taking in Regan's dismayed expression, he said to her, "No, Diane isn't out to get you. She's done better for you than I would have expected. This lady is Mathilda Baker. You've probably heard of her. She doesn't look impressive, but she wins. Consistently." He stood and gestured toward the cell. "If I'm going to take myself off for an hour or so, I'm going to have to lock you two in."

Perched on the cell's bunk beside Regan, Mathilda said to Matt, "That was a good job you did on the Denton case."

The hand turning the key paused only briefly. "Thanks," he said, shaking a bar of the cell door to test it. He turned away. "I'll be across the street. In case of fire, yell."

Both women were silent for a moment. The Denton case had been one of the uglier pages in Hayden's history. Bob Denton had been president of the town council when his teenage daughter, Connie, had gone to see Matt Olin, accusing her father of sexual abuse. Connie had been a troublemaker in the past, and a good percentage of the town had believed that she was making the whole thing up. When Matt had made the arrest anyway, it had almost cost him his job.

In court, however, it had come out that, in the midst of the uproar, Matt had quietly looked up Denton's older daughter, who lived in another state, on the assumption that what had happened to one of the girls would most likely have happened to the other as well. No one knew how he got her to talk, but it turned out that he had been right. Bob Denton was now in the state penitentiary.

Rather than admitting their error, many of the townspeople

still resented their police chief for being right. They watched him like a hawk, hoping for a slipup that would allow them to get rid of him.

"Matt is a good cop," Mathilda Baker said. "But one of the reasons he's still around is that your father took his side in that fracas. I hear Matt was at the party that night too. I think that could leave us an opening for questioning his objectivity."

"No," Regan said.

Mathilda glared at her. "*Why* was Matt Olin at that party? Is there something between you two?"

"No."

"You'd better not be lying to me because you're just the type a jury would fall all over themselves to convict. A spoiled little rich girl who kills Pop so he won't change his will, seduces the police chief on the side, and never a tear afterward. Unless you play it my way, they're going to love to hate you. Do you think you could blubber a little on the stand?"

"No."

Mathilda's aggressive manner dropped abruptly. "I have to admit you're good," she said with reluctant respect. "Those one-word answers are going to drive the prosecuting attorney crazy. It's when people try to explain themselves that they say way too much. But you don't want to come across as cold. If there's one thing a jury hates, it's cold. You don't want to live in a room like this for the next twenty years, do you?"

Regan looked around at the bars as if she'd just noticed them. "Right now, it hardly seems to matter."

Mathilda shrieked. Regan jumped.

"Why?" Mathilda moaned. "Why do they all have to do that? Just when I decide that they deserve whatever they're going to get, they say something pitiful and there I am, stuck with another impossible case." She did not sound very unhappy about it.

"Except for Sasha," Regan amended. "I can't ask Diane to look after her for more than a few days. And that war in Chevia doesn't seem close to ending. It can't be good for a child to have everybody she knows constantly going away from her. First her parents, then the nurses, then Daddy, and now me. She's the only one of us who showed any natural human emotion at that arrest, and I had to push her away. You have to get me out until time for the trial."

"Oh, yeah?" Mathilda said sarcastically. "You know how hard it is to get bail for a murder case and how steep it is if you do get it? Any other little thing you want while I'm at it? A ticket to Chevia maybe?"

"Two tickets," Regan said, "would be more to the point."

Mathilda looked sharply at her and grinned as if she had detected in that feeble attempt at humor a flicker of returning life.

"I don't think you'll have any trouble about the bail," Regan continued. "I asked him for help, and you are apparently it."

"Is there some guy," Mathilda asked, "that I haven't been told about here?"

"I was speaking of God. You aren't quite what I expected him to send."

"Figures," Mathilda said. "I'll do all the work, and you'll give him all the credit. I guess we'll have to go with the 'suffering in silence' gamut. Stiff upper lip and all that. We'll need a more intelligent jury for that one, people who can see beyond the obvious. And a smart jury is always risky. Oh, well. We can save that enticing Olin thing for a last resort."

"How," Regan inquired, "am I supposed to know when you're joking?"

"I never joke."

"In that case," Regan said politely, "perhaps I had better inform you that deceiving people is against my religion."

"I can see that you're going to be no fun at all. Is there anything else you don't do that I should be aware of?"

Regan seemed to take the question seriously and met Mathilda's gaze head-on. "Murder, for one."

CHAPTER 2

■ ■ ■

Pray you, love, remember.

When Matt walked into the small diner across the street from the borough building, curious faces turned his way. Several murmured, "Mornin', Chief." He kept his expression neutral and sat at the counter instead of a table.

"I'll have the special," he said to the white-aproned owner. "And coffee."

"Coming right up, Chief."

The diner was unusually quiet. He was aware of the speculative gazes boring into his back.

The special, beef and gravy over limp white bread with the inevitable coleslaw, arrived in record time. He really should eat better. It was what he thought every time he came into this place. Twice a day usually. But it beat dining at home alone.

"Busy morning?" the man beside him hazarded. The entire diner listened for the answer.

"So-so," Matt replied. He bent his head over his meal, discouraging further questions. Finally, the usual buzz of talk and clatter of silverware resumed.

No matter how friendly the greetings, there was a question in their glances. A cop was always, in some sense, a necessary evil, a buffer between society and the realities it would rather not face. The Flats. And because he was from the Flats himself, he was still a little suspect. Even after ten years.

He had lived in one of the cheap trailer parks where quarrels erupted frequently, especially on the weekends when most of the adults were drunk. The women tended to be single mothers with successions of live-in boyfriends. His own mother had been no better or worse than most of them.

She might have been pretty had she not used cheap hair dyes too light or dark for her complexion—and too much makeup. She yelled a lot, but she was not cruel. She read the women's magazines and made sporadic attempts at kindness, buying expensive cakes at birthdays, for example. She also developed occasional enthusiasms for finding employment, but none of the jobs lasted long; she got bored quickly. With men too. Undisciplined was perhaps the best way to describe her.

Matt had never known his father, who had been gone long before Matt grew to the point of remembering faces. But since his mother usually went for the sullen, self-centered type, he didn't think he'd missed much.

His mother's live-ins were largely indifferent to him and his little brother as long as they stayed out of the way. His mother craved drama, though, and loved to engage in loud arguments with the boyfriend, if one was handy, or with a neighbor, if one was not. This frequently ended with the town cop being called.

The chief then was Tom McNeil, a big, patient, slow-moving man in his fifties. He was the only constant male in Matt's life, and the little boy had been in awe of the uniform, the cruiser, the gun, and the man. McNeil seemed to bring his own circle of calm with him.

Matt had been about twelve when he stood in the shadows one night, near the police car, watching McNeil arbitrate a neighborhood dispute. This one had not required hauling anyone away in the back of the cruiser. "Evenin', Matt," the chief had said as he returned to his car. "How's every little thing with you?" McNeil always remembered names.

Encouraged by this acknowledgment and by the fact that nobody else was close enough to hear, Matt blurted, "I-I'm g-going to be a c-cop too."

Had the man laughed—or even smiled condescendingly—that might have been the end of that. But McNeil paused, taking off his hat to run his fingers through his hair as he eyed Matt thoughtfully. "I'm glad to hear that," he said. " 'Cause I hope to retire in another ten years or so. Think you can be ready by then?"

Matt nodded jerkily, scuffing at the ground with the toe of one dirty tennis shoe.

"Good," the chief said. "Well, you'll have to keep your grades up and stay out of trouble if you're going to get into the academy. You up to that?"

Matt nodded again, speechless at being taken so seriously.

"It's a deal then," McNeil promised, extending a hand. "You graduate from the academy; I retire and put in a good word for you. What do you say?"

Matt had shaken the hand, throat tight with the importance of it all. . . .

At the clink of china, he roused from his introspection to find a piece of apple pie à lâ mode on the counter in front of him.

"On the house, Chief," the counterman said with a grin.

"Thanks," Matt said, trying to match the smile. He wished he had McNeil's easy way with people. It came, he suspected, from treating everyone as having worth, as being important—even a grungy, stammering twelve-year-old.

He wished that he could consult McNeil about this case. The ex-chief was out West somewhere on a hunting trip. He had told Matt the name of the ranch, but Matt didn't remember now. Had the situation been reversed, he suspected that McNeil would have remembered. Time to take Regan Culver's official statement. As he got up from the stool, cautious stares followed him to the door. He suspected that a lot of other people were wishing for McNeil right now too.

■ ■ ■

"It was my father's birthday," Regan began. "We have a tradition that everyone comes to stay in the house for a night or two; we always have a big dinner. They all arrived on Friday. Diane was in the kitchen when I came down the next morning."

Diane had stood at the stove, making an omelet. "Good morning," she said. "I cut some of your herbs to use in this. I hope you don't mind."

"Of course not," Regan responded. There was no good reason for her to mind. Most of the chives and parsley were going to waste anyhow. It was really quite thoughtful of Diane to get her own breakfast. But Diane was like that. Just right about everything and scrupulously polite.

Regan lifted Sasha into her booster seat, scooped homemade granola from a glass canister into bowls for both of them, and got orange juice and milk from the refrigerator.

Agatha came into the kitchen and viewed the granola with distaste. "Don't you have any real cereal?" she asked. Although as elegant as her daughter, Agatha did not bother with the politeness.

Diane interrupted quickly. "I made you an omelet, Mother. You know you don't like cereal anyway."

Somehow Regan had suspected that Agatha wasn't really the Cheerios type.

Agatha poked ungratefully at the omelet. There wasn't much she could complain about there. Diane's cooking was as perfect as the rest of her.

"I don't know why you have to put all this greenery in it," Agatha said. "What if you got some of the poisonous herbs by mistake?"

Luke came into the kitchen behind Agatha and winked at Regan. "And how could you tell whether it was by mistake or not, Aunt Agatha?" he asked.

"Everybody knows parsley and chives, Mother," Diane said.

Luke scooped granola into a bowl, sat down beside his aunt, and reached for the milk. Agatha looked at him with the same distaste with which she had regarded the omelet, as if suspecting something undesirable in him as well. Luke worked at nothing but still contrived to live very well.

Agatha could console herself that he was not a blood relative, since he was her sister Gina's stepson. Regan had been surprised by his arrival the evening before, as had his father, Reid, with whom Luke was not on the best of terms.

He could hardly be excluded, however, since he was family. And because everybody was a little afraid of him. At least he wasn't a difficult guest.

Carrying a briefcase, Reid came into the room. A distinguished man in his fifties, he had an automatic smile that never reached his eyes, as if nothing really amused him. "I'll just have coffee," he said.

Regan jumped up. She hadn't thought of coffee. Neither she nor her father drank it. "There's some instant somewhere," she said.

Reid simply looked at her. He had an unnerving habit of pausing before he answered any remark. It always gave Regan the impression that he had found what she said inadequate and was waiting for more.

"Sit down, Regan," Luke said. "This isn't a restaurant, Dad. If you want coffee, get it yourself."

Diane, who was now eating granola too, said, "It's in the cupboard to the right of the sink."

"Never mind," Reid said. "I'll pick up some on the way." He had not looked at or even acknowledged the presence of his son.

Regan slumped in her seat, feeling as she always did in the presence of these people—insignificant and incompetent.

Alden Culver came into the room and smiled reassuringly at her. "Good morning, all." He had Paul Newman-blue eyes and finely drawn patrician features similar to Agatha's and Diane's. He winked at Sasha. She grinned and ducked her head. Despite his cheery greeting, he looked tired and preoccupied.

"Happy birthday, Grandfather," Diane said, and the others hastily seconded the salutation. He nodded thanks and began to fry himself an egg.

"Why don't you let Regan do that for you?" Agatha inquired silkily.

"I'll do it," Diane intervened. "Regan looks tired."

"I'm perfectly capable of getting my own breakfast, Agatha," Culver said. "I may be old, but I'm not helpless."

"Well, I do hope she remembered to get coffee for this evening," Agatha persisted. "Something other than instant, I mean."

"The party," Alden Culver said, "is going to be catered. I suspect that they will bring the coffee."

"Catered?" Agatha looked disapproving. "Won't that be expensive?"

"No doubt," her father said. "Tea anybody? Regan?"

"Yes, please."

Culver took a ring of keys from his pocket and used one to unlock the doors of a small wooden cabinet that stood in a corner beyond the end of the counter. He viewed the rows of glass canisters filled with dry herbs and asked, "What'll it be?"

Regan often drank rosemary tea in the morning for its stimulant properties. But now she thought that her nerves needed calming instead. "Chamomile, please."

"Coming up," he said. "I think I'll have some of the same. Anybody else?" When the others did not respond, he spooned daisylike flowers into two metal tea balls, shut the doors, and turned the key again.

"Is there any special reason for locking that?" Luke asked. "Other than keeping nosy guests out, I mean."

"Some herbs can be toxic in high doses," Culver replied, running tap water into a teakettle and returning to the stove to turn a burner on high. "And some of the ones we keep in here aren't meant to be taken internally. Like *arnica*—dogbane. Rosemary always thought it safer to lock the cabinet when there was a child in the house."

"Rosemary," Agatha said, "has been dead for ten years. How long are you going to keep up with all this, this"—her brusque gesture seemed to encompass the herbs, the gardens outside the window, perhaps even Regan herself—"organic stuff. Keeping up those gardens, the greenhouse, that herb farm. It can't be cheap. And are you really making anything?"

"I don't own the farm," Culver said mildly, dropping the tea balls into two separate cups and pushing one to Regan as he sat down across from her. "I have merely invested some money in it. It's starting to pay, especially since Regan uses it as a source of plants for her design business. Keeping up the gardens involves some expense, of course, but they were important to Rosemary and now to Regan. Her customers can get a good idea of her expertise by looking at them. Which is why," he concluded almost casually, "I have decided to leave the house and most of my savings to her. I know that she will keep up the place in the way that her mother would have wanted."

The shrill whistle of the teakettle cut the heavy silence that descended on the table. Agatha's face went white, then red. "I can't believe," she said in a shaking whisper which, like the kettle's whistle, rapidly escalated in volume, "that you are going to leave my mother's house to this, this . . ."

Diane was making shushing gestures with her hands, but she looked shaken herself.

"Interloper!" Agatha shrilled.

Luke rose to take the shrieking kettle off the burner. "Too bad one can't shut you up as easily, Auntie," he said, pouring steaming water into Regan's teacup and then her father's.

As Regan clasped her hands together in her lap in a futile effort to stop their trembling, Luke scooped up Sasha in one arm and her rabbit in the other and said, "Come along, you two," to Regan and Diane. "Seems to me we're eavesdropping on what should be a private discussion."

It said something for his way with females that two who didn't even like him meekly got up from their seats and followed his bidding. And that Sasha, who did not usually enjoy being picked up unless she initiated the action, rode along amiably enough with one hand clutching his hair for balance. He led the way to the living room at the front of the house, set Sasha down, and remained bent at the waist while he disentangled her fingers from his hair. No sooner was he done than Sasha giggled and made another grab, which he straightened up just in time to avoid.

"What I've never been able to understand about women," he commented, "is why you feel compelled to sit there and take whatever someone else sees fit to dish out."

"I'm sorry, Regan," Diane said. "Mother didn't mean—"

"Not to mention," Luke interrupted, "your compulsion to apologize for what somebody else does, which is just as stupid. One might wish that all this conscientiousness would extend to telling the truth, but I've yet to meet a female who wouldn't color the facts to match her outfit." He tossed the rabbit to Sasha before walking out.

Diane said, "I *am* sorry," and stood looking at Regan with frustrated bewilderment.

The rise and fall of Agatha's voice in the distance was the only background noise. *How many times*, Regan wondered, *have I sat at a safe distance, listening to that accusing tone? Not having to hear the words because the words are always the same?*

"Don't you feel sometimes," Regan said, "that we're stuck in this pattern, that somebody is going to have to do something new to break it?"

Diane looked taken aback. "What do you mean?"

Regan walked to a window to stand, looking through a screen of lace, at the gardens. Kierkegaard, whose journals she had been reading the night before, had had a morbid notion that his father's sin had doomed the whole family. But it wasn't a sin that her own father preferred his second wife to his first, or that, consequently, he favored his youngest daughter. Was it?

Maybe Agatha wouldn't have minded so much if Regan had left home after college. But she couldn't have abandoned her father so soon after her mother's death—or abandoned the gardens her mother had spent so many years creating. *I should be used to Agatha by now. But it's as if my reactions are programmed, as if we're destined to play the same scenes over and over again.*

She turned back to Diane. "Something Kierkegaard said. That knowing isn't enough. That you have to act."

"I don't know what you're talking about," Diane said. "Act on what? The rest of us will be out of here in a couple of days. Surely you can put up with Mother for that long. After all, you're going to get everything. You can afford to be patient."

"Can I? How far have any of us progressed in our attitudes since Mother died ten years ago? We're stuck."

Diane wrenched her fascinated gaze away and said huskily, "You're crazy."

"Not that we will do anything," Regan went on, heedless. "He said that women especially are victims of dread. That we have a craving for what we fear that renders us powerless. Kierkegaard said that, I mean. But Luke said it too, in another way. You know that it would never have occurred to either of us to walk out, left to ourselves. And you keep coming back,

Diane. Your mother treats you almost as badly as she does me. Why do you stand for it?"

"I don't know what's got into you, Regan." Diane backed toward the door. "Mother and I are going into town. She has a hair appointment. Don't expect us back for lunch."

When she was gone, Regan sat and drank the tea. Sasha wriggled up onto the couch beside her and leaned against her arm. *Why do we find the truth so disconcerting? Luke is right. So-called nice women can be the sweetest liars.*

It was strange being in the living room in the morning; it was more an evening, lamplight kind of room. The sun seemed too bold for it, showing up a fine film of dust on the coffee table. The ticking of the grandfather clock seemed unnaturally loud; she never noticed it in the evening. It seemed like a room that should be deserted.

■　■　■

"And did you think *you* were the one who should do something?"

At the question, Regan blinked her way out of the dusty silence of the living room to the sterile steel and linoleum neatness of the police station.

"*Did* you feel obliged to do something?" Matt Olin repeated, watching her eyes. It was hard to connect with her. She could be looking directly at him and yet seem to be sliding evasively away at the same time.

"Obliged?" she repeated, as if puzzled. "No, I would probably have waited things out as usual. It's the easiest way."

Matt remembered his interview with Diane.

"She was strange that morning," Diane said. "Of course, Regan is always a little strange, but this was different from usual. She was quoting some philosopher and seemed to be working herself up to something, as if she couldn't stand things anymore. I told her she could endure it for the weekend. She always had been able to before, after all. But she seemed to think that something drastic had to be done."

"Something as drastic as killing her father?" Matt asked.

"Oh, no!" Diane shook her head vehemently. "At least, I wouldn't have thought so. She loved him. But I don't understand her. I never have. She is different, you know. All that herbal stuff really irritates my mother. And Regan's job—making cottage-style gardens for rich people—is almost a contradiction in terms. They're all fascinated with her, you know. She seems to live in some romanticized version of the past. She has a taste for all those outdated theologians, most of whom were on the edge of madness themselves."

"So you think she's mentally off balance?" Matt concluded.

Diane looked at her hands, curling the fingers under one at a time, ticking off points. "No," she said finally. "She's on a different wavelength. If she did have a motive for killing him, it wouldn't be a usual one. No matter what my mother says, she wouldn't have done it for money. Some of the people she reads had peculiar ideas about sacrifice and suffering, you know."

Matt wondered if that was meant to imply that Regan could have killed her father as a drastic remedy for his dysfunctional family. Try selling that one to a jury!

■　■　■

He looked at Regan, who sat with hands clasped in her lap. It was more likely, he thought, that she had tired of carrying on the legacy of a dead woman and had wanted out. "Go on," he said.

"My father came in to say good-bye." She was looking over Matt's head at the wall behind him. "He was going into town."

■ ■ ■

She had almost fallen asleep, sitting with her feet in one of the squares of light, when her father came to stand in the doorway. "Are they gone?" she asked. Heavy against her arm, Sasha watched glittering dust motes drift.

"Yes," Alden Culver said. "They have appointments somewhere. I shouldn't have brought up the inheritance while you were in the room."

"It wouldn't have made any difference."

"I'm going into the city," he said. "Why don't you get some rest? You're not helping out at the farm today, are you?"

Regan winced and reached for the phone. "I hadn't thought about that. I hope Caroline isn't expecting me. This will be one of her busiest weekends."

"Tell her you can't make it. She can get along without you for once. Stay here and take it easy."

"All right. I'll try." Hand resting on the receiver, she said, "You look tired too. Is anything wrong? Besides Agatha, I mean."

He hesitated. "There is something, but it can wait until after the weekend; it's waited ten years already, after all. You let the caterers do all the work, you hear? It's what they get paid for." He grinned and snapped his fingers at Sasha. "What are you sitting around for? The lark's on the wing and the snail's on the thorn. Bring along Harold, and let's see the world." It didn't come close to rhyming, but he made it sound like it did.

Sasha giggled and clattered across to join him.

Caroline Stanton owned Thyme Will Tell, the herb farm

that supplied many of the plants for Regan's assignments. Caroline had been Rosemary's best friend. Her gruff, no-nonsense manner was belied by the sensitive herbal, *Rosemary for Remembrance,* which she had dedicated to her late friend and which had made Caroline and her farm famous. "No, I wasn't expecting you today," she said when Regan called. "What with the party tonight and all. How is your father getting along with the journals?"

Regan had almost forgotten about that. An editor who had read some of Rosemary's old columns somewhere had expressed interest in publishing the journals that were casually mentioned in one of those columns. Alden Culver had demurred at first, but he and Regan had finally decided that he should read the notebooks and edit out anything that he knew Rosemary wouldn't have wanted printed.

"All right, I hope," she responded. "He hasn't said much about it. I hope he doesn't find anything uncomplimentary about himself. They had their spats from time to time, like any married couple."

"It'd be a miracle if they hadn't," Caroline said, "as bullheaded as your father is. Always convinced that he knows best. Oh, well, all doctors think that they're God, I guess."

Regan was smiling when she said, "Bye. See you tonight." Alden Culver had never cared much for Caroline, and the feeling seemed to be mutual. He had been, Regan thought, more than a little jealous of his wife's friendships.

Caroline wasn't the only outsider invited to the party. Her manager, Dennis, would be along too. Regan wondered what she was going to do about Dennis. Dennis should be ideal. He liked plants and was good at growing them. He had even succeeded in germinating several sensitive varieties—like meconopsis—that Regan had never had much success with herself. He was good-looking and ambitious. He sent her rare and beautiful plants on holidays and whenever else he could manufacture a good excuse. She should have been quite enthusiastic about Dennis. There was always the suspicion, of course, that part of his interest was due to the fact that she would inherit her father's share of the herb farm. Dennis also tended to introduce her as "Rosemary Culver's daughter, you know."

She had gone out with Dennis once, and he persisted in believing that she was playing hard to get. During high school Diane had succeeded in collecting all the males in sight. Maybe she could do it again now.

Regan was just going out into the hall when the phone rang. She took it at the extension on the hall table. "Regan? Is your father there?" The male voice sounded vaguely familiar, but she couldn't quite place it.

"No, he's gone out. May I take a message?"

The caller hesitated. "This is Matt Olin. Your father invited me to the dinner tonight, but he wasn't specific about the time."

Regan's hesitation was a bit too long.

"Didn't he mention—" Matt began.

She interrupted quickly, overdoing the warmth. She didn't want him to know that he had taken her by surprise. "But of course, Matt! We're so happy that you can come. We're going to eat at six, but everyone's coming at five. Whichever is best for you. And no presents, please. Daddy says that at his age if he doesn't have it by now he doesn't want it."

"Okay." Matt seemed to relax a little at her friendly, matter-of-fact tone. "If this is going to be formal—"

"Oh, no," she said. "Semiformal, more like. And you can dispense with the tie, if you like. My father doesn't wear one."

"Okay," he said again. "Thanks. I guess I'll see you tonight then." He didn't sound altogether happy about it.

"I'll look forward to it," she gushed, aware that she sounded insincere. Or perhaps not.

As she hung up the phone, a voice close behind her said, "I hadn't realized that you were quite that friendly with the local constabulary."

She started convulsively. Luke had come quietly down the stairs while she was talking. "I'm not," she said. "We were all at school together—"

"Is that any reason to invite him to your father's birthday party?" Luke's tone was light, but his eyes were narrowed.

Since it would be awkward to admit that she hadn't invited Matt, Regan flushed and chose to ignore the question.

He leaned against the banister, contriving to look easygoing and expensive at the same time. As she went past him up the stairs, he murmured, "Slumming, darling?"

It was an obvious reference to Matt's lowly past, and Regan pretended that she hadn't heard it. When she was out of his sight, she stopped and leaned against a wall to think.

What had her father meant by inviting the police chief to his dinner? Was this thing he was worried about much more serious than she'd supposed? They all knew Matt casually; he had been in the same high school class with her and Luke and Diane. But they didn't know him well enough to invite him to what was essentially a family gathering. It was going to look strange. Everyone would be surprised to see him, and they would show it.

She shook her head and massaged her forehead with her

fingers. It wasn't Matt's fault that he reminded her too clearly of her mother's death.

It had been a warm June day much like this. Regan had just come up from the garden with a basketful of flowers, singing to herself the mournful English ballad "Barbara Allen" as she tended to do when she was happy. They had all been a bit giddy. Regan had graduated from college with a degree in horticulture. Caroline had opened her herb farm with Rosemary's help, and the three of them were excitedly discussing how they could combine their resources and talents. For a graduation gift, Alden Culver had presented Regan and her mother with tickets for a European garden tour. They were scheduled to leave at the end of the week.

The doorbell rang as she stepped into the living room from the terrace. Regan ran to answer it with a lightness and freedom usually foreign to her. Still clutching her basket, she was laughing and breathless. Matt had just become the little town's only policeman. He stood there with his hat in his hand, looking awkward and miserable. "I'm sorry," he said.

Regan turned abruptly and rapped at a door, behind which a TV muttered. She was invited to come in.

"Did you want any breakfast, Gina?" Regan asked. Her half sister, plump and girlish looking at forty-five, was propped up in bed, watching a game show on a portable television and eating sweet rolls.

"No thanks," Gina said, without shifting her gaze from the screen. "Brought my own." She waved a gooey roll by way of illustration and took a large bite.

That was like Gina. She didn't fuss. Knowing that there

would be no doughnuts or upstairs TVs in her father's house, she brought her own. That took considerably less energy than complaining. She never argued either. She would placidly agree with whomever she happened to be talking to at the time. It was easier that way. The only thing that bothered her was an argument among other people, from which, since she obviously couldn't agree with everybody, she would retreat as rapidly as possible. She was the only person Regan knew who had absolutely no ambition. Regan thought it must be restful.

"Okay," Regan said. "I'm going to be doing some cleaning. If you want anything . . ."

Someone else might have felt obliged to offer help. Not Gina. She would have trailed along, carrying a duster, if asked, but, since nobody was asking . . . Regan didn't mind. After Agatha, Gina's indifference was always a relief.

"Oh," Gina added, as Regan turned away, "don't bother with lunch for me. I'm supposed to meet Agatha in town." She did not sound enthusiastic at the prospect.

"All right," Regan said. "What are you going to drive?"

Gina dragged her attention away from the screen to look from her half sister to her sweet roll, as if expecting one of them to provide an answer.

"Would you like to borrow my car?" Regan encouraged.

"That would be nice," Gina said, her gaze darting back to the TV.

"The keys are on the hall table."

"Agatha says that Daddy is going to leave you everything in his will. Is that right?"

Regan stiffened as she turned back the second time, but Gina's face showed only its typical half-absent expression.

"Not quite everything," Regan said. "Most of it."

"I just wondered. Agatha gets so worked up about things."

Regan waited, but Gina had become immersed in her game show again and had nothing else to say.

■ ■ ■

"She didn't care?" Matt sounded skeptical.

"No, I don't believe she did. Reid is much richer than Daddy after all. Gina doesn't waste energy getting upset.

"She worked for one of Daddy's doctor friends for years. All the patients liked her because she always agreed with them. Everybody was quite surprised when she suddenly up and lost twenty pounds and snared the wealthiest widower in the county. They thought that was quite out of character for her. But I wasn't really surprised. By exerting a little energy that one time, she assured that she would never have to work for the rest of her life. And I imagine that Reid is satisfied with his part of the bargain. She gained all that weight back again, of course, but she's a very biddable sort of woman, and Reid is the authoritarian type. It is a good marriage in its way. Shall I go on?"

At his nod, she sank back again.

■ ■ ■

The rest of Friday morning, Regan devoted to cleaning. She did not like housekeeping and avoided it as much as possible. But once she had taken the plunge, she gave it the same careful attention that she afforded more agreeable tasks. In her father's study, the big loose-leaf binder that contained her mother's journals was lying on top of the desk. Regan dropped it into a drawer so that she could polish the desk's oak surface.

She had a salad for lunch, then did flower arrangements. Her footsteps echoed in the empty rooms.

Upstairs again, she washed her hair with a soapwort and rosemary shampoo. Then, wrapping her hair in a towel turban, she ran a bath, tossing in a tiny cheesecloth bag packed with lavender flowers.

As she luxuriated in the warm water, her mind drifted back to her unexpected guest.

Matt had showed up once again that fall ten years ago. Regan had canceled the European trip and spent the summer working hard in the gardens and at the farm. On the first evening that frost was predicted, she spent hours digging up tender plants to take into the conservatory. By the time she finished about midnight, her hair, skin, and clothes had absorbed the damp chill of the night. She brought in some things from the vegetable garden too, including a watermelon of the heirloom moon-and-stars type. Because she was too weary to go to bed, she cut it open. And then she remembered the big tubs with the bay and the myrtle and the fig. There was no way she could possibly move them herself. And her father was out of town on a book tour, the first time he'd been away since her mother's death.

She cried then, quite suddenly, with a cold piece of watermelon between her fingers. And as she cried, she ate—voraciously. Tears streamed from her eyes, and watermelon juice dripped from her chin. Her hands shook. When she finally stopped crying, a good third of the watermelon was gone, and she felt waterlogged but peaceful. That was when the doorbell rang.

When she saw Matt there, she laughed and said, "You again!" She must have looked strange, to say the least, with a tear-stained face and red, sticky chin, trembling and laughing at the same time.

"Your father asked me to look in and make sure you were all right," he said.

"Well, come in, then," she said. "Have some watermelon." And she giggled.

Matt turned up the thermostat, put his coat around her shoulders, and washed her face and hands as if she were a child. He poked around in the cupboards until he found some hot chocolate and made her drink it. Then he ordered her to go to bed, but she insisted that he bring her little trees into the greenhouse first.

When she started upstairs finally, he stood in the lower hallway, watching her. She said, "I'm going to take a hot bath and go to sleep. I'll be all right now." And she had been.

Stretching out in her current bath, Regan thought of how that night she'd almost been able to see her mother's droll woman-to-woman sideways glance. Hear her say, "Well, at least it was only watermelon, darling. No calories to feel guilty about in the morning."

Regan smiled. She could think of her mother now with warmth instead of aching loss. And maybe that had started on the night of the watermelon binge. Maybe she did owe Matt something.

The water was cooling. She climbed out of the tub, toweled herself dry, donned a white cotton robe, and went into her bedroom. The house was still quiet.

She opened the doors of the closet. The green dress was a bit too fussy with tucks and gathers. It added a good five pounds. Or, perhaps, she thought wryly, failed to conceal an extra five pounds. She preferred the slimming black, but it was not a summer color.

Yawning, she sat on the edge of the bed. Then again, black was a good color for her. Leaning back against the pillows, she recalled a line from an old country song. "Some women *do* look good in black." It had an ominous sound to it. If she remembered right, it had been about a funeral.

CHAPTER 3

And there is pansies, that's for thoughts.

Regan woke slowly to the sound of an angry voice in the distance. She thought for an illusive moment that she was still sitting in the living room downstairs with her feet in sunlight, listening to Agatha's harangue. Then she opened her eyes to find herself in bed with her cat, Gato, sleeping on her feet.

She looked at the clock. Ten to four. The caterers would be here any moment. She jumped up, shedding the robe as she went, and yanked open a dresser drawer. Within five minutes, she was in the black dress and twisting her hair into a loose knot. Now was a good time to be grateful that she had never learned to use makeup.

She took a final steadying look at herself in the mirror. On the dresser was a little bouquet of pansies that she had tucked into a perfume bottle. With a wry smile, Regan plucked one out from the back, and, keeping her eyes shut, tried to remember the children's game. Four lines for hope. Seven for constancy in love. Eight for fickleness. Nine for a change of heart. She ripped off a top petal and began to count the little purple veins. Eleven. Disappointment in love and an early death. She made a face and tossed the marred bloom at the wastebasket.

Regan went into the bathroom and took down a medicinal-looking brown bottle complete with dropper. Holding her nose, she dribbled coneflower extract down her throat. *Echinacea* boosted the immune system during periods of stress, and she had a feeling that she was going to need it.

On her way back through the bedroom, she glanced again at the whiskered pansy faces watching her from the dresser. They were supposed to be such innocent little flowers—heartsease—standing for pensées, thoughts. That all depended, she supposed, on how easing one's thoughts were.

She was still occupied with her own as she went out on the gallery and started down the stairs. Luke was on the phone in the lower hall, his back to her. His words penetrated her preoccupation only when she had come quietly down behind him.

"She's a bit too friendly with the local cop for my comfort," he was saying. "She's invited him out here tonight, in fact, which she wouldn't do unless it was serious."

In response to a question from the other end, he went on, "Considering his background, I think he would be more impressed by cash, but she has that too, you know. One way or another, he's going to be a pain."

Another pause. Luke laughed. "Regan a user? Nah."

He began to get irritated again. "I'm supposed to be hiding out here a while, you know. These people are my family, after all."

The doorbell bonged, sending a startled shudder through

Regan's body. "I've gotta go," Luke said. "I'll call you later, but I don't like it. Remember that."

As he dropped the receiver and turned, he became aware of Regan's silent, staring presence. His face twisted. He grabbed her arm. "How long have you been there. What did you hear?"

She simply looked at him.

"Your car wasn't here!"

She looked down at his hand and said, "Your stepmother borrowed it." The doorbell bonged again. "The caterers are here, Luke. Let me go."

■ ■ ■

The two women at the door looked nervously eager. "Miss Culver?" The older one tried to be brisk, but confidence faltered. "We're the caterers. Your father—"

"Yes," Regan said with a reassuring smile. "Here, let me help you carry things."

She went out with them, leaving the door open, without another glance at the man in the hallway behind her.

When the three returned, laden with boxes, Luke stepped forward. "Regan, can I speak to you for a moment?"

"Not now," she said.

She saw the two women glance at each other. They could feel the tension.

From their nervous chatter, she deduced that this was their first job. She was afraid that their cooking would be amateurish too, but the dishes they produced for her inspection looked impressive. The plump younger one unpacked the china and some place cards done in calligraphy, while the other, who appeared to be in charge, worked with the food.

"You'll have to do one more of those," Regan said of the cards. "We're going to have another guest."

"But I didn't bring my pen. Your father gave us a list."

"Then I'm afraid we'll have to skip them," Regan said. As the other looked on the verge of tears, she added hastily, "Then again, I have some pens and ink in my studio. Maybe I can find some card stock like that too; just a minute."

Gato had gotten frustrated with following Regan back and forth and was sitting on the stairs out of the way of clumsy human feet. Except for him, the hallway was empty as she hurried back to the room that adjoined the conservatory. Sooner or later she had to try to make some sense out of Luke's words, but there wasn't time now.

She scrabbled through the drawers of the supply chest next to her drawing table. Clutching a handful of pens, an ink bottle, and a half dozen different shades of thick paper, she started back to the kitchen. As she passed the study door, Luke stepped out and grasped her arm.

"Luke, leave me alone!" she said, more loudly than she should have apparently, because when she shook off his hold and pushed into the kitchen, the two caterers were looking at her with startled expressions.

"You should find what you need here," Regan said agitatedly, dumping her load on the table. "The name is *Matt Olin. Matthew*, I suppose."

They lifted a large cake out of its box and took off the dome cover to exhibit it, with justifiable pride. The cake was a veritable mountain of pristine, glistening angel food. "Your father said he liked sponge cake without too much frosting," the leader explained. "We have some candles here somewhere." She turned—and tripped over the cat.

Her hands flew up; the cake hit the edge of a box on the counter and broke into airy chunks. One woman moaned. The other simply stood—staring.

And all the king's horses, Regan thought, *and all the king's men and all the birthday parties in the world are never going to stick this family together.*

Hearing voices in the hall, she called out, "Diane, may I see you for a moment?"

Diane looked pale, and she pressed her lips too tightly together as she studied the debris of cake. Regan suspected that she wasn't really seeing or understanding. But then Diane began moving, opening doors, looking in the cupboards, the refrigerator, the caterers' boxes. "All right," she said finally, and began assembling things on the counter. A pudding mix, a carton of heavy cream, a jar of spreadable fruit. "Find me a deep glass bowl, Regan. We'll do English trifle. It's easy, but it looks impressive. And ladyfingers are just pieces of sponge cake after all. We'll pipe the whipped cream around the top like frosting and put the candles in that."

Within twenty minutes, Diane had turned disaster into an elegant dessert and had gone upstairs to change. Regan stayed in the kitchen to watch the caterers, even though she could hear people gathering in the living room.

Diane and I are alike in at least one way, Regan thought. *We don't want anything to happen.* That sounded like a quote from something and Regan tried to remember from what. Oh, yes, Eliot's play about Becket. *Murder in the Cathedral.* The women of Canterbury. "We do not wish anything to happen. Seven years we have lived quietly, Succeeded in avoiding notice, Living and partly living . . . do not ask us to stand to the doom on the house . . ." *What is wrong with Diane?* she asked herself. *No, I won't think about that. I've got to think about what Luke said. And it seems to me that there was something else . . .*

But her thoughts veered back to the play. "We have not been happy, my Lord, we have not been too happy. We are not ignorant women, we know what we must expect and not expect. . . . Picking together the pieces . . ."

Sasha scurried into the room, stopping at the sight of the two strangers then detouring wide around them to reach Regan. "Look what we got. Uncle Aldy says I can wear it to dinner."

It was a frilly white dress. With a glance at the clock, Regan said, "We'd better get you into it now. Did you have fun?"

"We went to the farm," Sasha said as they started up the stairs. "And to a office with a sun. And one with a moon. And to a cafeteria."

All big buildings were offices to Sasha and all restaurants were cafeterias, after the one at the hospital. It was a good thing she had had a bath the night before because there wasn't time for one now. Even as Regan knelt to zip her up and smooth down the tufts of hair with a wet comb, she could hear voices in the hallway—Caroline and Dennis.

The little girl stood stiffly with her hands away from her sides. Her expression was hopeful. "Am I pretty?"

"Gorgeous!"

"You just say that because you love me," Sasha said, looking pleased nonetheless. She was, Regan knew, self-conscious about how strange her hair looked as it grew back in.

"Everybody's beautiful when they are loved," Regan said, tickling her. "That's why you should love as many people as you can."

"What do *you* want?" Agatha was saying to someone. And Regan, still on her knees, suddenly remembered. Matt!

She scrambled up and out into the upstairs hall where she could see Agatha below, holding the front door open but blocking the police chief's path. Hastily Regan called, "Oh, Matt, come in. We're so glad you could make it!" Wearing a broad, stiff smile, she tottered down the steps as rapidly as she could manage on unaccustomed high heels.

Maybe her acting was better than she realized. Matt looked surprised but gratified when she hobbled to a stop beside him and beamed up into his face. Out of uniform, he still appeared to loom. But without the sunglasses and gun belt, he seemed considerably more vulnerable.

The others looked surprised too, but far from gratified. From their speculative stares, she realized that they had made the same mistake Luke had, assuming that Matt was her guest. Even the caterers were peeking at her around the kitchen doors.

Sasha, cross at being so abruptly abandoned, stomped to the head of the stairs and demanded, "Who's that?"

Carrying the green loose-leaf notebook under his arm, Alden Culver came out of his study. He looked with mild surprise at the assembly in the hallway. "I didn't realize it was so late," he said. "I'll be down in a minute." The guest of honor stumped upstairs.

A half hour later, Regan stood hemmed in front of the fireplace by three young males and tried to be vivacious. She had never been the femme fatale type, and this sudden popularity made her claustrophobic. Sasha clung to the back of her skirt.

Matt probably felt obliged to stick to her after her warm

welcome. Luke was determined that she not be alone with the police chief to tell him what she'd overheard. Dennis resented the competition.

Regan looked around for her niece, but Diane showed no inclination to come to the rescue this time. Diane was talking to Gina. Actually Gina was obligingly carrying on the whole conversation while Diane stared into space and muttered a polite monosyllable from time to time.

Agatha had cornered Alden at the far end of the room. Caroline had brought knitting—probably, Regan thought, so the evening wouldn't be a *total* waste—and was politely listening to Reid talk about the stock market.

"How's your brother doing these days, Matt?" Regan asked.

"Pretty good," Matt said. "He's a research scientist at Chemco."

Regan's friendly smile congealed. She had recently written a scathing indictment of Chemco for an organic gardening magazine. Dennis snickered.

"Have you ever considered getting out of Hayden too?" Luke asked. "It can't be that exciting for you—a sleepy little town like this. Not much crime here, I imagine."

"You'd be surprised," Matt said. "Or maybe you wouldn't."

"Sasha, honey," Regan said, "you're pinching."

Sasha slipped around to glare at Dennis. "He called me a cunning little beast."

Dennis's mouth dropped open. "Hey, that was weeks ago."

Regan flexed one of the ankles that was tightly strapped into a high-heeled sandal and sighed.

She caught a sympathetic grin from Matt. "Do you know what *cunning* means, Sasha?" he asked.

"It means sneaky, like a fox."

"Yes, but it can also mean *pretty* or *cute*."

"Really?" Sasha looked at Regan for confirmation.

"He's right."

Sasha turned to Dennis.

"Exactly what I meant," he said with a charming grin. "Cunning little beaut. You heard me wrong."

Sasha didn't look convinced. "Is supper ready?"

"Let's just go see, shall we?" Regan said with relief as she escaped to the kitchen. She had barely reached it, though, when Dennis pushed his way in after her. The caterers exchanged a glance.

"Say, Regan," Dennis said. "What's the idea of inviting Olin anyway?" He ignored the other two women. "Not trying to make me jealous, are you?"

Even he could hardly mistake her amazed expression. "I'm busy, Dennis."

"Don't be that way," he said. "I didn't say I was mad about it, did I? Invite anybody you like."

"Thank you," she replied. "I don't recall asking for your permission."

He was surprised and annoyed, but managed to smooth the twist of his lips into a placating grin. "Okay, okay," he said, backing out. "I'll talk to you later when you're not so tense."

"Sorry about that," Regan said to the caterers. Dennis had never acknowledged their existence.

Regan began to wish that she had done the cooking herself before the meal was long underway. Agatha was critical of everything, and the younger caterer, who was serving, got paler and clumsier with each course. Dennis flirted determinedly with Diane, who just as determinedly ignored him. Luke and Matt both ate silently and answered in monosyllables when addressed. The guest of honor seemed preoccupied.

During the salad course, Sasha apparently decided that the conversation had languished long enough. "When I came from the hospital," she announced to the table at large, "we ate dandelion flowers." Everyone turned toward her with relief.

"You did?" Diane said with a questioning glance at Regan.

"Yes," Regan supplied. "Batter fried. Not very nutritious cooked that way, but they do taste good."

Sasha seemed pleased to be the center of attention. "I saw a mantis eating a grasshopper," she continued. "It crunched. Like this." She bit down on a crouton. The caterer turned green, and Diane quietly laid down her salad fork. "I watched to make sure it didn't eat any good bugs," Sasha concluded virtuously.

"There are good bugs?" That was Gina.

"Oh, yes," Regan said quickly. "The ones that are not vegetarian, actually. Because they eat the ones that are. Uh, Sasha, maybe we shouldn't talk about bugs at the table." Agatha was regarding her salad as if she expected something to crawl out of it.

"Here's your tea," the caterer said to Diane, reaching around her to pour.

"We made noor tea," Sasha announced.

"Really?" Diane said. "I don't believe I've heard of that one. What kind of herb is noor?"

Regan noticed that Matt Olin was grinning. He at least seemed to know what was coming.

"Noor," Sasha insisted, giving Diane a scornful look. "Out of cows."

"Well, actually," Regan said apologetically, "it was out of horses. She's talking about manure tea. We use it as a fertilizer."

Diane, who had picked up her teacup, set it carefully back down again.

"You suspend it in a loosely woven cloth inside a barrel of water and let it, er . . . brew. Then you water the plants with it. If you use composted manure, it doesn't smell too bad."

"Fish smells," Sasha said with simple conviction.

"Fish emulsion," Regan interpreted. "Yes, that does smell. Speaking of tea—"

"How do they make fish emulsion?" Matt asked in a deceptively innocent tone.

Regan barely refrained from glaring at him. "I wouldn't know—exactly. It's sludgy and often mixed with kelp. I suppose they somehow liquefy . . ." She faltered.

"Probably heads and tails," her father supplied, becoming interested in the conversation. "Whatever is left over from fillets."

Sasha giggled. "They squish the eyes."

Even Agatha was beginning to look a bit pale about the gills. "Organic gardening is organic," Regan said. "What can I say?"

"But you'll hear it from the customers if they smell anything rank," Caroline contributed. "I'm convinced that most of them haven't the foggiest idea what organic means."

"They're probably better off," Agatha said with a shudder. "If we might change the subject before we all get nauseous . . ."

The conversation turned into safer channels. Sasha lost interest and began to nod shortly after the main course.

Diane said to Alden Culver, "How are you coming with Rosemary's journals?"

Regan felt a sudden tension descend. Looking around at faces that were politely expectant or frankly indifferent, she told herself that she was imagining things.

She realized that she had missed her father's answer to Diane's question. She tuned back in to hear him say, "Surprises? Yes, there were surprises. One, anyway."

He didn't look at anyone as he spoke, and further questions were forestalled by the caterer bringing in the trifle, aglow with candles.

Later, while Diane carried a coffee tray into the living room, Regan carried a sleepy Sasha upstairs. By the time the child was tucked in her own bed in Regan's room, she was wide awake again and demanding a story. "Okay," Regan said, sitting down on the edge of the bed. "How about Uncle Aldy's story about the pig and the pelican?" Sasha shook her head. "Well, my mother had one about the flower children who—" Sasha shook her head again in the same implacably negative motion.

"Tell me one of yours."

"Mine? Well, I don't really have any. I'm not very good at stories. How about *The Velveteen Rabbit*? You always like that one."

Sasha's arms were crossed imperiously. "Make one up," she said.

Regan shrugged and plunged. "Once there was little girl who hated ice cream . . ."

By the time Regan returned downstairs, the caterers had packed up and gone. In the living room Caroline was chatting with Gina. Luke and his father were arguing in low tones. Dennis was still pestering Diane, who was still not listening. Alden Culver and Matt were both missing.

Regan decided to slip along to the greenhouse for a moment to see the night-blooming cereus. On the terrace, she paused to lean against the stone balustrade and looked down over the gardens. In a few days, the night air would be thickly sweet with the sensual scent of roses.

Now though, it was clean and fresh with only a hint of spice. Or maybe she was just smelling her own lavender perfume. The old maid's fragrance.

She had been surprised by her own balking at Sasha's request for an original story. *Probably because children are so honest. If Sasha didn't like the story, she wouldn't bother to pretend otherwise. Somewhere along the way, I've become frightened of honesty.*

Regan remembered another incident, just after the child had arrived. "I'll show you my mother's garden," Regan had said.

Sasha had looked bewildered. She seemed to be watching for something—or someone. "Where is she?" the little girl had blurted finally. And, at Regan's puzzled look, "Your mother. Where is she?"

"Oh, she isn't here," Regan had replied quickly. "She died—years and years ago."

That had earned her a scornful look. "Then how can it be her garden?"

How indeed?

"Tired?" Her father came quietly up the far steps from the garden and stood beside her. There was a humorous note to the query, as if he knew that she was experiencing one of what Rosemary used to indulgently call "Regan's antisocial spells."

"Mmm," Regan replied noncommittally, and added, "I was thinking how English manor all of this looks. We could be in an Agatha Christie novel."

"Yes. You like mystery, don't you?" he said.

"Yes," she responded, "but only if there is an answer. Maybe that's why they call those books cozy, because there is always an answer. Is something wrong, Daddy? Why is Matt here?"

He ignored the question. "I'm an old man," he said, "and I'm beginning to think that I failed some people. I was never there for Agatha and Gina, you know." He raised a hand to her protest. "I didn't get along with their mother, so I stayed away as much as I could. Being a doctor, I always had good excuses. I thought at the time that they didn't really need me. Diane too. She never knew her father; she should have at least had a grandfather."

It was getting dark. Regan watched the shadows creep out from the rose garden walls and said, "Diane is pretty self-sufficient."

"I suppose she's had to be. Don't make the mistake that I did, Regan. When I'm gone, they're all you'll have."

"I don't need many people," Regan said. "You know that. I'll survive."

"Yes," he said. "I know. You have your plants and your animals. They are safer. You almost always know what they'll do. You can trust them."

It should have been comforting, but it sounded like a reproof. "I've tried, Daddy."

"I know," he said again. "But I do want you to do better than just surviving. It's a little late for fixing things now, isn't it? Ten years too late. Maybe sometimes there aren't any correct answers. Your mother was a merciful woman, but sometimes mercy isn't merciful."

Regan looked at him blankly. "What are you talking about?"

"Later," he said. "I haven't decided whether I should tell you yet. Whether I should tell anybody."

■ ■ ■

Regan had been talking for a long time in the same quiet tone. Matt had finished jotting down the phrase about mercy not being merciful when she stopped and looked at him. "You know the next part," she said. "Shall I go over it?"

"No," he answered. "I remember."

Alden Culver had suggested that Matt take a stroll around the gardens. It had been too dark to see much, but as Matt approached the terrace, he heard the voices of the doctor and his daughter, then silence. Thinking that they both had gone inside, he came quickly up the steps and collided with someone hurrying the other way.

He caught at the person's arms and heard Regan say, "Sorry!" breathlessly. "Is that you, Matt? I was going down to the greenhouse for a minute. Do you want to come?"

Matt wanted nothing more than to be out of this house and away from these people altogether, but he found himself saying "Sure" and trying not to tread on her heels in the dark.

As she entered the glassed-in octagonal enclosure, she

flicked on an overhead light. The greenhouse was actually what the English would call a conservatory. All white wrought-iron and glass, it described an arc on its free side and was a jungle of tropical plants and wicker furniture. The overhead glass had been whitewashed recently to screen out some of the summer heat. An opening in the wall of plants to the west led to a studio. Matt could dimly see a computer and drawing tables.

Regan proceeded to the center of the room and sat down beside a table that supported a gangly cactus. The cactus, in turn, supported a huge exotic white flower. Matt stood by the terrace door and watched her.

"Night-blooming cereus," she said. "Pretty, isn't it?"

"Quite." He thought that there must be a door somewhere leading into the rear of the house—perhaps from the studio. But, circled by lush greenery with only the hum of the light to break the awkward silence, they seemed quite separated from the party.

Regan looked nervously sidelong at him. She knew, he thought, that she should ask him to sit down but didn't really want him to stay.

Enough already of tugging at the forelock and "yes, milady, no milady!"

"You didn't know that I was coming tonight, did you?" he demanded.

"No," she said. "But it didn't really matter. Daddy often forgets to tell me his plans."

"And did he forget to mention *why* he invited me?"

"He said we would talk about it later. Is it important?"

"He wouldn't tell me," Matt said. "He said that he'd decided it wasn't a police matter after all, but something he'd have to take care of himself."

"Oh." She seemed bewildered by the edge to his voice and drew away, half of her averted face in shadow. "I'm sorry that he got you out here for nothing."

The flower had a sweet tropical scent. He hadn't noticed it when they first came in, but now it hung heavy in the air around him, cloying, infuriating. *What's wrong with you, Olin? She's trying to be nice to you.*

But his reasonable voice was swamped, drowned under a renewed rush of anger. And she had to work very hard at it, didn't she? He didn't belong here. The harder she tried to cover that up, the more obvious it was. The out-and-out snobs were easier to take. *Get back to your own side of the tracks, Matt. The air up here is too thin and this*—his gaze raked her remote features—*is one exotic that's way too expensive for the likes of you.*

"Well," he said in a tightly controlled tone, "I'll be going then. See you around."

"Good-bye."

Her look then had been perplexed. Now it was just stoic.

In the clinical atmosphere of the police station, it was hard to recapture the anger he had felt. It seemed ridiculous— childish, in fact. "Go on from there," he said.

She nodded.

■　■　■

She was surprised by his attitude, but too tired to worry about it much. *Everybody is mad at me, even the ones who hardly know me.*

She stroked the satiny curve of the flower. It was peaceful there, with the faint buzz of the light the only sound.

She remembered the first time she'd seen a cereus blossom. She'd been five or six at the time. Her mother had got her out of bed in the dead of night and carried her downstairs to the greenhouse. "It won't last till morning," Rosemary had said. "And you have to catch beauty on its own time."

Regan had gaped in amazement at what seemed an exorbitant flower. "It's so pretty," she had whispered. "It hurts my heart."

Her mother had hugged her in complete understanding. "There's always a little bit of pain in all perfect joy," Rosemary had agreed. "Because we know it can't last. But it's worth it. Always remember that, dear. Flowers and love require a lot of effort. And they can both hurt you sometimes." She had gone silent for a moment then. Looking back on it, Regan wondered if Rosemary had been thinking of all the futile attempts she'd made to be accepted by her husband's family, all the strains of adapting to another social class. "But it's worth it," she had concluded fiercely, squeezing her daughter tight. "It's *worth* it."

Where did we go wrong? Regan crossed her arms on the table and pillowed her head on them. *We tried not to bother anyone. Why do they all dislike me so much?*

They'd tried to hold themselves aloof from Rosemary too. But they hadn't quite been able to. Rosemary had drawn people like butterflies to nectar.

Though Regan had inherited her mother's dark hair and eyes, she knew that her personality was more like her father's. Despite all his careless charities, Alden Culver was a private person.

He wouldn't speak until he was ready to.

She remembered now his evasiveness that morning. He had said, "It's waited for ten years after all." What had waited for ten years? And why should it be so important?

There was only one day ten years ago that she remembered at all clearly, but she could recreate that one with excruciating vividness, because of what had happened late in the afternoon.

She closed her eyes. The sound of the light was like the whir of a film projector. The picture began to run, first jerkily, then smoothing out: a veil of shadowy leaves, the arbor, then the leaves fading out of focus as her mind's eye centered on the terrace, which was as sunnily lit as any stage.

CHAPTER 4

A document in madness, thoughts and remembrance fitted.

Regan had slipped out to the arbor that day to read, taking pillows with her. It was too fine a day to be inside. Her father was lunching in the city with a publisher. Her mother was addressing a garden club somewhere and would grocery shop for their houseguests on the way home.

Regan had come down with the flu during finals week, and everything had seemed more difficult than it should have. But now college—graduation—was done. A few weeks of relaxing—reading, walking, driving around the back roads— had restored her to health, and there was everything to look forward to. Not only the upcoming trip to Europe, but, afterward, a career of doing what she loved best. Rosemary, too, was in an ebullient mood, singing to herself and surreptitiously winking at Regan whenever Agatha came up with one of her zingers.

Regan plucked a rose on her way to the arbor. Turning the stem in her fingers, she regarded it with wonder.

It was the ancient "Rosa Mundi" with its mutant striping.

It looked unlikely somehow. *"A flower is a vision because it isn't only a vision, because it isn't a dream." That's what Chesterton said. If we weren't so accustomed to things, we might realize how unlikely they are, how close we come to heaven without realizing it, how this is Eden still, if we could see it.*

She tucked the flower behind her ear and settled back against the cushions and into her book.

The story she was reading was an old one in a collection of other old ones. Regan was unimpressed by modern authors; she tended to prefer those of the twenties and thirties—or even earlier. Her father often asserted that modern literature catered to seared palates, that it depended on sex and sensationalism so much because modern readers could taste nothing else.

Regan preferred the understated style of bygone times—the expertise that could create a sense of creeping horror without mentioning bloodshed or sensuality without explicit sexual details.

This short story was called "The Library Window," by someone who signed herself only as Mrs. Oliphant. It was about a nervy, imaginative girl—not unlike Regan—who was spending a summer with her aunt in Scotland. The girl, apparently recovering from some ailment, spent the long summer days reading and dreaming in her aunt's window seat. And debating what her aunt's elderly friends debated in a friendly way among themselves, whether the end window in a row of library windows opposite was real or simply painted. Eventually the girl was able to see furniture at a certain time late in the evening in the room beyond that window.

The story was unexpectedly absorbing, and Regan surfaced from it abruptly, as confused as if roused from heavy slumber, by the sound of voices on the terrace. She looked through the veil of leaves beside her with the same vagueness that the girl in the story afforded to the aunt's visitors.

Agatha and Diane. They did not see her. The arbor was heavily draped with rose canes and honeysuckle vines and afforded only a few small peepholes.

"And what is wrong with Strathmore, might I ask?" Agatha was saying. "It's a very exclusive school; you're lucky to get on there."

"Nothing is wrong with it, Mother." Diane sounded tired of the subject. She stood with her palms flat on top of the terrace wall and her back to her mother, looking down at the garden. "Except that the salaries seem aimed at keeping the staff in their proper places—several steps below the students."

"What did you expect? There are more teachers than positions these days; they can afford to be choosy. You're lucky to have got on anywhere."

"Thank you for that vote of confidence." Diane leaned on her elbows in a bent-over position that looked extremely awkward, as if to get as far away from Agatha as possible.

"What do you want from me?" Agatha's voice rose querulously. "Under the circumstances, you can't expect me to pay for graduate school."

"I don't expect anything from you, Mother." Diane's voice had grown, if possible, wearier. There could be more than one interpretation to that, which Agatha realized.

"Oh?" she shrilled. "Maybe you'd prefer to have had a different mother. Rosemary, perhaps? You seem to get along fine with her!"

"Please, don't start," Diane said.

"Then you could live here, quite spoiled, like Regan,"

Agatha plunged on, heedless. "That would be much more to your liking, wouldn't it?"

Diane didn't answer.

Agatha wheeled away. "Sorry you had to get stuck with me!" Her voice quavered. Regan was surprised; she had never seen Agatha close to tears before.

"Mother," Diane said, pushing up, "I didn't . . ." but Agatha had already gone back into the house. After hesitating and debating whether to follow her, Diane shrugged and dropped into a wicker chaise lounge. She shut her eyes and turned her face to the sun, running her fingers through a pot of thyme beside her.

Regan had begun to submerge herself in the story again when a male voice jerked her reluctant attention back to the terrace.

It was Luke. He had come quietly out to stand, looking down at Diane. He said without preamble, "If you want to go on to graduate school, I'll pay for it. I've decided against law school myself, but—"

He didn't get to finish. Diane swung her feet to the stones on the other side of the chair, got up, and went inside without saying a word.

Regan frowned. Luke and Diane had always been friends. They hadn't dated precisely, but they'd often been together in high school. That had frustrated the other girls, who couldn't determine whether Luke was taken or not. There had been some snide remarks about "kissing cousins," though the two were related only by marriage.

What could have occurred that Agatha must punish her daughter by refusing to pay for her education, that Luke should give up law school? If it were any other couple, Regan could have come up with a worst-case scenario, but Luke and Diane were both mature, controlled sorts, not the types to get pregnant, for example, unless they intended it. And even that wouldn't have been disastrous. There was no reason they couldn't marry. Luke had money, inherited from his mother.

With a little uneasiness prickling at the edges of her own security, Regan decided that the real-life drama was too jerky and incomprehensible. The story she was reading was better, and she had just gotten to the place where the girl could see a man sitting, writing, behind the disputed window.

But the real-life drama was going to run to more than a couple of acts. For no sooner had Diane disappeared than Luke's father, Reid, popped out, as if on cue, to replace her. He must have just arrived from the city. "What's this Gina tells me about you not going to law school?" he demanded.

Luke was still standing, hands in pockets, looking down at the now-empty chaise. "I'm not going to law school," he said, without turning. "What's so hard to understand about that?"

"But why?" Reid sounded more bewildered than angry.

"Because I don't want to."

"But that's not a reason!"

Luke lifted an eyebrow. "It isn't? I'd say it was a pretty good one myself. I've decided I don't want to stay for this party either. Give Rosemary my regrets, won't you?"

Reid followed him back through the french doors into the house, expostulating, "But what are you going to do? You can't just do nothing!"

Luke's lazy tones floated back, "But I can. Just watch me!"

Regan watched the open doors for a few moments to make sure the men weren't coming back. She wasn't sorry to see Luke go. She found that unshakable self-possession of his incomprehensible. She couldn't really call it vanity. Vain people were more insecure. If necessary, Luke would use his good looks with the same matter-of-factness that he used any other of his assets; otherwise, she doubted that he gave them much thought. No, Luke wasn't vain, but if pride was a refusal to be dependent, then he was definitely proud and had been since his early teens. She dreaded the inevitable fall and hoped that she wouldn't be around when it happened. She found anyone's humiliation difficult to endure.

She dropped her gaze to her book and ran her finger down the page.

"What are you doing here?"

Regan jumped. It was Agatha's voice, and Regan thought for a confused instant that it was directed at her.

But when she looked wildly around, she saw Caroline standing on the terrace. Agatha was on the balcony above her—the one from Diane's room. Diane herself came out to stand behind her mother.

"You've got your nerve, just walking in here like this!"

Caroline looked square and cool and sensible. "I didn't," she responded calmly. "Luke let me in on his way out. Is Rosemary here?"

"No, she's not, and it's just as well. I know your type. You're not really fond of her. You're using her for her money. We'd see how quickly your attitude would change if you found out you weren't getting any more."

Caroline looked bewildered at Agatha's emotional outburst. Regan understood it a little better. Those histrionics weren't really directed at Caroline, but at someone else.

Diane, however, didn't seem to realize that she was the target. "I'm sorry, Miss Stanton," she said. "Mother's not herself this afternoon."

Ha! Regan thought.

"Rosemary has gone grocery shopping," Diane continued. "May I take a message? I think Regan's around somewhere."

"Never mind," Caroline said. "I was going to drop something off for Rosemary, but I'll wait till Monday. I wanted to talk to her about it anyway. Good-bye." She nodded at Reid and Gina, who had come out behind her, and went back into the house.

Reid barely waited until she was gone. "Does anybody know anything about that woman?" he asked. "Why is Alden financing an herb farm for her?"

"She's a friend of Rosemary's. Rosemary is going to help her with it." That was Diane.

"Caroline's brother was that veterinarian," Gina inserted helpfully. "The one down by the feed mill that nobody ever went to because everybody likes Dr. Pauli. He died. The brother did, I mean. And she'd helped him out there, but obviously she couldn't anymore, so—"

"So Rosemary felt sorry for her, I suppose," Reid finished dryly. "Not much to base a business on, is it? How much does this woman know about plants?"

"Rosemary's name will carry her," Diane said. "Rosemary is well known in certain circles."

"Yes," Gina agreed, strolling to the terrace wall to look approvingly down over the gardens, "It will probably be very successful. Things always work out for Rosemary." At the sudden silence of the others, she looked back to add, "Don't they?

I mean, her cancer went away and she married Daddy, and now she's become almost as famous as he is."

Agatha turned and went back into Diane's room. "Agatha never liked her," Gina continued. "That's only natural, I expect. But Rosemary is a nice person. You've got to admit that." It wasn't clear to whom she was speaking. Diane opened her mouth as if to say something, changed her mind, and followed her mother into the bedroom.

"She's also probably going to cop the lot," Reid said. "Her and Regan. Your father's not a young man anymore, you know."

"That won't matter, will it?" Gina hopped up on the wall and sat, swinging her legs like a child. "We have plenty, and Agatha's got her shop."

"I hate to see so much going to some complete stranger like that Stanton woman," Reid grumbled.

"You would be a stranger if you hadn't married me," Gina said. "Of course, you were Agatha's boyfriend before, but that didn't exactly give you any family status."

Reid looked at her sharply, but there was no malice in Gina's voice. "What did Luke say?" she asked. "About law school?"

"Just what he usually says. Nothing." Reid paced moodily. "There was some talk after that roommate of his died. About drugs."

"Pooh," Gina said. "Luke isn't on anything."

"Not about him being a user. Dealing."

"It doesn't sound likely to me," Gina said. "Why would he have to? He's got money."

"That's his problem, if you ask me." Reid kicked at a

flowerpot. "If Anne hadn't left him a small fortune, he wouldn't be able to thumb his nose at the world."

"At you, you mean," Gina said. "You can't blame him, can you, darling? You weren't around much while he was growing up."

Reid gave her a hard look. "C'mon, let's go somewhere. I'm not sitting around here all afternoon."

Gina hopped down. "That was always the problem, you know, that you can't just sit."

He laughed. "Like Regan, you mean. There's one kid who does enough sitting for ten people. Agatha is right; she is spoiled."

"Just sitting is not that easy," Gina said. "You're too twitchy for it. Regan is an intelligent girl. She has to have time to think. It's what intelligent people do."

"Aha," Reid said. "So that's why you sit in front of the tube all day. You're thinking."

"No." Gina's sunny expression hadn't altered. "What I like about TV is that you don't have to think."

They all left then, and Regan was allowed to slip peacefully beneath the surface of reality again. Down—far down—this time into another country and time, and she only floated leisurely up again when the words ran out.

There had been, to the fictional girl's anguished bewilderment, no window after all—or only a bricked-over one. And the question of what she had discerned was left up to the reader's imagination.

There was the quite real possibility that dreamy adolescent girls, after all, will see what they want to see. The author never really suggested that, except in the knowing looks of the aunt's elderly friends, but then old-time authors could rely a little more on their readers' perception.

It was not a depressing story so much as a wistful one. And very good, Regan thought, stretching blissfully, for a quiet June afternoon when a lifetime of possibilities—like months of summer—stretched ahead.

She meandered out of the arbor toward another favorite seat. It was an indentation carved into the bank that went down from the terrace, and was turfed, as in the Middle Ages, with chamomile. Regan probed the herb gently with her toes to make sure that there were no bees in the small white blossoms before she sat down.

She nestled into the applelike scent and let the warmth of the sun soak into her. Around four, she went through the open french doors into the empty house to find a basket and scissors. Back in the garden, she sang softly to herself. She had filled her basket with flowers and was just strolling back up the path toward the terrace, humming, when the doorbell rang. She scrambled up the steps and ran across the living room . . .

Looking back on it later, that haste of hers was something horrible. Better that she had loitered on the way or not heard the bell at all so that she might have had at least a few more moments of innocent joy. But the tape rolled relentlessly on to the opening of the front door and Matt Olin's strained white face.

In the conservatory, the girl in the black evening dress stirred slightly but did not lift her head. Instead, she speeded up the tape as she had learned to do, fast-forwarding through what followed.

Matt took the flower basket from her unresisting fingers, led her to a seat, and called to the unresponsive house, "Is anybody else here?"

But there hadn't been. Regan sat quite still on the sofa with her hands clasped while he discovered that emptiness. Finally, not wanting to leave her alone, he took her with him in the patrol car. There were things he had to do, witnesses to interview. It was, she realized afterward, his first accident; it was a nasty one to be the first.

There was the old man at the corner. He came to the passenger door of the cruiser to peer in at her, to say in a cracking voice. "She waved to me, Miss Culver. She waved to me, and then she didn't look before she pulled out. If only I hadn't been out here, maybe she would have remembered to look."

"No," Regan said. "It wasn't your fault. She does—did it all the time. She never remembered. She was always lucky before; she said she must have a special angel."

Regan's voice stopped on her, and Matt tried to ease the old man away. "She was happy, miss," the man persisted. "Just remember that. She was singing."

They drove on to the other places Matt had to go. And everywhere people looked in at her and patted her and said awkward, ineffectual things. Nowhere did they find her relatives, so finally they drove back to the house to discover the others had returned in her absence. They were all standing by their cars out front and looked curiously around as the cruiser drove up.

Her father was not there even then. It was Gina who, tears

running down her chubby cheeks, took Regan from Matt with an "I think she'll probably want to be alone" and led her upstairs.

"I'm so sorry," Gina said, stumbling on the steps. "I don't believe this. It's madness. It just isn't possible. She was so alive."

She kept up that running commentary on into Regan's bedroom. "Here we are then. Sit down." Gina got awkwardly down on the floor in her tight skirt to wrest off Regan's shoes. "I don't know how we're going to tell Daddy. This will kill him. It really will. All right, dear. Lie down. Lie down. You should cry. It doesn't take away the pain, but it does take away the lump in your throat. You're so young to have to go through this."

Gina went on like that for much of the week that followed, leading Regan from one place to another, making her bathe and dress and eat. But then letting her alone. And sometimes at night, Regan's father came in and sat beside her bed and held her hand as he had done when she was sick as a child.

He did not say much. There was not much that either of them were capable of saying at the time. The only thing she could say to God was an endless and unanswered *Why?*

At the funeral home, Gina seated Regan beside Diane on an overstuffed couch with a shiny chintz surface. Regan would always recall the horridness of its striped pattern. "I'll talk to them," Gina said. "I can always talk. This is a barbaric custom. I've always thought so. Making all the mourners stand here to be gaped at and patted. If you want to leave, just tell Diane, and she'll take you home."

Regan sat stiffly through it all, enduring having her hand

squeezed and saying over and over, "Thank you." She knew that people were trying to be kind, to help. Though she could not manage to return their embraces more than perfunctorily, she also felt unable to leave.

Every now and then, Gina scurried to Regan's side with a glass of water, smoothed her hair into place, and replaced the crumpled tissue in her clenched fist with a fresh one. Not that she used them. She didn't cry—then.

Even Agatha was subdued, as if the sudden drastic removal of her adversary had left her bereft. And Caroline Stanton looked smaller somehow, shrunken and bewildered. "We'll go on with it, Regan, you and me," she said. "I don't know how, but we will."

Eventually her father sent the others away. And one July afternoon Regan walked away from the house. She walked for hours, but ended up sitting on the hillside of an abandoned farm and looking down on Hayden as dusk settled and lights winked on. A police car glided to the berm of the road below her and Matt Olin got out, big in the twilight. "Regan, your father's getting worried."

"Did he send you to bring me back?"

"No." He climbed the bank, dropping casually down beside her. "He wanted me to make sure that you are all right. Peaceful up here, isn't it?"

Fireflies glinted over the dampening grass.

"She wouldn't have wanted this from you, you know," he said, as if continuing some earlier conversation. "She was so proud of you. Remember the night we graduated?"

"Yes." She had been valedictorian and he salutatorian of their high school class. They were both to give speeches, and she was terrified. It didn't help that she had to wait backstage with Matt, the football star she scarcely knew. But he had talked to her in the same slow, quiet way he was doing now. "Hey," he had said, "at least you don't have to worry that you'll start stuttering partway through."

"It's all those faces," she had said. The senior class would occupy the first row in the auditorium; all of her classmates would stare expectantly up at her.

"I'm not intimidating, am I? I'll be right there in the middle after I finish. Just look at me and you'll be fine." He had lowered his voice to a theatrical growl. "It's payback time! These are the ones who teased us when we were kids. Now we're up here and they're not. Are we going to let them ruin that for us? Revenge has a steadying effect."

She had laughed and relaxed. And she had delivered her speech to Matt Olin, who grinned in all the right places and nodded seriously in others.

"I never thanked you," she said now.

"That's okay. I should thank you. I was too busy worrying about you to be nervous myself. Remember how your mother looked that night? McNeil sat next to her, and he says she was literally bobbing in her seat the whole time. She could hardly contain herself. That woman loved you so much. She still does."

"I don't know why." Regan's voice was hoarse. "I'm not thinking of anybody else. I'm worrying Daddy."

"I never heard that love was something you had to earn."

Remembering that his mother had *not* been at graduation, she looked at him in the darkness.

"Don't bottle it up," he said. "Talk about her. People will

try to avoid the subject. Don't let them. Dodging the truth never helps. Look in her face. Ask her what she wants you to do now."

Regan gave a small giggle. "I know what she would say. Weed the garden already! It's such a little thing. I wanted to do big things for her. I know she must have been disappointed sometimes. I was insecure and shy and not like her at all. I was never going to be able to reach out to people like she did. But I always hoped that maybe I could find something that might be almost as good. But there wasn't enough time!" Her voice had been shaking more and more. It cracked there, and her tears welled up through her frustration.

He put his arms around her then, and she cried on his broad, safe shoulder until all the tightness was out of her throat and stomach.

It was quite dark when he finally helped her down the dew-slick bank and onto the front seat of the patrol car. He handed her a tissue, and they drove in silence until he pulled into her driveway.

"I'm sorry," she said then, twisting the tissue embarrassedly in her fingers.

He touched her shoulder. "Nothing to be sorry about. Your mother didn't need the big things to be proud of you. I saw her face that night. I know."

She arose early the next morning. When her father came down he found her kneeling among the flowers in a weeding frenzy.

The tape in her mind rustled to an end. The light crackled above her; it was a crotchety light. Her shoulders felt stiff. She sat up, the white flower brushing her cheek, to look around in a dazed sort of way. She wondered how late it was. Out here, it was impossible to tell.

They were kind to me back then—Gina, Diane, and the others. I was ungrateful, sunk in my own selfish grief. It's no wonder they don't like me.

I thought you were punishing me because I was too happy. I realize that now. Because I sat snugly apart in my flowery bower that afternoon, watching but not comprehending the misery of others. Mother and I were too happy, and we were punished. I never had the courage to speak that, but I acted on it. I decided it was not wise, not safe, to be too happy. The plunge from that height is shattering.

She had settled for what Louis Evely called "lonely comfort" and muted her emotions. She hadn't even gotten really angry in years. She had been contented enough. Until tonight.

She wasn't sure what caused her restlessness now. Perhaps it was the sudden grab of a man's hands at her arms when she thought she was alone, the scorn with which he had regarded her in her Edenic bower of plants.

Matt Olin had changed from the big kind kid he had been. This time his touch had roused quite different sensations in her. So all of this agitation probably had a very obvious reason. It would, she hoped, prove as ephemeral as the mysterious man in the story, who had only acknowledged the girl's presence once, waved, and was gone.

Perhaps that had been the attraction for the girl, that the man was almost always turned away from her, constantly at that little distance.

A raw March wind had seemed to blow briefly through Regan's sheltered world. Strange how spring winds were so much sharper than any that winter managed.

It's probably a good thing that I'm not likely to see him again, except in our old roles of the most casual acquaintances.

"Lucky for you, Matt Olin," she said softly aloud into the constantly warm, still air of the conservatory. "Lucky for you."

CHAPTER 5

There's fennel for you . . .

"What's lucky for him?"

Luke stood in the doorway to the studio just out of the shadow. It was impossible to tell how long he'd been there. From a couple of steps back, he could have watched her conversation with Matt without being seen. Not that he would have heard anything that mattered. She had, she realized, quite forgotten to tell the police chief about the phone call she'd overheard.

Apparently Luke didn't expect an answer. "I'm only going to warn you once," he said, with both hands in his pockets in that casual way he had. "I wouldn't bother except I know how much Alden dotes on you, and I don't think he deserves to be disillusioned. You have no idea what you're getting into. Clean up your act, Regan, or be prepared to face the consequences."

He turned and was gone.

Regan blinked. Could she have fallen asleep and dreamed that? It made no sense at all. A straight-out threat she could understand, but he seemed to imply that she was in the wrong. Of course a really convoluted criminal mind might see any association with the police as betrayal. But he couldn't imagine that Alden Culver would view it that way.

She shook her head and decided to go around by the terrace just in case he was still lurking in the studio somewhere.

When Regan came back into the living room, it was empty. A chill crawled up her back. She lifted her gaze to the mirror over the fireplace. She looked very small in the large room.

She always got overly imaginative when she was exhausted. She had a peculiar, lightheaded sensation of being on the verge of tears.

Gina came into the room and said, "Oh, there you are."

"Where is everybody?" Regan asked, surprised at the steadiness of her own voice.

Gina considered. "Here and there. Agatha is with Father in the study. Diane had a headache and went upstairs. Reid is arguing with Luke somewhere. Dennis left. I'm afraid, you know, that he thought you'd gone off with Matt." Gina cocked her head to one side.

Regan ignored the implied question, so Gina continued. "Your friend Caroline stayed to say good-bye to you. She's gone up to use the bathroom. And I haven't seen Matt lately." Again there was a rising inflection at the end that suggested a question mark.

"He's gone," Regan said, making her tone neutral. "I'd better find Caroline." She went out into the hall. Caroline was standing at the bottom of the stairs, looking back over her shoulder as if listening to something from above.

"Is anything wrong?" Regan asked.

Caroline started, then moved her shoulders as if shrugging

off uneasiness. "Not really. Agatha has just pursued your father upstairs. You might want to go rescue him."

"My presence would probably make things worse," Regan replied. "I'm sorry this has been such a lousy party."

Caroline shrugged again and smiled. "I only have to endure them for one evening. None of them seem happy—or to like each other very much." She tucked her knitting bag neatly under her arm. "But it's probably just this house. Sometimes it gives me the creeps. I know you're fond of it, but it's too big and quiet. Give me a modern little bungalow any day. I had better be going."

"Come on out to the kitchen with me for a moment," Regan said. "I'll make Daddy some bedtime tea. Maybe Agatha will get the hint."

"Any hint less hefty than a sledgehammer is going to be lost on that woman," Caroline commented, but she followed Regan and stood just inside the swinging doors, watching.

Regan ran water into the teakettle. As she reached to switch on a burner, her gaze swept the rows of cooking herbs racked at the rear of a counter. "Perhaps I'm like fennel," she suggested. "They say, you know, that it inhibits the growth of other plants just by its presence."

Caroline's square, plain face looked skeptical. "The only way you're inhibiting them," she said, "is by preventing them from getting their hands on Alden Culver's money. And none of them particularly need it. That doesn't keep them from wanting it, though. You'll just have to get used to the fact that the favored ones are always resented. Look at Cinderella."

Unlocking the herb cabinet, Regan laughed. "I don't think I'm quite up to the Cinderella standard."

"You're not beautiful," Caroline agreed forthrightly, "but

you are striking. Both Dennis and Matt appear quite impressed. Although," she added, "being an heiress, you could do much better. That's the nice thing about money. It expands one's options."

Regan wondered if she was imagining a hint of envy there. Caroline had had to struggle for everything.

Fortunately, she had been befriended by Rosemary Culver, who had devised the plan to open an herb farm together. Alden Culver had, of course, provided a good percentage of the capital. Then, when things finally seemed to be going right for Caroline for a change, Rosemary had died. Since Alden had not been enthusiastic about the farm to begin with, it had taken much coaxing from Regan to prevent her father's prompt withdrawal from the venture altogether.

But now she was being proved right. The farm was beginning to prosper. And Caroline was certainly entitled to a little bitterness over Regan's own easy access to wealth. Only it wasn't that easy.

The favored ones were not, as a rule, carefree. As she scooped some of the bedtime mix into a tea ball, Regan thought of Joseph in the Old Testament. *Nothing comes free. One way or another, you pay.*

■ ■ ■

In the upstairs hallway, Diane loitered near Alden Culver's door. She looked sick; perhaps she really had a headache. When she saw Regan with the tray, Diane said, "The dutiful daughter. You have the wrong name, you know. You should really have been Cordelia. Though that wouldn't fit either, would it, since Cordelia got absolutely nothing in reward for that virtue. You, it seems, are going to bag the lot."

She spoke jerkily, almost absently, turning toward her own room. With her hand on the knob, she added, "Forget that. Sorry. I'm not myself tonight."

Regan stood quite still in the silent hallway after she had gone. Diane had always been polite before. But the apology this time had not been sincere. Dislike, anger, and something close to despair had been in her voice.

Although not an expert on literature, Regan knew that Diane had referred to Shakespeare's *King Lear*. The Regan in it had been one of the older, conniving daughters. Cordelia had been the good one, and in Regan's opinion, something of a bore.

No sounds came to her from behind any of the doors. Regan's hands trembled. She did not want to endure Agatha now and break that silence. She was briefly tempted to take the cup to her own room and drain it herself. Things wouldn't seem so bad after she had slept.

Instead, she rapped on the door. "I've brought your tea, Daddy."

They were sitting in armchairs in front of the cold fireplace. Seeing Regan, Agatha got up and left the room without a word. Her features looked pinched and sunken.

When Regan circled her father's wing chair to set the tray on a stand by his elbow, she was shocked at a closer glimpse of his face. He was *old*. Of course, she knew that her father was eighty-five, but knowing and realizing it were quite different.

In one sense, her father had always been old; he had been fifty-three when she was born. But he had carried those years so lightly; he had been a walking role model for the natural health methods he espoused. Tonight he looked his age. There was that same stubborn set to his mouth that she recognized, but his eyes and movements were strangely uncertain.

He sensed her concern and smiled feebly. "I don't know the answers anymore, Regan. Does that mean I'm getting senile?"

"Perhaps it means you're mellowing," she suggested, removing the saucer, beaded with condensation, and slipping it under the cup. "Like fine wine."

"Fine *old* wine," he said, taking the cup between his palms as if to warm them.

"It's been a long day," she said, perching on the arm of his chair. "All of us are feeling a bit antique tonight, I think. Daddy, do you notice anything wrong with Diane?"

He drank before replying. "Not only with Diane," he said finally. "There's tension all around, I think. Maybe we've been a little too removed from it all here. We haven't realized—"

"Leave them the money, Daddy," she said. "That's only fair. If I get the house, they should get the rest. I'll have what I make from my business."

He shook his head. "You've sacrificed a good part of your youth to staying with me—"

But Regan was shaking her head just as vehemently. "Here," she said, "is where I've always wanted to be. I haven't had to give up anything. I'm doing what I love. Don't start painting me as the poor deprived spinster. I don't fit."

Setting down the empty cup in its saucer, Alden Culver grinned. "Not with all the fellows hanging all over you," he agreed. "I'm afraid I've put you on the spot, Regan. Agatha is convinced that Matt is your boyfriend. And I didn't disillusion her. I don't want to have to explain yet why I invited him. I suppose he wasn't too happy about being dragged up here for nothing."

"He wasn't exactly brimming over with good will," Regan said. "But then carrying such a large chip on his shoulder must get tiring, don't you think?"

Some of the deep-graven lines in her father's face softened as he laughed. He cast her an oddly speculative look. "You could do worse, you know."

Regan stood and stretched. "Don't get your hopes up. He doesn't like me." She was about to add, "That seems to be a common attitude right now," but desisted. It would only worry him.

As she reached for the cup and saucer, her father said, "Leave that and go to bed. I'll bring it down in the morning. And I'll lock the door behind you. I have to think about some things, and I can't do that if Agatha comes back."

"All right," she said. "But don't think too long. You need your sleep too." On sudden impulse, she leaned to kiss him on the forehead. It was an unusual gesture for her; neither of them were demonstrative. "Happy birthday, Daddy. I love you more than I can say."

He caught her hand and held it for a moment against his cheek.

She started away, then turned to say with elaborate casualness. "Oh, your gift is behind the screen in the fireplace there."

He shot her a glance of mock reproof, stood, bent over to look, and froze in place. "A plant. It looks like . . ." He turned, a new animation wiping out the lines in his face. "Is it—"

"*Una de gato,*" she finished for him. "Cat's claw. You were so worried about the natural supply being wiped out that

Caroline and I decided to start cultivating it at Thyme Will Tell. The shipment just came in today. I asked her to smuggle one in for me in her knitting bag and sneak it up here when you weren't looking."

He lifted the pot out of its hiding place and turned it reverently in his hands to study the vine with its curling claws. "This could well be the most important anticancer herb yet. And it goes to show why protecting the Amazon forest is so essential—"

"You don't need to convince me." She was pleased to see that he no longer looked aged. "And we both know who's going to be in the thick of the research and preservation effort."

He grinned. "Eighty-five isn't old. Abraham didn't have his first child until he was eighty-six."

"And Sarah was probably still wowing pharaohs when she was that age." Regan sighed.

"I wish I could figure out why they lived so much longer back then," her father said. "Especially before the flood. You'll notice that the life span began to shrink drastically afterward."

He was drifting toward his bookshelves as he spoke, and Regan slipped out quietly, smiling.

She felt much better as she prepared for bed, tossing her dress across a chair, dragging a white cotton gown over her head, slipping, with a sigh of relief, between the lavender-scented sheets. She plummeted instantly into a dreamless sleep. There were no forebodings.

■　■　■

As Regan's narrative faltered to a stop, Matt asked brisk, bracing questions. "You only saw three other people besides your father after you made the tea—Caroline, Diane, and Agatha?"

"That's right."

"And none of them were ever close enough to you to put anything in the cup?"

"No. Caroline was standing over by the door the whole time I was making it. Agatha and Diane were at least two or three yards away. Besides, the cup was covered with the saucer when I saw them."

"Caroline couldn't have put something in the kettle instead?"

"Of course not!" It was the first trace of animation Regan had shown since the handcuff incident. "I told you, she was clear across the room. Besides, why should she? They might not have liked each other very well, but she could only lose by my father's death. He was one of the biggest investors in her farm."

"Yes, but you won't withdraw those investments, will you? And you are more amicably disposed toward her than your father was. She might have needed that."

"If you're implying," Regan said, "that she might have been misusing Daddy's money, you can put that thought right out of your head. Caroline is scrupulous about careful book-keeping and frequent audits."

Caroline had been, Matt recalled, just as vigorous in Regan's defense.

"I watched her make that tea," the herb farmer had stated flatly, sitting behind her bare desk in an office as square and practical as she was. "The whole process. She didn't add anything extra."

It did no good to point out that the something extra could have been added after Regan was out of Caroline's sight—or to the herb mixture itself hours, even days, before. Caroline's mouth set stubbornly. "She loved her father. Alden Culver was bullheaded and arrogant, but she worshiped the ground he walked on. It was one of those others. They're a nasty, vindictive bunch, and this is their way of getting rid of Regan."

"Why wouldn't they just have poisoned her?" Matt asked sensibly. "None of them gain much from Culver's death. Agatha and Gina and Diane each get twenty-five thousand dollars. That's chicken feed to people like them."

"If Regan is convicted, they'll get the rest," Caroline insisted. "There's some law that says you aren't allowed to profit from your crime. One of them put something in his glass at dinner that evening."

"The state police lab found aconite in the teacup dregs," Matt said.

"All right. So one of them went to his room after Regan left."

"He locked the door behind her. It was still locked in the morning. And she says that he drank all of the tea while she was there."

"And would she admit that," Caroline demanded triumphantly, "if she was guilty? Not on your life! I know. One of them put dried aconite in that herb mix while it was in the cupboard."

"Regan and her father had the only keys to that cupboard."

"Keys can be copied. The key to his door could have been copied for that matter. Or, more likely, he simply unlocked it for somebody. Your case is full of holes."

"Both of the keys are antiques. It wouldn't have been easy to have copies made. Regan herself would have had the best chance of putting aconite in that canister. We haven't got the analysis yet. But the expert we consulted thinks it unlikely that the toxin is in there. To be sure of killing someone, a heavily concentrated extract—a distillation—is needed. And any liquid mixed into a dry mix would be easy to see. It's more likely that the toxin was added directly to the water."

Caroline's eyes narrowed. "Well, it wasn't. And that's what I'll testify to. Regan was wearing a black evening gown, as you should recall, since you were ogling her pretty closely. And I doubt very much that it had pockets. Where did she conceal this poison, may I ask. Under her tongue?"

Matt kept his temper in check with difficulty. "She may not have gone directly to her father's room."

"But she did. She met Diane in the upstairs hall, remember? And Diane is not going to lie her pretty little head off for her dear auntie, believe me! I watched Regan up the stairs, and Diane watched her along the hall."

"Diane went into her own bedroom before Regan entered Culver's."

"You are determined to convict Regan, aren't you?" Caroline said. "I wonder why that is. You seemed pretty chummy with her at the party. Did she repulse your advances and hurt your pride maybe? Are you sure you're really objective enough to investigate this case, Mr. Olin?"

Matt moved with deliberate slowness, folding his notebook shut and tucking his pen into his pocket. "Thank you for your help, Miss Stanton. I understand your loyalty to Miss Culver, so I won't take offense at that."

Caroline was not pacified. "Get this!" she said, standing and leaning forward over the desk. "I'm where I am today because of Rosemary and Alden Culver. Regan was everything to them. You bring her to court, mister, and I'm going to tell her lawyer to ask why you were at that party—and why you had a private conversation with Alden outside. Nobody saw you leave. How do we know that the poison didn't get into that cup *after* it was in police hands?"

Steady, steady. Matt talked to his temper much as he might talk to a fractious horse.

She wasn't the only one who had brought up that point, although Agatha had approached it from a different angle.

"Because of your friendship with Regan, Mr. Olin," she had said coolly, "you will, of course, disqualify yourself from this case?"

"I am not," he had said truthfully, "particularly friendly with Miss Culver."

"No?" Agatha Creighton's impeccably coifed silvery head moved in a slow, hypnotic fashion from side to side. "I was on the point of convincing my father to change his will. She knew that, and that's why she killed him. Don't let that nicey-nice façade fool you. She was an unnatural, reclusive child, and she has always hated all of us."

Agatha leaned forward, speaking in the same well-articulated syllables. "You let her get away with my father's murder, Chief Olin, and you're done in this town. Whatever it takes, I'll have your badge, believe me."

Matt did.

Now, looking across at Regan, he wondered how this quiet, unobtrusive female could provoke so much rage, one way and another. From what he had seen, she never attempted any response to Agatha's attacks. Passive resistance it was called. Agatha could rant and rage against that wall of irreproachable meekness all she wanted; she would only make herself look bad. And Agatha was the type who wouldn't learn, who would continue to be bewildered and defeated by a foe who wouldn't fight.

After ten years of police work, Matt had developed an instinct for detecting guilt from innocence. But this time he couldn't even guess. It was often the quiet, private types who were psychotic. They also, he had heard, made the best saints.

"Tell me about finding your father's body."

■ ■ ■

When Regan had gone downstairs with Sasha at nine-thirty Saturday morning, she found everybody in the kitchen. Everybody. Including Caroline and Dennis. Caroline had stopped to drop off some of Rosemary's letters that Alden Culver had asked to see. She and Dennis were on their way to one of the big nurseries in Boston to pick up some tropicals that they couldn't grow themselves.

"I guess he must be thinking of publishing excerpts from her letters as well as from the journals," Caroline explained. "But I didn't have many." She produced a small bundle of envelopes from her bag. "But then, she wasn't away that often."

"Daddy should be down in a few minutes, if you can wait," Regan said. "I know he'll want to thank you." She was beginning to wonder if her father was looking for something more than publishable passages. What had he meant by that comment about its being ten years too late?

The others did not appear particularly interested. Somebody had found the instant coffee. Several of them were drinking it and loitering over their cups much longer than seemed necessary. Since it was the weekend, they had no place they had to be.

With the exception of Caroline and Dennis, most of them

lived in or near Boston. Agatha had her boutique there. Diane spent most of the year teaching at an exclusive girl's boarding school in Connecticut, but she usually stayed with her mother for a couple of months during the summer. Reid kept the family home in Hayden, though it was shut up for most of the fall and winter. It was being aired out now; Gina would move into it after this weekend and Reid would commute to and from the city. Luke was usually in New York, though he got around a lot. He could often be seen in tabloid photos, squiring some famous beauty in California. Regan wondered if he kept those famous beauties supplied with cocaine and, if so, what she could be expected to do about it.

"Shouldn't Father be down by now?" Agatha demanded, pushing her cup away.

Glancing at the clock, Regan saw that it was almost ten. That *was* late for Alden Culver, even on a weekend. He was usually up before Regan to take a stroll around the gardens or, if it was raining, putter about in his study before breakfast.

Sasha had finished her granola and gone out into the kitchen garden, where she was picking, shelling, and eating peas, watched by the curious cat. She seemed safe enough for the moment.

"I'll go see," Regan said. The study was empty, the gardens peaceful and deserted in the sunlight of a perfect June morning—an abandoned Eden. Regan felt uneasy. As she climbed the stairs, she was reminded of Caroline's comment the night before—too big and quiet. Gina had joined the others downstairs, so even the faint murmur of the television was absent this morning. The Saturday morning programs were mostly for children.

Regan was again reluctant to disturb the silence. She

knocked lightly, calling, "Daddy? Are you coming down? Caroline brought over the letters you wanted."

There was no reply. Perhaps he was in the shower with the water running. But she could usually hear the water. It roared out of the old pipes. She tilted her head toward the door and listened intently. Nothing. Or maybe . . . Strange how straining the hearing in a deep silence could produce an impression like a soft roar in the ears.

She raised her voice. "Daddy! Are you all right?" She grasped the knob and turned it, and it stopped hard. Locked, still locked. The roaring in her ears intensified.

She began to pound on the door with her fist. "Daddy! Answer me!"

"Regan, what's wrong?" She sagged against the door in relief before realizing that the answer came from the wrong direction. She turned her head to see the others at the head of the stairs. Luke was the one who had spoken.

"It's locked," she said, as if that explained everything. The roaring was returning like the breathy sound from a seashell. She stepped back. "Somebody open it. Please!"

Dennis came willingly enough to throw his shoulder against the panels—and to wince at the impact.

"You'd need a battering ram for these doors," Luke said. "Diane, get me a paper and a nail file. That always seemed to work in the old books. If the key was left in the lock, that is."

"Daddy said he was going to lock it after me," Regan said.

Luke gave her a sharp glance. "He didn't trust his dear family? Can't say I blame him. Don't panic yet. He's an old man; he might just be overly tired."

He's an old man. That was the part that Regan caught. *I*

didn't believe that until last night. But he is an old man, and old men . . .

Diane had come back with the requested items. Luke slid the paper under the door, knelt in front of the key hole, and probed with the nail file.

None of the others, watching, heard the key fall, but he said "It's gone" and started tugging the paper toward him. There wasn't room. They all seemed to see that at once, and to chorus it with pointing fingers. There was barely space for the paper under the door, none for a thick, heavy key. The paper jerked out empty.

Luke crumpled it and threw it to one side. "This house," he said, almost conversationally, "is too well made. Get out of the way."

They scurried to the side as he put his back to the opposite wall, pushed off, took a couple steps, and, balancing on one leg, kicked the door viciously just below the knob. It barely shuddered.

"There's the balcony," Diane said suddenly, turning toward her own room. "All along that side. Glass doors—"

Luke was already ahead of her, and the others streamed after. The french doors from Alden Culver's room to the balcony were also locked—and curtained. But they were old—and not safety glass. Luke picked up a small clay flowerpot and, as they all pressed back against the railing, lobbed the pot at a pane near the lock.

It went in with a smash. He reached through to yank the latch up, and shove the doors open. They all paused then, as if listening. That noise should have woken the soundest sleeper. But there was no stirring except a morning breeze catching at the torn lace curtain.

Regan picked her way over the glass. On the side table by the fireplace, the china teacup gleamed in the sunlight let in through the open doors.

The bed was still in shadow, mercifully so. Alden Culver lay rigidly on his back, lips swollen, eyes protruding. The roaring in Regan's ears drowned out any cries from those around her. Her lips mouthed *Daddy* silently, hopeless to rise above that roaring. Her knees became water and refused to hold her as she reached and reached and couldn't find him, would never find him again.

■   ■   ■

Diane stood frozen. He looked so terrible, stiff, staring in pain.

"Diane," Caroline ordered. "Get her out of here." She pointed at Regan, who was groping for her dead father's hand.

Obediently Diane grabbed her aunt and pulled her backward. "You don't want to see him like that," Diane panted in her ear. And, irrationally, "Let go, Regan. Let go," as if that blind grasping were actually impeding their progress.

Regan ceased struggling, but she remained turned toward the bed so that Diane had to back in the direction of the hall door, veering off course, almost into the fireplace. Glancing down, Diane took in the pearly gleam of the teacup beside an old book bound in worn leather. A pretty tableau.

Looking back at the scene by the bed, Diane thought how ridiculously pretty that was too. The room looked east over the wash of color on the terrace and gardens. The morning sun limned in fuzzy gold the figures silhouetted against the windows, and gleamed on wooden floorboards polished by age. Petals from the shattered geranium that had been in the pot shone like rubies. The bed was in shadow, and the figures seemed to incline toward it in the luminescent stillness of a Rembrandt painting.

Something clinked behind her. Her heel had kicked the key up against the door. Keeping a grasp on Regan's wrist, she bent to retrieve it.

"He's dead," Regan said.

Diane straightened, inserted the key carefully into the lock, and turned it until the door gave gracefully before her. "Yes," she said, leaving the key where it was. "Come on. You had better lie down."

"There was nothing wrong with him." Regan's gaze was fixed, blind. "He was an old man, but nothing was wrong with him. He was a doctor; he would have known."

"No," Diane said, "yes," no longer sure what she was answering. It had not looked like a natural death to her. But she had never seen death when it was not sanitized and embalmed. Perhaps there was always the struggle, the contortion, the last futile resistance.

"He shouldn't have died," Regan repeated. "There was no reason."

. . . and columbines.

Regan's official statement ended with the finding of her father's body. Although she had been collected enough in her recital of facts up to that point, she began to tremble in her chair then like a patient coming out of anesthesia too soon. Mathilda, who had watched quietly from the background throughout, got up to put hands on her client's shoulders and say curtly to Matt, "That's all you need, isn't it?"

It was. He knew well enough what had followed. It had been Luke who called to report the murder. "They're all in there. You'd better get out here fast if you want to preserve any evidence." Matt had summoned a state police forensic team, cordoned off the murder room, asked the proper questions, and got answers that all seemed to circle inevitably back to Alden's youngest daughter. Regan had been her own most damaging witness, continuing to assert with automatonlike regularity that she had made the tea and watched her father drink it.

So when Diane had said privately to Matt, "At least wait

until after the funeral; she won't go anywhere," he hadn't had to ask what she was talking about.

■ ■ ■

"We're going to waive the preliminary hearing," Mathilda told Regan, meeting her at the elevator in the courthouse. "In return, the DA's office has agreed to cooperate on bail. The hearing would have been just a formality anyhow, with your statement that you were the only one with access to that tea. Yours were the only fingerprints on the cup, too, besides your father's."

They walked along a hallway, their heels ringing on marble. A female deputy held Regan's right arm. Mathilda had the other, despite the deputy's disapproving glare. Mathilda's garish handbag all but hid the handcuffs. The deputy did not remonstrate. Regan suspected she had had run-ins with the attorney in the past.

"We do have one advantage," Mathilda said. "I think that editor, Jean Francis, is leaning toward our side, largely because Agatha hung up on her. It is never smart to antagonize the press. Her story will imply, I imagine, that you are a sweet young thing, beloved of children and animals, who is being railroaded by envious and greedy relatives."

Regan frowned. "But that's not true."

They entered the courtroom. The deputy pulled out a chair for Regan. "I have to leave the cuffs on, Miss Culver," she explained, "until the judge sets your bail. That's departmental policy. I'll be back here if you need to take a break."

"That's all right." Regan smiled. "Thank you."

The woman nodded.

"I am not," Regan reminded her lawyer, "all that young

and sweet anymore. My relatives don't like me much, granted, but only Agatha really wants me in jail. And animals and children are not discriminating; they usually like anybody who likes them."

"That deputy has bought it anyway," Mathilda said. "The idea that you need protecting, I mean. I've been in jail a couple of times, and I never got treated that well."

"Gardening is her hobby," Regan explained shortly. "She attended one of my classes once. What were you in jail for?"

"Contempt of court," Mathilda said with a wink. "I always refused to pay the fines."

She eyed Regan's dress—a cleverly cut, moss green two-piece—disapprovingly. "Too haute couture," she said in a fierce whisper as they rose for the justice's entrance. "It's okay for now, but I'll choose your clothes for the trial. For now, just sit still and look meek."

Regan managed a smile. "Oh, I'm very good at that."

■ ■ ■

That afternoon Regan and Mathilda sat in Alden Culver's room, the police having finished with it, in wing chairs before the fireplace. The weather was gray and misty, but Regan had opened the french doors to the balcony and the room was filled with the odors of the damp garden.

"Sasha's out there weeding," Diane had said when they arrived. "She seems to think that she has to take care of your flowers."

The little girl appeared in the doorway, looking damp, and shuffled around the lawyer to Regan's chair.

"You remember Mathilda, don't you?" Regan lifted the child onto her lap.

"I broke it off." Sasha dejectedly held out a stalk of something with graceful fan-shaped leaves.

"That's okay," Regan soothed. "That's columbine. It's done blooming for this year anyway. It will come back again. It's a perennial."

"I couldn't get the marshmallows up." Sasha pursued her depressing litany.

"It doesn't matter. I have a hard time digging those myself. We'll do it another day." Regan smiled at Mathilda's incredulous look. "Yes, Virginia, there *are* marshmallow plants, and they *were* used at one time to make the candy. Sasha and I are going to try it as soon as I can find a recipe that shows how it's done. Marshmallow grows wild in swampy places, and I should never have planted it in the garden because now we have it all over. It's as bad as tansy or comfrey or sweet rocket. The worst weeds are always the ones you introduce yourself. I'm sure Daddy would have found a lesson in that somewhere." Her smile faltered, and a shadow crossed her eyes.

"We can go somewhere else to talk if you'd rather," Mathilda suggested gruffly.

Regan gave her a surprised look. "No, that's all right. Daddy always said that it was best to face things at once and get them over. He thought that avoiding objects because of unhappy associations with them was mere superstition. It's you that makes you unhappy, he would say. Not things or other people. Unless you let them."

"Smart guy," Mathilda said. "Did he have any enemies?"

Regan considered. "He didn't worry much about what people thought of him. That irritated some of them. He was a little different that last night, though. He seemed to be having regrets."

"Was he depressed enough to kill himself?" Mathilda asked.

"What?"

"It's the obvious answer," Mathilda said impatiently, "and the easiest to build reasonable doubt on if we can't get around those locked doors. He knew as much about plants as you did, I presume?"

"Certainly. Quite enough to have known that aconite is not a pleasant way to die. He wouldn't have killed himself. I told you he believed in facing things."

"Even if he had a fatal disease, say?"

Regan smiled faintly. "You didn't know him. He would have seen a terminal illness as a great opportunity for experimentation. He would have gotten at least one more book out of it. Father adored challenges. Besides, for all his unconventional medical views, he was religiously orthodox. He would not have presumed to forestall God."

Mathilda raised her brows. "A holistic healer who wasn't New Age?"

Regan's smile broadened. "That would have earned you a real lecture. Daddy's main complaint about the New Age movement was that it skips the concept of original sin altogether. The bit about the heart being 'deceitful and desperately wicked.' Daddy believed, with Chesterton, that it's the only optimistic view."

"I don't dispute the deceitful and wicked part," Mathilda said. "If you'd had to deal with some of the minds I have . . . But that's optimistic?"

"Of course. If you believe that people are naturally good, you're always going to be disenchanted. If you believe that there's a rottenness at the core, but that a cure has been provided, then you have hope. He also believed that for every physical disease, a natural remedy has been supplied. 'Seek and you shall find' was one of his favorite dictums."

In the curve of Regan's arm, Sasha had fallen into an exhausted sleep almost at once. "What are her folks like?" Mathilda asked.

"Strong," Regan said, looking down at the sleeping face. "Strong and poor. She is everything to them, but they knew they would have to send her away to keep her. That's what the locket is for. She has worn it ever since she left Chevia. Their pictures are in it, so she won't forget them."

"If they love her that much, you might suggest to them that she is better off with you."

Regan shook her head emphatically. "Sasha comes from a line of people who have suffered for their faith. Those people know what is important and what isn't. Do you think I could give her anything that would match that?"

"No," Mathilda said slowly. "I suppose not."

"I think sometimes that I may be weakening her by keeping her here."

"Why was Olin here that night?" Mathilda changed the subject abruptly.

"Father invited him." Regan scanned the room. "That was surprising." She rose, lay Sasha on the chair, and crossed to the shelves on the right of the fireplace. "To me, anyway."

"What are you looking for?" Mathilda asked.

"My mother's journal. It's in a big green binder. You don't see it anywhere, do you?"

Without moving from her chair, Mathilda raked the shelves with her eagle-eyed stare, then turned her attention to the rest of the room. "No notebook," she concluded.

Regan tugged at the drawer in the little stand. "That's strange. He brought the journal upstairs with him just before dinner that night."

She wandered around the perimeter of the room, even checking under the bed, and continued into the bathroom.

"Is it important?" Mathilda asked.

"I don't know." Regan's voice came faintly from the other room. "He was talking that night about something that had happened ten years ago. I assumed he must have read about it in the journal. He wasn't very specific. He made some strange comment about mercy sometimes not being merciful. I took it to imply that Mother had or would have forgiven whatever it was, but that he didn't know whether he should or not."

She came back into the room, looking perplexed. "Well, it isn't here. He must have taken it downstairs again after all."

Mathilda was on her feet with a gleam in her eye. "Or perhaps somebody else took it," she said. "Like his murderer. Are the others all still around?"

"Yes. Reid and Gina will be moving out as soon as they get their house opened up. Why?"

"We can search their rooms. After all, this is your place now, isn't it? Or it will be after probate. But that's one little detail we won't bring up."

"Well, actually it's my house now," Regan said conscientiously. "Daddy put everything into joint accounts and ownership a few months ago. Something to do with inheritance taxes, I think."

Mathilda stood stock-still, staring at her. "Do you mean to tell me," she asked incredulously, "that he made over your inheritance to you before he died?"

"Yes. He was thinking about taking another trip to South America. I think he wanted everything settled, just in case—"

"You don't have a motive!" Mathilda exclaimed.

Regan raised her eyebrows. "Well, actually, I never thought I did. Everybody else seemed to differ with me on that, though."

"Does Olin know about this?" Mathilda demanded.

"I think he talked to the lawyer," Regan said doubtfully. "Or to one of them, anyway. The one that handled most of Daddy's business is out of town now. The partner may not have known about the joint accounts. The will was very short. It simply said that Agatha and Gina and Diane were to get twenty-five thousand each and that everything else was to go to me. It didn't mention that most of it already had."

There was something a shade too ingenuous in her inquiring look.

Mathilda was beginning to grin. "You know darned well that you should have mentioned it."

"He didn't ask. I'm not required to volunteer information, am I? After all, I needed to reserve something for my defense. I didn't know then that I was going to have such a brilliant lawyer looking after my interests."

Mathilda could not detect a trace of irony in that limpid gaze. "You're kind of like that whatdidyacallit—columbine. Tougher than you look."

"Oh, I'm a perennial all right. Better make that chamomile,

though. It can spring back after being walked on. Columbine is elegant, but not entirely predictable."

"Not a bad comparison at that," Mathilda said. "About this notebook. While the others aren't up here, we might wander around the guest rooms looking for it."

"No," Regan said. "It's probably down in his study. You just want an excuse to snoop."

Mathilda glared wearily. "It might save me all the money—your money, mind you—that will have to go to a private eye. So who do I tell him to start on? Agatha?"

"No!" Regan was emphatic.

"I thought you didn't like her."

"That's why you have to leave her alone," Regan said contradictorily. "It wouldn't be fair—"

"Okay," Mathilda said. "When in doubt, go for the pretty blond. She's hiding something. That I know for a fact."

"Not Diane either," Regan objected. "She's been nice to me—"

"Regan, Regan," Mathilda enunciated with careful clearness. "If we eliminate everybody who is nice to you and everybody who isn't, whom do we have left?"

Her client looked mulish.

"We're on a Russian bobsled here," Mathilda said. "The wolves are slavering at our heels, and Leningrad is miles away. Quick, who gets tossed?"

"Luke, I expect," Regan said. "I overheard part of a phone conversation the other evening, and he almost took my arm off."

Mathilda settled back into her chair and produced a notebook. "Do tell," she said invitingly.

■ ■ ■

Matt Olin was also thinking about Luke Hayden. A nervous prosecutor had warned him that he had better find out ahead of time just what ammunition Mathilda Baker was likely to come up with. "Not that it'll do much good," the prosecutor had concluded. "That woman doesn't know what fighting fair means. Shoots you in the back every time. Women never have understood the concept of honor."

On the other hand, Matt Olin thought wryly, women very rarely started conflicts. That could be left to the men and their concept of honor.

He had a feeling that she would begin with Luke, who would make the most convincing killer. Matt reached for the phone, dialed an agent in DEA for whom he had intercepted a suspect a couple of years earlier.

"Luke Hayden?" the agent repeated. "Haven't heard of him myself, but I'll ask around. No apparent source of income, huh? You'd be surprised. Had one of those shifty types under suspicion once. Turned out he wrote romance novels. Under several aliases. Poor guy doesn't know how close he came to being facedown with a knee in his back and a search warrant in his face."

The agent did not sound as cheerful when he called back. He was decidedly unhappy, in fact. "Sorry, Olin," he said. "You've hit a nerve somewhere. DEA wants you to lay off this Hayden character."

"Why?" Matt asked.

"Nobody would explain that. I'd guess they're tracking him to get at somebody bigger, and they don't fancy seeing him taken out of action right now. What do you want him for, anyway?"

"I'm working on a homicide," Matt said.

Silence. "Uh, what's the name of that burg of yours again?"

"Hayden."

Another pause. Then "Afraid I can't help you, buddy," a sharp click, and Matt was listening to a dial tone.

CHAPTER 7

∎ ∎ ∎

There's rue for you . . .

When Matt Olin arrived at the Culver house and asked to speak to Regan, Diane showed him into the study and departed. Mathilda Baker was sitting with her feet up on the desk. Regan was wandering around the room, poking at books on the shelves.

"We're looking for Mother's journal," Regan explained at once. "It seems to have disappeared."

"Regan, honey," Mathilda Baker said, "remember what we agreed about telling things to the police?"

"I need that notebook," Regan said. "It was my mother's and nobody else has any right to it."

"Probably burned by now," Mathilda opined cheerfully. "It'll make a good subject to bring up at the trial, don't you think, Chief? Mysterious journal disappears. What was in a dead woman's diaries? The jury will love it. Just like Perry Mason."

"Relevance?" Matt leaned a shoulder against the closed door and watched Regan.

"Why, I think you'll be the best witness to that," Mathilda purred. "My client thinks you might have overheard her father remark on it when they were talking on the terrace. Ten years ago—and all that."

"He didn't mention the journal then."

"Not specifically. But earlier—at the table?"

"What," Matt asked Regan, "has the DEA got to do with this case?"

Mathilda stiffened. "Don't answer that."

Regan was on her knees, pulling several large books off a bottom shelf. She inserted her head to peer behind them, sneezed, and said matter-of-factly, "Luke, I expect. I overheard a strange conversation of his the other night and he didn't like it one little bit. It was almost certainly about drugs. That's why he was so attentive at the party that night. He was afraid I would tell you."

"And why didn't you?" Matt demanded.

Regan sat back on her heels and dusted off her hands. "Mainly because you were fuming at me over something, and it slipped my mind."

"Your father," Matt said carefully, feeling his way, "believed in plants as alternative medicines. How did he feel about—"

"Recreational drug use? He didn't approve of it. He thought that it abused the purpose for which the plants were created. It was one of his hobbyhorses. He thought that modern society was so pleasure-mad because it had lost the guts to be happy without artificial stimulation. If he had found evidence that Luke was dealing drugs, he would have turned him in."

"What happened ten years ago?" Matt asked.

Regan did not appear ruffled by these sudden jumps in subject. She was still on her knees, her frowning gaze searching the room. She spied the wastebasket and hitched across to it, then upended its contents onto the floor. "Mother died ten years ago," she said, pawing through the wastepaper. "We were all graduating from college about then—Luke, Diane, and me, that is. Mother and Caroline had just opened the herb farm. It was a happy time—until the accident."

She paused. "Or at least it was for some of us. Now that I think of it, Diane wasn't particularly cheerful. Everyone had expected her to go on to graduate school, but she took that teaching job instead. Luke had been accepted at a law school, but he never went either. Agatha sold her house here and moved to Boston about then."

"Any reason for that?"

Regan was looking at the papers and dumping them, one at a time, back into the basket. "I don't know," she said. "Agatha had been dating Reid before he married Gina. Maybe she didn't like seeing her sister living in the Hayden mansion."

"You didn't tell *me* that," Mathilda reproved.

"It wasn't relevant. Their dating was a good five years earlier. We were all still in high school when Reid married Gina. Agatha wouldn't speak to Gina for a while, but she got over it." Regan was reading a cream-colored sheet of paper as she spoke and tugging thoughtfully at her lower lip. After a pause, she added, "It would never have worked between Reid and Agatha. They're both aggressive types. Actually, I think Agatha was on the verge of breaking the whole thing off before Gina interfered."

"What's that?" Matt asked. Looking up cloudily and realizing that he was referring to the paper she was holding, Regan said, "Nothing you'd care about. Part of a letter from Selene Books. Apparently they were the ones who were going to publish Mother's journals. 'If possible, we would like to see a complete manuscript by September.' No chance of that now." She stuffed the paper in her pocket. "That's why I've got to find that notebook. I'll have to take over from Daddy. It's mostly an editing job, and I think I can handle that."

"The girl has a one-track mind," Mathilda said to Matt. "If Alden Culver was like that, it's no wonder somebody got annoyed."

Regan was sitting back on her heels again, frowning. "Did you see it?" she demanded of Matt. "When you were searching his room? A green, leather-bound binder full of notebook paper, all with handwriting on it?"

As Matt shook his head in a silent negative, Mathilda said, "We need that notebook for another reason. Don't you want to know who killed your father?"

"What good would that do?" Regan said. "It can't resurrect him." She stood and shook out her skirts.

"What did I tell you?" Agatha stood in the side doorway that connected with the living room. "She doesn't care. What is it going to take to get her out of this house?"

Mathilda's eyes narrowed. Before she could speak, Regan said, "You might as well give it up, Agatha. Daddy made the house over to me before he died—along with the rest of my inheritance. It's already mine."

Mathilda had already taken in Matt's tensing. The lawyer's expression wavered between irritation and triumph. "Regan didn't have a motive for murder. When I put somebody from the bank on the stand, your case will be blown to kingdom come."

Matt's mouth was dry. He should have found this out earlier. The prosecutor was going to make that all too abundantly clear. Regan was watching him. He yanked off his sunglasses and strode over to her, crossed his arms, and glowered down into her face.

He thought he saw a gleam of amusement in her dark, heavy-lidded gaze. Agatha shrilled furiously in the background, and Mathilda enthusiastically responded in kind. "Is there anything *else* you haven't told me?" Matt asked.

Regan's eyes widened. Those eyes were her best feature, the irises limned with smoky gray shading to a rich hazel around the pupils. There was a strange translucency there too and specks of something darker. He was reminded of a mountain stream. Clear but with the depths tantalizingly obscured by flickering shadows. And only the reflection of sunlight dancing mockingly over the surface.

"But I answered all your questions," she said.

There was a challenge there, and he couldn't help feeling a momentary response to it. But then he said flatly, "It's not a game," aware that he was speaking in cliché.

Her gaze was momentarily obscured by a thicket of lashes. When she looked up again, they were simply brown eyes. "Nobody ever said it was," she murmured. "The consequences are a bit extreme for that, aren't they? If you'll excuse me . . ."

When she had reached the door, she turned suddenly and said, "I *don't* want to know." Her compelling tone stopped Agatha and Mathilda in mid-spate. Agatha had left the door on the south wall open, and those in the living room who had been pretending that they weren't listening now turned their heads.

"Whatever pitiful reason one of you had for killing my father," Regan went on, "I don't want to know about it. It can't begin to be—" Her fists clenched; she struggled. "Adequate," she finished tightly, "for what you have done. He would have wanted justice because holding people responsible was, to him, the ultimate mercy. But I don't want to know."

Out in the dim hallway, she headed for the stairs, but was stopped by a hand on her arm. It was Reid. "You might want to tell your lawyer," he suggested in an undertone, those humorless eyes uncomfortably close, "that Agatha was in that herb cabinet of yours on the night of the party. After you went outside and the caterers left, I saw her. She had the doors open."

He turned and walked away before Regan could respond. She thought there had been a hint of satisfaction in his voice. Perhaps it *had* been Agatha then who had broken off that relationship. Perhaps the male ego still smarted. Regan went slowly up the stairs, thinking hard. Agatha?

She spent the afternoon in the room that had been her father's. She curled up in the seat of one of the wing chairs, arms around her knees, staring into the dead fireplace. Caroline had phoned to see how she was doing and to express some reservations over Regan's choice of a lawyer.

"Mathilda Baker's the flashy, sensational type. Couldn't you have got someone a bit more respectable?"

"She's okay," Regan said. "It might take somebody like her. Mother's journal is missing, Caroline. You remember Father taking it upstairs with him that evening, don't you? Did he ever bring it back down?"

"Not that I saw. Is it important—now?"

"Father wanted it published. I'll have to keep looking.

Mathilda thinks there might have been something in it that somebody didn't want to come to light. But it doesn't seem likely to me; Mother wrote it so long ago. Do you still have those letters? May I see them?"

A pause. "I suppose so," Caroline said finally. "Though I shouldn't encourage you. If one of your charming relatives killed Alden because of something he found out, you'll be putting yourself in danger. Let your lawyer handle it; it's what she gets paid for. I don't want to lose you too. Leave it alone, Regan. *Please.*"

"I want that journal published," Regan said. "My mother deserves a book. I'm sure it's here somewhere."

Caroline sighed. "You're as obstinate as your father was. Be careful, then. Don't tell anyone if you do find it. I'll drop the letters off the next time I'm in town."

Feeling too dispirited to make the effort herself, Regan hoped that Diane was getting supper. A wind was rising outside, billowing the lace curtains on the open french doors. Regan got out of her chair and went across to the shelves. There at eye level were Alden Culver's books and those written by acquaintances. Regan reached for the tallest one of the lot, *Rosemary for Remembrance* by Caroline Stanton, and carried it back to her chair.

The publisher had made the format large to accommodate the photos and gotten permission from Alden Culver to take pictures of the late Rosemary's garden.

Only the first chapter was written as a direct tribute to Rosemary, and it was probably the least well done. But Caroline was never articulate about her emotions, and Regan found this awkwardness touching. The rest of the book was not how-to, rather it was simply a commentary on gardening and the changing seasons, stirring without being maudlin. Even Alden Culver had to concede that Caroline could write, though it had been his grumpy opinion that her style owed a lot to her late friend.

Regan paused at a favorite passage:

Gardening is a microcosm of what it means to be human. Some plants won't flourish in the most fertile soil; others thrive on sand and rock. Some days are aphid-eaten; some burgeon like Eden. Eventually you come to realize that the idyllic June hours would not be as intense without the raw February afternoon you spent stamping roots back into the stiffening ground.

Eventually you learn that you are not God, just a gardener. That no life of any kind can really belong to you. That you can encourage it from the outside, but only he can animate it from within. And, when he wants it back, you give it up without complaint. Knowing that, imbued with his essence, it never really ends.

Regan's eyes stung, and she paged on quickly, studying the pictures, noting which plants had gotten much larger and which hadn't survived. A garden was never the same from one year to the next. Except for a few things—like the rock walls—that only grew more weathered, the pictured garden was no longer recognizable. Her mother was slipping away from her. How much of what Regan recalled of Rosemary now was true and how much had she added or subtracted, as she had added or subtracted plants in the garden?

She reached the end of the book. She sat for several minutes, staring absently at a sheaf of notepaper tucked into the back cover before she really saw it. Then she grabbed at those handwritten pages. This, at least, was really Rosemary.

It wasn't all of the journal, of course, or even most of it. But her father had apparently taken some of the pages out of the binder, hiding them in this book that was big enough to conceal—

Someone rapped at the door, and Regan slammed the back cover quickly shut over the papers just as Diane opened the door. "Dinner's ready."

"All right," Regan said, without moving. "I'll be down."

Diane hesitated, shrugged, then pulled the door shut behind her.

Regan stayed where she was, holding the book tightly closed. Her heart had lurched at the interruption, but more from surprise than alarm. She looked down the room to where a torn curtain fluttered over a cardboard pane. Caroline was right; she should be afraid.

She was alone now, watched from all sides by critical eyes. *I should have cried at the funeral. I shouldn't have taken my arrest so calmly. I should desperately desire that the real murderer be caught. The jury isn't going to like me. I'm not playing my role correctly. God, you're the only one who really understands me. Even Daddy didn't always, but he took my side anyway.*

Maybe that was the problem. Since I never defended myself, he always felt obliged to do it for me. Maybe subconsciously I wanted it that way. By not fighting back, I made myself the mar-

tyr—*the injured one. And the martyrs almost always win. You can't fight martyrs.*

That turning the other cheek thing is supposed to be Christian, but I suspect there are times when it is anything but.

She wasn't liking herself too well these days. Maybe that was why she'd let those facts slip to Matt this afternoon. So that they could both start on equal ground. A fair contest.

That was all she wanted. The system might let her off easy because she had a lot of wealthy clients and an expensive lawyer. But she didn't want let off easy. *I don't want to be the protected little girl any longer, Daddy. I want—*She turned toward his empty chair and shook under a gust of silent grief. The dam cracked, buckled. A tidal wave of sorrow roared over her.

Tossed and whirled helplessly on a sea of anguish, she thought that the dark water would drag her under, drown her, break her. Surely her mind, her nerves would give. She cried silently to her other father, like Peter from the storm, *Help me!*

When she surfaced, she was hunched forward in the chair, fists clenched, shivering violently, the book fallen at her feet, the loose papers fluttering like flailing wings. Gato appeared suddenly on the balcony rail, jumped down into the room, and rushed past her with a preoccupied air. He had been in the plants again; he carried with him the bitter pungency of rue. A voice said in her mind, *You are stronger than you know. If I am in you, you cannot sink.*

I'm sick of shadows, she replied. *Of always sidestepping, trying to placate, keep things down. So let the unholy mess boil, come to a head, and do its worst!*

■ ■ ■

The atmosphere at the supper table was subdued. Agatha did not speak at all. Regan followed that example, feeling a strange sense of release—almost of power. As if sensing some difference in her, the others kept casting furtive glances her way. The only sound besides the clink of silverware was Gina's light rambling voice, going on about everything and nothing.

Afterward, Diane, Agatha, and Gina left on individual pursuits. Where Luke was, was anybody's guess. Reid had not yet returned from Boston.

Regan read to Sasha until the little girl feel asleep. Gently unhooking the locket to lay it on the nightstand, Regan noticed that an edge of paper was sticking out. Perhaps the picture was coming loose. She carried the piece of jewelry with her as she strolled through the garden, the cat at her heels.

It was going to rain. Swollen blue-black clouds rushed in from the west. She had always loved the hot, urgent wind that preceded a storm. She stood on the bridge above the wildflower field with her eyes closed, swaying slightly as if dancing. Her father had always teased her about not having enough sense to come in out of the rain. He would never tease her about anything again.

She dropped onto the floor of the bridge then, and sobbed with her hands over her eyes, her shoulders shaking, and the cat curved like a question mark against her knees.

When she was done, she wiped at her wet cheeks with her fingertips and smiled shakily at the cat's puzzled, gleaming gaze.

Gato climbed into her lap, and she sat for a while, cross-legged with one of the bridge rails against her back, stroking smooth fur, and watching the water churn. She was not, after all, alone.

She clicked open the locket. It was not the photo of Sasha's parents that was loose, but a new one. Regan's own face looked up at her, snipped from a newspaper picture. Sasha must have done the cutting herself; the edges were uneven. Next to the police chief's burly build, the woman in the photo looked frail, defenseless. *That,* Regan thought, *is not me.*

She jumped up, shoved the pendant into her pocket, and strode up the hill toward the house, warm with anger. Anger that Sasha should have to keep such a picture in case her Aunt Regan was taken away again, just like everybody else in her young life had been taken away.

By the time Regan reached the flower beds, the wind had dropped. Only a warm, insinuating breeze remained to grope intimately under the hair at the nape of her neck. Although she could only dimly see the flowers and herbs in the twilight, their scents were stirred up tonight, restless, jostling for position—sweet, spicy, sharp, cloying, aloof, brazen, evasive—all in a discordant clash of personalities.

How ancient most of these plants were. Indifferent spectators of history's triumphs and tragedies. Used to scent, to soothe, to heal . . . to poison.

She half-ran up the path, through the pergola, wanting, for the first time in her life, to get away from them. The cat loped, smooth as a shadow, in her wake.

When she came out on the lawn, she saw that the western horizon was smeared with pale orange fading to blazing white in the south. That light glared off the roof of the car parked in the drive and silhouetted the man who had paused beside it to look across at her.

He had seen her. There was no use dodging back into the

uneasy arch of rose and honeysuckle where she had evaded his notice that first time.

The wind rose again like her anger. Anger that this man had thought she was the type to go quietly. Behind her, the plants whispered urgently.

As quickly as the wind and her anger had risen, they subsided into something steadier, more resolute. She stepped forward onto the bright lawn.

■ ■ ■

Watching her come toward him as if on a lighted stage, Olin was convinced that he should have waited until morning. He was as susceptible to atmosphere as anybody, and this was the kind of weather that prodded at the subconscious mind, that caused him to look quickly over his shoulder for no reason at all, that raised in him a restless half-dread, half-anticipation.

His words were quick, forced, as if they were prescripted, inevitable. "I knocked, but nobody answered."

A slight smile stirred her lips. "Tell them that I came and nobody answered. That I kept my word, he said."

A chill ran up his spine. The wind was turning cold.

Then, "A poem," she explained. "What you said reminded me of it. Walter de la Mare, I think. Nobody else is home." She turned toward the front door, then glanced back at him. Her lips moved, but her words were lost in the sudden gust that flipped his hat from his head and peppered his skin with fine bits of gravel.

He scrambled after the hat, looked up from his crouch, feeling bulky and clumsy, to find her watching him from the porch with that same bland patience. "Are you coming?" she asked, the words seeming unnaturally loud in a sudden lull.

He should say, "It's not important," but the wind was rising again, shrieking the length of the porch, flapping her skirt and whipping hair into her eyes. She turned away without waiting for an answer, opened the door, and groped for a light switch. As he came up behind her, the draft eddying down the dark hall swirled her skirt against his legs. The light bloomed, a homey, yellow glow, and, at a noise like a distant rifle shot, was as abruptly extinguished. Another clap of sound much nearer was the door slamming shut behind them to a simultaneous crash of thunder.

Regan started and grabbed at his arm. She trembled to the tuneless vibration of glass near them in the darkness. When the quivers in the air had ceased, she muttered, " A tree down on the wires, I suppose. Wait here. I'll try to find us some light."

She was gone before he quite realized that she was going, the warm pressure fading from his arm, a cool breeze wafting around his ankles. Even now, he should call after her, "Never mind," and go, but he didn't.

The old house creaked and groaned around him like a ship in heavy seas. He heard something fall and roll across a hardwood floor above. A window must have been left open. He could imagine curtains streaming inward on an empty room, perhaps the room where Culver had died.

When his eyes grew accustomed to the dark, he saw that a faint illumination was seeping in through the window in the door behind him. But that faded away just before he caught a gleam at the back of the hall.

She held an oil lamp at waist level, its bowl cupped between her hands. It was quiet enough that he could hear the intermittent snap of the lamp's burning wick. "We might as well go into the living room," she said.

He moved thankfully. His holster jostled the hall table beside him, and he managed to grab a vase before it toppled to the floor. There was something like a spark of amusement in her eyes again, or perhaps it was only the reflection of the flame.

In the other room, she sat in the middle of the couch and put the lamp on a coffee table in front of her. He went wide around her to take a chair opposite.

She folded her hands in her lap and waited. The cat jumped up beside her and looked at him with the same patient expectation. And he couldn't remember what he'd come to talk to her about.

He felt a tight constricting band around his head and looked down at his hat to make sure that he had taken it off.

He would have welcomed the thunder now, but the room was ominously quiet. A drape wafted away from the wall and settled back again with muted rustlings. Regan's eyes seemed to absorb the light much as did the onyx brooch at her throat.

He rubbed at his forehead and muttered, "Sorry, headache."

"Oh," she said, "I can get you something for that."

She was gone again before he could protest that that wasn't necessary. It was not a headache really, and he doubted that aspirin would do it any good. She had taken the lamp with her, but the cat had stayed, prowling up and down the sofa. A hard-driven gust of rain rattled against the window like thrown pebbles, and he started. He felt the cat stop and turn to look at him.

A glow preceded Regan's entrance. The lamp rested on a tray between two antique china teacups and saucers. He looked at the cups with a brief puzzlement, then a shock of realization. She set the tray carefully down on the table between them. As she leaned over it, she raised her head to look into his face. "I always turn the kettle on—on low—before I go out on my evening rounds of the garden," she explained. "So I have hot water waiting when I get back."

The voice was soft. The eyes were not. She was no longer intimidated by him, if she ever had been.

"That's our headache formula," she explained in the same gentle tone, picking up her own cup and sinking comfortably back onto the couch. "It's very good actually. There's honey too, if you would like to sweeten it."

He looked down at the pretty china, the greenish liquid wafting up its herbal steam. Seemingly so cozy, so harmless. It was the bedtime formula that had killed her father.

She was just playing with him. She wouldn't really—

The cat sat and watched him. Its gaze was not as knowing as hers was, simply curious.

"You'd better drink it," Regan chided, "before it gets cold."

. . . and here's some for me.

The blare of a car horn and an angry squeal of brakes jerked Diane back to reality. The trail had ended and she had nearly stepped out onto the blacktop in front of an oncoming car. She mouthed a weak "Sorry" and stepped back.

The man in the car was inclined to be conciliatory when he saw that she was blond and female. He gave a magnanimous wave and watched her in the rearview mirror as he drove off. His parking lights were on. Dusk was settling in, she realized with a shock, and a storm was brewing. She had been vaguely aware of the wind as she walked, but since most of the trail ran through thick brush and trees, she had been sheltered from the brunt of it. She began to walk again, slowly and uncertainly, along the edge of the road as she tried to remember where the trail came out. She had not meant to follow it to its end. Ten miles! She had walked ten miles without even thinking about it. Only now was she aware of an ache in her hips and calves.

Which meant, she realized with another shock, that she

was ten miles from the house. There was no way that she could grope back down that trail in the dark, even had she the strength to do another ten miles. And since the trail cut across country, the distance was much farther by the road.

She would have to find a phone and call someone to come and get her. *What is it with you anymore?* she asked herself angrily. *Why can't you pay attention to what you're doing?*

She shuffled on with her arms crossed tightly in front of her. There were no houses in sight. What could she say, anyway—"I need to use your phone because I walked too far and can't get back"?

A car was coming up behind her. She heard it slowing and moved farther over onto the berm. Instead of passing, the car pulled up beside her and stopped.

She turned to face it and backed away, the hairs on her bare forearms prickling. The thrum of the car's engine was barely audible above the swoop of the wind. It was dark enough that she couldn't see the driver clearly. He seemed to be sitting still, looking at her. Then he leaned across, shoved open the passenger door, and the interior light blinked on. "Ride, lady?"

She opened her mouth to deliver a freezing rejoinder before she realized that the voice and the face were familiar.

Weak with relief, she made herself walk with casual offhandedness to the open door and dropped onto the seat. "Thanks. I walked a little too far, I guess." When she clicked the door shut, the roar of the wind dropped to a distant drone.

"I guess," Luke said. "Worried about something?" He asked the question with the same impersonal ease with which he shifted the car rapidly through its gears. Diane supposed that that manner might be intriguing to some of the women in his crowd. Actresses and society lights weren't used to being met with disinterest. But it was off-putting to her.

She didn't feel up to exerting the effort it always took these days to make conversation with him. But since he was giving her a ride, it wouldn't be prudent to ignore him.

"Well, shouldn't we be?" she said. "Are you quite comfortable with the idea of Regan spending the rest of her life in jail?"

"Is that it?" he said. "I thought it might be losing your job that was bugging you."

She continued to look straight forward, the road winding smoothly back under them like the mechanical forward rush of a computer game. "How did you know that?" she asked finally.

"I didn't," he said, "until right now. But I figured that if deep-freeze Diane was frazzling at the edges over something, it had to be money. Then this solicitousness toward Regan seems a bit suspect, since your attitude toward her has always been distant at best."

He spoke with amused indifference, as if commenting on the characters in a book or movie.

When she didn't respond, he added, "But I wouldn't worry about Regan if I were you. I have a feeling that she'll never see the inside of a cell.'

"Why?" she asked. "You're not underestimating Matt, are you? He may be slow, but he's thorough."

"No," he said, "it wouldn't do to underestimate Matt."

■ ■ ■

Gato's gleaming eyes reflected the lamp flame. The animal sat upright with the tip of its tail curling neatly around one foot, as if in imitation of its mistress's prim pose.

Matt realized that he should have made some excuse right away, said that he didn't drink tea, which was true enough. But the longer he waited, the more awkward it became.

Playing for time, he picked up the honey stick and drizzled some of the amber liquid into the tea. "Smart move, Olin," he thought immediately. "If it was bitter, you won't be able to tell now."

She smiled, as if she knew what he was thinking.

Why couldn't he just make some excuse and leave? It was a long chance that the tea was any more than what she had said, but a smart cop never took any unnecessary chances.

And she didn't expect him to. That was what that Mona Lisa expression implied. She knew that he wasn't going to drink it. She would watch his halting attempts at an excuse, his equally blundering try at getting out of the room with some dignity still intact, with that same enigmatic quirk of her lips.

"Don't you like tea, Matt?" she said.

There. She was even providing him an out. Flinging it down under his nose just in case he was too dumb to figure one out for himself.

It was suddenly unendurable, as unendurable as the speculative looks he still got from many of the townspeople. Looks that read, "Oh, we know you're doing okay so far. But blood will tell, you know."

As unendurable as the anticipatory smirks of his tormentors at school who had known only too well what it would take to make him lash out in futile rage.

He grabbed for the cup so suddenly that he almost knocked it over. Steadying it by cupping his big hand over the top, he stared back at her, the steam forming warm droplets on his palm. Then he plucked the cup up and drained it in several quick swallows. "Th-thank you," he said with only the slightest of slurs, and, pausing to draw a steadying breath, "I'll be going now. It's late."

The cat watched all this with the same alert attention. But the smile had frozen on Regan's face as she had frozen in place, her own cup halfway to her mouth. He pictured her still sitting like that as he felt his way down the hall and out into the windy darkness.

■ ■ ■

"Have you noticed," Luke asked Diane, "that the careful, practical ones usually end up making blundering idiots of themselves over the wrong kind of woman?"

The car surged on through the night, disdainful of the wind and rain. Diane half-drowsed on the butter-smooth leather to the equally smooth sound of Luke's voice.

His light-colored eyes combined with his coldly handsome features to make Luke look the quintessential drug lord villain. The type who would say, "Kill him," while playing idly with some expensive bauble. But she couldn't really believe that of someone she knew.

Or could she? She had more or less believed it at one time . . .

She and Luke had attended the same Ivy League college. They had been on good terms back then, had gone about together in a cousinly sort of way. Luke had a prelaw major and was doing very well; he always did well at whatever he chose. That had been before Jamie died.

Jamie, Luke's roommate, had been a writing major. Imaginative, enthusiastic, eager to please, vulnerable. Everybody had liked him.

There had been rumors about Luke before that, but she had always ignored them, thinking them inspired by jealousy. He came from a wealthy family, after all; he could be expected to have lots of money.

Then Jamie died. The first time she saw Luke after that, she was walking from the library to her off-campus apartment. He fell in beside her with an abrupt, "You shouldn't be out alone after dark."

She made an attempt at condolences. "Luke, I'm so sorry! Jamie . . . He was so eager . . . It doesn't seem fair. Does anyone know where he got the stuff?"

They came to a rustic wooden bridge spanning a creek. She turned toward Luke for his answer to find his expression cold, unresponsive. "Jamie was a big boy," Luke said. "What he chose to do wasn't anybody's fault but his own."

It had been like one of those jolting dreams where one turns for comfort to a friend to find him wearing a stranger's face. As she searched that face for some softening, some relenting, she realized that she had never really known him at all. Earlier that week, Diane had received an equally staggering letter from her mother. She felt lightheaded standing there, somehow feeling the empty space under the boards, the empty space under everything she had known. There was nothing there, nothing at all.

She turned and walked away from him without another word, her heels echoing over that emptiness.

Luke did not go to law school. Perhaps she had always wanted to believe his playboy role because that would be better than . . . Luke was not the type to be satisfied with doing nothing; he would require a challenge of some sort.

What if Rosemary had found out? Jamie had visited Luke several times and had been in the Culver house. A vivid memory rose in Diane's mind. Everybody sitting out on the terrace, Jamie leaning forward, gesturing excitedly with his hands, as he described to Rosemary the plot of a story he was writing. It was all mixed up in Diane's mind with the tart taste of lemonade garnished with the pungency of mint, ice-jingling glasses beaded with condensation. Diane herself had been lying on a chaise lounge, watching Jamie's face lazily from under her straw hat and enjoying his enthusiasm but not really listening to his words. Luke had been perched on the terrace wall close to her. That would have been the summer before Jamie died.

She and Luke had been quite comfortable with each other then. It had been a comfortable afternoon, probably because her mother wasn't there.

Now she could not remember anything that Jamie had said. But Rosemary would have been listening to the words. Perhaps she got some hint from the plot of his story, even. Writers did include so much of themselves in their stories. Subconsciously, sometimes. Jamie had been awfully twitchy, but then his had been a restless personality.

Perhaps Rosemary had written her suspicions in her journal, not having any proof to act on them. "He is a little too excitable," she might have recorded. "I do believe he is on something—and that he is getting it from Luke." But Rosemary would have been reluctant to create trouble for Gina's stepson. There was enough tension in the family already. She might have let it go, telling herself that she had no proof, after all, that she could be wrong. If, that is, she did have no proof . . .

For an instant, Diane yearned after the innocence of lemonade and the comfortableness of a summer afternoon, back when she didn't realize that it might be hiding something corrupt . . .

Corruption. She opened her eyes and looked at Luke's coldly handsome profile.

With his intelligence and his academic brilliance, law school would have been almost easy. Perhaps too easy. Minds like his were often plagued with boredom. Maybe he had thought that afternoon unbearably tedious. It was always impossible to tell what he was thinking.

If only the risk of defying the system was enough to whet his jaded appetite, what might that not lead him to? Jamie was dead. Rosemary was dead. And now Rosemary's husband was dead too.

Diane fought down a rising panic. Rosemary's death was clearly, irrevocably an accident. There were witnesses. But she could not fight down the sickening sense that she had, after all, been picked up by a stranger.

■ ■ ■

Regan carried the tray back into the kitchen, the cat trailing in her wake. Leaving the tray on the counter, she took the lamp upstairs into her father's dark room, and set it on the mantel. A candlestick had fallen to the floor, and she picked it up automatically, restoring it to its place before crossing to the still-open french doors. The curtains were damp under the slash of wind and rain.

She pulled the doors shut and latched them, then followed the cat out into the hall.

Back in her own room, she set the oil lamp on the dresser and glanced at the child. Sasha was curled up on her side, hugging her rabbit, with her eyes shut. But as Regan started to turn away, she realized that there was no deep, easy breathing to signify sleep. The thin arms clenched the stuffed animal. The eyes were squinched.

"Sasha?" Regan said. "Are you awake?"

The child flew upright, dropping the rabbit and clutching Regan around the neck with something like a drowning grip. Regan was dismayed to discover that the frail body was trembling. "There was somebody there," Sasha whispered. "In Uncle Aldy's room."

Regan patted Sasha's back soothingly. "That was just me. I went in to shut the balcony windows."

"Not now," Sasha said. "Before. Then they came in here. I kept my eyes shut and didn't move. Then they went back there again."

"Are you sure it wasn't the wind? The wind makes strange noises sometimes."

That scornful look. "It was a person. I heard a man talking downstairs too."

"That was just Matt." She wished he were here now.

The wind was quieter, more subtle, a cold swirling at ankle level that caused muted rustlings and sly stirrings in dark corners.

Had somebody been looking for those journal entries? Whoever had the notebook might have noticed that there were some pages missing. Perhaps it hadn't been the wind that knocked that candlestick off the mantel. Had there been someone watching from the dark bathroom when she closed those doors? Was that somebody standing on the other side of the wall, as still as she was, listening?

Fear hit her then like a shock of extreme cold. Her heart labored. There was a cramp in her leg, but she didn't move.

The nearest phone was out in the dark hall, between her room and her father's. Partway between her and what? Would Matt come back if she called him? Would she be *allowed* to call him?

Regan lifted her reluctant gaze to the dresser mirror, to their images, pale and darkly shadowed above the flicker of the lamp, to the open door also reflected there—the open door *behind* them. She could not bring herself to turn. The question thudded through her mind in rhythm with her heartbeat. Which one? Which one? Which one?

Which familiar face? Luke would be dispassionate; it was nothing personal with him, Reid self-justifying, Diane distant, Agatha angry. The anger might be the easiest to take, being human, being, in a sense, warm. And with Gina? The same amiable smile on the same soft, placid face? That would be the most horrifying. No, Matt would be worst. It could be that her father had invited Matt not to consult him, but to confront him. It made a wild kind of sense. Matt could have run upstairs while she was searching for the lamp and matches. Why else had he come?

Matt had been angry the night of the dinner party. He had asked her how much she knew. Tonight he had drunk the tea. Would he do that unless he was sure she wasn't guilty? And how could he be sure unless he was guilty himself?

If he were to appear in that mirrored doorway, what would she do? The arms that had held her when she cried for her mother, the hands sworn to protect . . . Regan felt faint and sick.

She was frightening Sasha. The little face looking up for reassurance and not finding any was crumbling on the verge of tears. Anger surged back in Regan, warming, steadying. She tried to put Sasha down, but the child would not release her grip. In a loudly cheerful tone, Regan said, "Aren't we being scaredy-cats? There's nobody there, Sasha. I'll just show you." Shifting the child's weight onto one arm, she picked up a heavy brass candlestick from the dresser, tramped loudly toward the door, hearing nothing out in the darkness but the echo of her own footsteps funneling down the stairwell.

She caught the edge of the door with her foot, kicked it shut, and dropped the candlestick to turn the key in the lock. "You'll have to help me, Sasha," she said. "We'll drag the washstand across." This time, the child got down willingly, and set small hands to the side of the wooden antique. Wood scraped on wood and the pitcher rattled in its bowl.

"There," Regan said breathlessly. "Nobody can get in now." Secretly, she thought it likely that if she could move the washstand, somebody else could too. But at least she would be warned by the noise. Dusting her unsteady hands in a "That's that" gesture, she went to check the bolt on the french doors.

Even when they were securely locked in, Sasha insisted on crawling into bed with Regan. Long after the child was asleep, Regan lay, staring tensely into the darkness, repeating softly the only reassurance that she still trusted. "He shall cover thee with his feathers, and under his wings shalt thou trust: his truth shall be thy shield and buckler. Thou shalt not be afraid for the terror by night . . ." After all, the journal entries were in here. She had simply switched them to her own copy of Caroline's book.

Regan did not know when the others returned. The wind

made sounds that could have been footsteps and closing doors or nothing but air.

■ ■ ■

The following morning Matt reached for the phone. He was not optimistic that anyone would answer on a Saturday. He was not optimistic about anything at the moment. He had been called out in the early morning to a domestic quarrel. As a result, he had gotten hardly any sleep; his jaw was swollen and throbbing, and he ached all over.

Gabriel Johnson had been there in the background—with his usual mocking smirk. Gabe was Matt's latest problem. There were always problems. Many of them might seem insignificant to city cops, but they were often harder to solve than bigger issues. For instance, Cujo. It had patently not been Matt's responsibility to find a home for a massive dog after its master died. But the relatives hadn't wanted it, and the old man had made Matt promise.

Then there had been little Miss Burke, a frail elderly woman who could be counted on to call at three in the morning at least once a week, convinced intruders were breaking into her cottage. The whole time he was angrily rolling out of bed and dressing, Matt would be promising himself that he would really come down hard on her this time. But when he was actually there and her trembling hands were fumbling with the bolt, when her voice was quavering with relief and he saw how frightened she really had been, somehow he never delivered more than a mild rebuke.

He had solved those two problems by combining them, so to speak. It hadn't been easy. Miss Burke was as scared of dogs as she was of everything else. Fortunately, she had never read anything by Stephen King, and when Matt pointed out that no burglar would dare brave a dog that came up to his waist, she falteringly agreed to give Cujo a try.

The dog had solved the problem of Miss Burke in more ways than one. He had to be taken out, of course. And by the time Cujo finished walking Miss Burke all over town, she had made many new friends and had quite forgotten to jump at her own shadow.

Few successes were so unequivocal. There was still Old John, who insisted on shoplifting from the local grocery every Monday promptly at two and had to be intercepted and gently deprived of his booty.

And there was Gabe Johnson, a brawny black kid with an attitude. Gabe's aunt, Lily, was one of Matt's staunchest supporters. She kept a matriarchal eye on everything that went on in the Flats and kept the chief informed. She was the one who had called the previous night about the quarrel happening right next door to her. "Isn't there any way you can keep him in jail longer than overnight?" she had asked over the phone.

"Not unless she presses charges."

"How about if he hits somebody who will press charges?"

"Lily," he had said. "Don't you dare—"

Lily contrived to keep almost everyone in line—except her own nephew. Him, she seemed to regard with baffled despair.

When Lily's sister, Rose, had got cancer, she had come to stay with Lily, bringing Gabe along. The two had lived in the city up to that point, but Rose had been determined that her son not return to that environment. She had summoned Matt Olin to her bedside. "I want you to keep an eye on Gabe," the haggard woman had said. Her eyes had burned in her dark face like the last embers of a dying fire, while Lily hovered in the background. "I'm only asking you to keep him out of trouble until he gets to be eighteen. I think I can make him promise to stay here with his aunt until he graduates. Lily tells me that you keep things in line in this town. Don't let those city friends of his hang around. Get him on that team of yours. I'm not asking for miracles. Just that he graduates. Then, if he wants to go back to the city you'll have to let him."

It had been not so much a request as an order, and Matt had promised to do what he could.

The team she had spoken of was the school football squad. Matt had started coaching when the district ran out of money to hire someone to do it. He had talked several kids from the Flats into joining and convinced Bob Fisher to give them jobs at his grocery store so they could pay for their uniforms. He also required all players to maintain a high grade average and a healthy lifestyle—no smoking, drinking, or drugs.

After the team started winning, he had no trouble convincing kids to join. Especially after they'd gone to the state championships two years in a row. Everyone was convinced that the coming year would be the one when they took that championship.

Now McNeil, Fisher, and a couple of fathers took over for Matt when he couldn't be at the practices. The team had become a town effort. It had also cut the juvenile crime rate significantly.

One of the few holdouts had been Gabe Johnson. He had said, "No thanks, Chief," with his perennially mocking grin that implied he knew just what Matt was up to—and had no intention of being reformed. Not that he'd actually done anything to be reformed from. Or anything that Matt had caught him at, anyway. But that taunting grin promised that it was only a matter of time. This fall Gabe would be a senior.

But there were other things to worry about at the moment. Gingerly stretching his legs under the desk, Matt dialed and was surprised to hear a cultured baritone voice answer, "Dean Harris speaking. I'm afraid none of the secretaries are here, but," the voice continued almost apologetically, "can I help you?"

"Good morning, Dean," Matt responded. "This is Chief Olin of the Hayden, Massachusetts Police Department. I'm making some inquiries about a student who used to go to your school. I don't suppose you would have been there ten years ago?"

"Well, yes," the voice conceded. "I was. Been here twenty years, actually. Please don't tell me that one of our illustrious alumni has run afoul of the law." His humorous tone made that contingency so unlikely as to be laughable.

"You probably won't remember him after all this time," Matt said. "Luke Hayden?"

Another one of those telling silences. "Yes," the dean finally said with seeming reluctance. "I remember Luke quite well. There was an incident. His roommate died—"

"Of a drug overdose," Matt interrupted. "Yes, I know that. There were rumors at the time that Luke had provided the drugs. I would like you to tell me how much credence you gave to those rumors. Was he a dealer?"

Again the hesitation. "The students seemed to think so. They're usually right about things like that. They have more of an in than we staff members, you understand."

"If you don't mind"—Matt was insistent—"I would like to know what *you* thought."

The dean sighed. "I was trying to avoid that. Luke had a brilliant mind. I had great hopes for him. But he was almost too mature for his years. College students, you know, still tend toward insecurity and self-consciousness. Luke wasn't like that, and I think they resented his assurance. He was popular, but he had few close friends, if you can understand that. I confronted him about those rumors, and he made me feel ridiculous; he could do *that* very easily too. But he didn't deny it."

"And Diane Creighton?"

"She dropped him rather abruptly after Jamie's death. That's what made many of the students believe . . . She was, I think, closer to him than anyone. She disappointed me by her decision not to go to graduate school. But she was insistent. Said she was tired of college and wanted to start working. I got her that job at Strathmore. She seemed to fit in well there. I was shocked to hear that she'd resigned so suddenly after ten years."

Matt was careful not to show any surprise. People who assumed that he knew more than he did tended to clam up when they found out differently. "Gossip has it that her resignation was not entirely voluntary?" He had found that he could get away with almost any wild guess by attributing it to gossip.

"I can't comment on that, I'm sure." The dean's tone had gone distinctly frosty. "You might keep in mind that the new administration at that school is not what I would call sound. The fault may very well have been on their side, not on hers."

"Quite possibly." Matt discovered that he was taking on the other's refined, detached mode of speech. He dropped it to demand bluntly, "Did you like Luke?"

Speaking in a deliberate tone that suggested he was picking his words carefully, the dean said, "It is difficult to say. He was quite at ease in social situations, but he gave little about himself away. He assumed, I imagine, that his emotions were nobody else's business. I would guess that he grew up in a home where he had to look after himself from an early age. That is not uncommon with wealthy kids. Their parents are often otherwise occupied. I never felt quite comfortable around him, but that could be occasioned, I think, by my resentment over the fact . . ." Seeming to become tied up in his own verbiage, the dean paused and concluded abruptly, "He could run circles around me in the smarts department, Chief. That's hard to take from a student. Might I ask why you're interested in him?'

"I'm working on a murder case."

"I see. In that case, I doubt if Luke is the man you're looking for. I don't say he wouldn't be capable of killing. I just don't think he would ever be *reduced* to it."

"I get you. Those smarts would always help him find another option. You may be right. Thanks for your time."

■ ■ ■

When Diane went out on the terrace after breakfast, Sasha was playing with the Peter Rabbit house. Diane remembered it well. Alden Culver had made it for Regan when she was a child. It was fashioned from a piece of hollow log that stood upright on a flat base. Inside were pieces of furniture made out of twigs and pots and pans fashioned from acorns. Diane remembered especially the basket carved from a peach seed;

she had been jealous of Regan for her possession of that house. Or perhaps simply for her possession of a father's love.

Sasha was fully occupied with what she was doing, talking to herself as she dropped round black seeds one by one into a minuscule bowl. Diane sat on the edge of the chaise and watched her. Regan had been like that as a child too, absorbed in her own world.

"Hello," Diane said. "Who are you talking to? Harold?"

Sasha could not resist the chance to correct an adult. "God," she said. And, looking up, "Regan says that God doesn't see your outside, but right into where you think."

"Oh," Diane said. "Does he talk back to you?"

With her childish immunity to boredom, Sasha began transferring the seeds one at a time to the peach-pit basket. "Yes. God has lots of time to talk. All the time in forever."

Diane leaned forward. "What does he say?"

Again that grave gaze lifted to her face. "He says that you're very pretty."

Sudden tears stung Diane's eyes.

■ ■ ■

After breakfast, Regan went back up to her room. Her fears of the night now seemed exaggerated, those about Matt especially ridiculous. There had probably been no one there at all. Still she locked her door again before she sat cross-legged on the bed to read the journal entries.

Their familiar voice almost had her believing that if she raised her head from that vivacious scrawl she might see her mother smiling in at her from the old wicker chair on the balcony. On June mornings when Regan was a teen, Rosemary would come breezing into this room about nine, carrying a tray, with a blithe, "Up and at 'em, slugabed!"

It had been idyllic. When you are a teenager in June, anything seems possible. The idea of both your parents dying violently before they should have . . .

Regan shivered and looked up to see if the sun had gone behind a cloud. But it was still shining serenely.

She felt an intolerable sense of oppression. There was nothing in the handwritten pages to have brought it on. They were mostly about gardening. Rosemary's occasional references to people, by initial, were kind. Regan jumped up, slammed the papers shut in the book again, as if imprisoning something, and shoved the volume back on its shelf. Hurrying to the door, she fumbled with the lock. She would finish later. Just now, there was something awful about being barricaded alone . . .

She rushed downstairs, through the living room, and out to the terrace, where she leaned against the low wall, breathing hard. "Later," her father had said. There hadn't been any later. "You like mystery." She didn't like it anymore.

"Is something wrong?"

Regan looked around to see Diane lying in a lounge chair and Sasha playing quietly in a corner.

"No, I'm okay." Regan moved her shoulders as if shrugging off something. Her emotions had certainly returned with a vengeance. She was already turning toward the steps. "I'm way behind on my weeding." She paused. Diane too appeared haunted. "I don't suppose you'd want to help?"

When there was no reply, Regan looked back to find her niece staring at her. "Never mind. You're not dressed for—"

"That doesn't matter!" Diane jumped up, negating her white sundress with a wave of the hand. "It'll wash. I was just surprised. I've been itching to go down there and putter around myself, but I thought you might not like it."

Regan laughed. "Putter all you want. I'll be grateful. This is all really too much for one person to take care of. Hats and gloves are down in the shed." The heaviness had lifted somewhat. Perhaps it was simple loneliness after all, not a warning . . .

■ ■ ■

Early that afternoon, Matt pulled up to the big house again, got out, and regarded it with bleary resentment. The stormy night had been succeeded by a balmy, seventyish day, but he was in no mood to appreciate it. His jaw was still throbbing.

"I'm out here," a soft voice said. He turned his head to see Regan standing under the arbor. She was wearing a faded khaki shirt, a full denim skirt, and leather work gloves. She had not even, he noted sourly, bothered to ask if he was looking for her. As he approached, she turned and went back into the garden. He followed to find her kneeling in the grass path beside one of the flower beds, transferring seedlings from a flat to a bare patch of earth.

"I'll finish this if you don't mind," she said, gesturing with her trowel toward a bench on the opposite side of the path. "Have a seat."

She was acting as if the events of the previous night had never happened. She seemed, if anything, a little more relaxed. Perhaps that storm had cleared the air a little.

He sank to the bench, rubbed at his face, and winced as he brushed the swollen jaw.

"Who hit you?" she asked.

He moved his big shoulders uncomfortably. "A guy who

beats up on his wife routinely. She won't even press charges, but I will. Assaulting an officer is a felony. It'll put him away for a few months."

There was that faint glint of amusement in her expression. It reminded Matt of Gabe Johnson's sardonic grin of the evening before as the kid lounged in the background, taking in the whole scene as if it were staged for his entertainment.

"So you provoked him into taking a swing at you, I suppose?" she said.

"I reckon I can stand it better than she can. It's my job." He thought, but didn't say, that it was better him than Lily Johnson too. Despite her big mouth, Lily was a slight little thing. "There's a rose down there you might be interested in, by the way. Runs wild all over the porch."

"Oh?" Regan turned toward him, alert. "What does it look like?"

"It's pink and it's pretty," he said. "What else is there?"

She smiled. "That would only cover about three-fourths of the roses in the world. Where is it?"

"Third and Pine. In," he added deliberately, "the Flats."

She raised her brows. Again that flash of some secret laughter. "As if that would stop me? I don't think you understand me very well, Matt."

He didn't tackle that one, just sat and watched her work. The warmth of sunlight and the spicy scent of herbs were soothing, the buzzing of bees around the flowers soporific. The cat strolled up the path to lie on the edge of Regan's skirt, its sleek black coat gleaming in the sun. Up on the bank, Sasha was sleeping in the chamomile seat.

A primitive bronze cross was strung from Regan's neck by a leather cord and swayed idly with her movements. She had stripped off the gloves, and he found himself watching the long, slender hands, the smooth curve of forearms under rolled-up sleeves.

He tore his gaze away to look down the lush aisles of plants. This was a kind of escape that people from his world could not afford, could not even, perhaps, imagine. But he could not deny its effect. The throbbing in his jaw had eased; the muscles in the back of his neck were beginning to relax.

Actually, living in the Flats hadn't been so bad once he'd made up his mind to get out.

Matt had taken that pact with McNeil seriously and had applied himself to his studies. As soon as he was in high school, he got a job stocking shelves at the Fisher grocery store when Bob's father was still running it. His size won him a spot on the football team. He had little free time, going directly from school to practice to work and staying up late to study. His mother regarded him with bewilderment. His stoic determination was beyond her.

Timmy, five years younger, a quiet little kid with big glasses, was in awe of his big brother and trailed him like a timid puppy when Matt was actually at home.

When Matt was eighteen, his mother decided to leave town with her current boyfriend. "I'm not going," Matt said flatly, and he got an apartment over one of the shops downtown. After he graduated, he planned to get a swing-shift job at a factory and attend day classes at a local college until he was old enough for police training.

A timid rapping on the door of his apartment woke him the morning after his mother had bid him an emotional farewell. Timmy stood on the landing, looking scared, with his book bag on his back and a single suitcase in his hand. "They dropped me off," he said, desperate gaze fixed on his brother's face.

Fortunately, Matt had learned to control his temper by then, right down to his facial expressions.

It was something that she would do, he realized with more resignation than anger. She had convinced herself that Timmy was better off with his big brother, which was probably true. Matt rearranged his schedule in his mind. If he could find a day job that coincided with Timmy's school schedule and take college classes in the evenings . . . It wouldn't do to leave a twelve-year-old alone in the apartment at night.

That was the way it worked out. Timmy immediately took over the cooking and cleaning. In the evenings, Matt dropped him off at the college library on the way to class and picked him up there afterward.

No one interfered. McNeil had a lot of influence in Hayden, and Matt suspected that he used it on their behalf. To make up for the tightness of their schedules during the week, Matt always tried to take Timmy somewhere on the weekends: fishing or hiking, skiing during the winter. That got harder to do after he became police chief.

Their schedules hadn't left Matt with much time for a social life. He found most of the women he dated to be unfocused, almost lazy, their chatter trivial. Too, they didn't appreciate having dates interrupted by his beeper. After a while, he hadn't made the effort.

McNeil worried about him. "You've overreacted to your past, Matt," he said. "You've become too disciplined, too tightly controlled. You need some kind of life of your own. One of these days, you're going to snap."

Matt dragged his gaze back to the present to find Regan watching him. "Don't you think it's unfair to the kid?" he asked abruptly. "Getting her used to all this when she has to go back?"

Regan stood and dusted her hands off on her skirt. The cat rolled off onto the grass, lay on his back, and waggled his paws reproachfully at her. She crossed the path to stand, looking down at Matt, and put a smudgy hand to his chin. He flinched, more from surprise than pain because the touch was featherlight.

"Swelling and bruising both," she said. She leaned to snap some heart-shaped leaves from a low-growing plant under the bench and dropped them in his lap. "*Arnica.* Make a tea out of those; soak a cold compress in it. But *don't* drink it; its common name is dogbane—for good reason."

She perched on the edge of the bench beside him. He scooped up the leaves and stood, as if trying to regain control of the situation. "An up-to-date wise woman?" he asked.

She laughed and toyed with the bronze cross. "It was really the monks and nuns who kept early medicine alive. I might have made a good nun, the contemplative type, not the modern good-works sort. There used to be an idea that there should be a few people whose only occupation was to pray for the rest of the world. Well, my occupation is to create places where people can hear themselves think—or hear God speak."

"A nice ideal," he said, "for those who can afford it."

"So it's my wealth that irritates you." Her relaxed tone had tautened again.

"I am getting just a teensy bit tired of people trying to shovel guilt of one sort or another into my lap. My mother was loaded down with it too. She scrimped and saved all of her life just so nobody could say that she was wasting my father's money. It used to make him very upset. Looking back on it makes me upset too. My father earned that money, and was perfectly within his rights to give it—or to leave it—to whomever he chose. Now, I suppose I should apologize for last night, but I don't intend to. You've been asking for it. With that constant wary, disapproving expression as if you think I'm the classic rich brat. It makes the temptation to act the part almost irresistible. I wanted to find out what you really believed, and I did. You wouldn't have drunk that tea if you thought I was a killer. Admit it."

Matt had been standing stiffly, turning a dull red throughout this harangue. But then he seated himself at a careful distance and growled, "Feel better?"

"Much," she said with that same glint. And demurely, "What did you wish to talk to me about, Chief Olin?"

CHAPTER 9

■ ■ ■

We may call it herb of grace o' Sundays.

It took Matt considerable effort to drag his mind back to the case. There was something tantalizing about those brief, secret flashes of levity.

"Why," he asked finally, "didn't you tell me that Diane had lost her job and that she and her mother were in desperate need of an inheritance?"

The amused expression was wiped from Regan's face. "What?" she said.

"You mean you didn't know?"

Her bewilderment was palpable. "I don't believe it! The way they both dress—"

"Agatha's business has been in trouble for years," he said. "She just kept borrowing. She finally had to sell her house to pay off her creditors. She's been living in a cheap motel. Diane's in the same trap, since she went in with her mother after the other partner absconded. The fifty thousand they inherit between them isn't going to get them out of the hole they're in. *Listen*," he insisted, as Regan seemed on the verge of interrupting. "Think back carefully. When your father said that he was going to change his will in your favor, did he make clear that he had already done it?"

Regan gripped her cross. "I think—" she began, then stopped. "He said, 'I am going to leave the house and most of my savings to Regan.' Something like that. But you can't really believe—"

"*Am* going to," he quoted. "You're sure of that? He didn't say, '*I have* left the house,' et cetera?"

She shook her head dazedly. "I'm sure he didn't put it that way. But they must have understood—Why did Diane lose her job?"

He shook his head. "You'd better ask her yourself. I shouldn't have mentioned this much, but I assumed you knew. Has Diane been acting strange lately?"

"She wouldn't kill him. Not for twenty-five thousand ea—"

"If you're desperate," Matt said, "twenty-five thousand can seem like a lot of money. People have been murdered over far less than that. If she framed you, she might get considerably more. Did your father know about any of this?"

"No! I'm sure he didn't. I mentioned to him that Diane seemed upset. But if he knew that Agatha was in trouble, he would have done *something*."

Matt stood. "The members of your family don't communicate very well, do they?"

"No," Regan said. "I guess we don't."

He left through the arbor, and she continued to sit on the bench for several minutes, staring at nothing. The cat curled up in her lap. Unaware of it, Regan jumped up and hurried toward the terrace. The unfortunate animal flailed and managed to land with a thump on its stomach. It glared, yowled once, licked angrily at a paw, then went to sleep where it lay.

Inside, Regan paused at the bottom of the stairs to catch her breath. Then setting her mouth and shoulders in an attitude reminiscent of her father's, she went up the steps and rapped on Diane's door. There was a momentary silence, perhaps a surprised silence, then a cautious, "Come in."

"I need to talk to you," Regan said, pushing the door open. Diane was curled up in a wicker chair near the french doors. A magazine was open in her lap.

"Why didn't you tell us," Regan came right to the point, "that you'd lost your job?"

Diane's shoulders slumped. "It didn't take her very long to find out, did it? I suppose she won't be able to resist using something like that?"

"Her?" Regan said. "Matt told me just now. He didn't tell me why, though. Will you?"

Diane tossed the magazine onto the bed, stood, and walked over to the lace-blinded windows. Then, with an almost defiant stiffening of posture, she turned. "Mental problems. I started having amnesiac episodes—and sleepwalking. The campus cop found me trying to get into my classroom one night, without a key, in my nightclothes. He was a nice guy, said he wouldn't report it, but suggested that I get some psychiatric help. Then I started walking out of classes when the period was only half over and turning up in places I didn't remember going to. The new principal had never liked me. She said that if I didn't agree to resign, they'd have to make an issue of it, and that I might as well face the fact that my mind was failing."

"There must have been a reason," Regan exclaimed.

"Of course there was. I finally got scared enough to see a psychiatrist—once. He thought it was disassociation and said that it was plain I hated my job and was under too much stress. My mind had had enough and was just blanking some of it out. He thought the episodes would stop if I quit my job. And they did. At least," she added, "I *think* they did." She turned frightened eyes to Regan. "But how can I be sure? Maybe I was sleepwalking the night Grandfather was murdered. Maybe I did it and I just don't remember."

"I refuse to believe," Regan said firmly, "that you can poison anybody in your sleep. Besides, Daddy had already drunk the tea before I left that room, remember? You hated teaching?"

"Yes. I found that I wasn't cut out for it right after I started. But we needed the money. I couldn't quit. It wasn't too bad until this current principal took over. You know how they say a school will change to match its administrator? She's a vindictive, jealous, highly competitive type who has her favorites and her not-so-favorites. The backstabbing started almost at once. The problems with Mother's store were getting worse too; it took her a long time to admit defeat. Finally she had to close, but then there were the creditors. We should have declared bankruptcy, of course, but mother decided instead to go to one of those places that offer to consolidate all your debts. The interest rates are monstrous, and they get abusive when you can't pay. Do you know how horrible it is," she asked, voice shaking, "to hear yourself reviled on your answering machine day after day? I had to listen to the messages, of course, in case there was something important. After a while, you start believing that you are what they say you are."

"For heaven's sake, Diane, why didn't either of you tell any of this to Father?"

"We were trying," Diane said. "We were really trying. Mother just couldn't admit to being a failure. Not when you were so successful."

"*Me?*" Regan asked. "What do *I* have to do with—"

"Everything," Diane interrupted. "It was always the three of you. You, Rosemary, Grandfather. You had your own cozy little circle with everybody else excluded. *I* resented it, and I'm not his daughter. I'm very fond of plants myself, and I had a nice little garden at Mother's house every summer. But I could never talk about that here. You three had a monopoly on the subject."

Regan was shaking her head. "That's wrong," she said. "That's completely backward. Mother and I were the outsiders—the intruders. You all resented us." She stopped. "Oh."

"Of course we resented you!" Diane flared. "We're only human. And then when Grandfather said that he was going to leave you everything, it was just too much. You've got to see that!" She began to cry.

Regan shook her head again, not in answer to the question, but as if to clear it. "If Agatha hadn't been so loud all the time, so dramatizing—"

"Mother only says what she feels," Diane insisted through her tears. "You don't. You're dishonest, Regan; you always have been. You hated us too, but you were never straightforward enough to say so. So it was always Mother who looked bad. I explained that to her, but she was never able to hide her emotions like you do."

Regan had a hand over her eyes to shield them from the

light as she peered up at Diane. "I'm not going to argue with you," she said. "I know you're right. Except that I never really hated any of you. I just wanted to be left alone."

"Why?"

"Why?" Regan shrugged. "As a kid, I avoided people because I didn't think they would want to be bothered with me. By the time I became an adult, I was so comfortable being alone that I began to prefer it, especially after Mother died."

Her voice caught. She stopped a moment, then went on. "I never wanted to hurt like that again. Mother had always been able to coax me out. But Daddy tried to protect me. It wasn't his fault. It was mine. I'm sorry."

Regan wiped at her eyes with the back of her hand. Diane, sniffling, reached for a tissue, then passed the box to her aunt. They looked at each other and laughed. "When we finally do get emotional, we do a bang-up job, don't we?" Diane commented.

"Both you and Agatha dress so well," Regan said.

"Haven't you ever noticed that most of those clothes are ones we've had for years? Fortunately, well-made classics age well. Never mind, Regan. I was just looking for somebody to blame. It's not really your problem. Mother would rather starve than accept charity from you."

"How about you?" Regan demanded.

"Me?" Diane laughed shakily, dropping back into the chair. "I'm not quite so proud. Do you think I'd make a good waitress? That's all I'm likely to get now. Any teaching job I apply for, they're going to want to know why I quit such a good position so abruptly—and why I haven't any references."

"That's easily solved." Regan became briskly matter-of-fact. "Caroline has been talking for months about adding a tea-and-craft shop to the farm. And she's been bugging me to find someone to get it going. It demands a creative imagination and, above all, excellent taste. We want historically accurate, not cutesy, stuff. We've been thinking nosegays, strewing herbs, Parma violets. For the tea shop, crumpets and scones and such. Most of our customers are great admirers of all things British. You'd have to come up with the ideas and oversee the cooks and clerks and waitresses. At a manager's salary, of course. Do you want the job?"

Diane raised her head and regarded her aunt with incredulity. When Regan had finished, Diane struggled to sit up straight. "Yes. Yes, I do. Are you sure? Caroline doesn't seem to like me very much."

"Caroline never lets her prejudices interfere with good business," Regan replied. "She'll realize that you're ideal. You and Agatha can stay here. There's plenty of room."

"Yes," Diane said, still dazed, "but I don't think that Mother will—"

They became aware at the same time of a raised voice from downstairs—an unfamiliar male voice. "You thought you'd got away from me, didn't you? Sneaking off up here like this. Well, I got news for you, lady. You're not going to get rid of me until you pay up! You ain't fooling nobody. If you've got relatives who live in a joint like this, you can sure afford—"

By that time, Regan and Diane were at the head of the stairs. The front door stood open. In the hallway below, a burly man in a T-shirt and jeans had Agatha backed up against the wall. He was doing his yelling inches from her averted face.

"Who are you and what are you doing in my house?" Regan's voice was no louder than usual, but there was an intensity that sliced right through the intruder's harangue. He turned to look up at them.

"He's a bill collector," Diane said. "His name's Wayne."

"Nice to see you again too, beautiful," Wayne said, unabashed. He turned his bold gaze on Regan, "More to the point, who are you?"

"Diane," Regan said, without shifting her attention from the man below, "will you go into Daddy's room and get the strongbox that's on the closet shelf?"

"Hey, now, that's more like it," Wayne said. "A reasonable woman for a change." He approached the foot of the stairs, but Regan's cool stare stopped his advance.

She turned to twirl the dial on the box, as Diane held it. The clicking spin was quite audible in the sudden silence, as was the purr of a car and the crunch of gravel outside.

Wayne looked over his shoulder, then back at Regan. She reached into the box and lifted out a pistol. "Hey," he said, taking a couple of steps back.

Regan paid no attention. She broke open the revolver to make sure that it was loaded.

"Mathilda," she said. "You're just in time. I need to ask you something."

Wayne whirled and stood sideways, trying to keep both Regan and the lawyer in view. A balding young man with wire-rimmed glasses followed Mathilda and raised his eyebrows at the scene.

"This man has forced his way into my home and threatened my sister," Regan said. "That means that I can legally shoot him. Right?"

Mathilda pursed her lips. "Fine by me, but kindly wait until we're out of the line of fire." She pushed Agatha before her into the doorway of the living room. "What do you think, Harry?"

"I doubt that any American jury would give her more than manslaughter on it," Harry said. "Since she's already up for murder one, she doesn't have much to lose. If I were you, Miss Culver, I would shoot to kill. Otherwise, they almost always sue."

Wayne tried to grin. "All right, you've had your little joke."

"No joke," said another voice behind him. Luke lounged in the open doorway. "The lady *has* been indicted, pal. If I were you, I'd beat it before she decides she might as well have two for the price of one."

Regan guessed afterward that it was Luke, not the gun, that was the clincher. Because Luke looked so much like what he was.

"Hey." Wayne extended his hands, palms out. "No offense, people. My argument ain't with you, but with the other lady." He looked around, but Agatha had disappeared. "It can wait." He slipped around Luke and out the door. His pickup roared away down the drive, spewing gravel.

Luke proceeded calmly up the stairs, saying to Regan as he passed, "You've still got the safety on."

Regan plopped the gun back in the box that Diane held and spun the dial to lock it again. Diane carried it back into Alden Culver's bedroom.

"If you two will come with me," Regan said to Mathilda and Harry. She led them up to her room, went out onto the balcony, and turned.

"I was angry," she said simply. "If Agatha has had to put up with that on a regular basis, it's no wonder that she's . . ."

Mathilda had seated herself comfortably in one of the balcony's wicker chairs. "Harry's an intern from my old firm," she said. "I've borrowed him. That was a very pretty bluff. It *was* a bluff, wasn't it?"

"Of course. I've never fired that thing in my life, and I understand that it isn't easy to hit anything with a handgun." She regarded them thoughtfully. "You've been investigating everybody. You would know how much Agatha owes and who she owes it to."

Mathilda turned her head. "Harry?"

He flipped open his notebook. "That guy was probably hired by Acme Credit. They're a sleazy outfit that promises to consolidate all your debts. They then charge an exorbitant rate of interest."

He read off the amount owed, and Regan did not flinch. "Get me the president."

"What?"

"The president of that credit place. I want to talk to him. Can you get him on the phone for me?"

Harry appeared doubtful. "Well, this is the weekend . . ." He looked at Mathilda.

"She's employing us," Mathilda said. "Go dig the guy up for her." When Harry went out to the hall to use the phone, she said to Regan, "What do you plan to do?"

"Pay it all off. They'll have to wait until Monday when I can make some arrangements at the bank."

Mathilda shrugged. "Like I said, you're the boss. As long as you have enough left to pay me, I'm not going to argue with you. Just don't expect her to love you for it."

Regan turned to look down over the gardens again. "There is enough," she said strangely. "As long as you keep using it, there is always enough. It's when you try to hoard it that it rots."

"Money?"

"And love, time, talent, flour, oil. I'll have to talk to Agatha."

"Where is she?"

"Down by the lily pond."

Mathilda shot Regan a concerned look. "She wouldn't—"

Regan shook her head. "Not with Sasha there. Sasha loves the pond, but she isn't allowed near it unless there's somebody with her. Whenever she sees anyone heading in that direction, she follows. I wonder sometimes if she was sent here to help us, instead of the other way around."

■ ■ ■

"I talked to the president of Acme Credit."

Agatha did not look up. She was sitting under a tree at the edge of the wildflower meadow, holding one end of the daisy chain that Sasha was braiding.

"Mathilda and I were pretty severe with him, actually. Mathilda hinted that we could sue over his employee's conduct. Acme will be glad to see the last of your account. And I don't think Wayne will have a job come Monday. I'm prepared to transfer the money then."

Agatha continued to watch Sasha's fingers.

"If you had only asked Daddy for help when you first needed it!" Regan went on. "You don't think I could have got my business going without him, do you?"

A bee bumbled into one of the flowers on the chain and glinted off to the clover-scented west. "You shouldn't be mad at her," Sasha said. "She's sad."

Regan smiled crookedly at the little girl. "Daddy would

have been so happy to help you if he'd known, Agatha. Like God. He can't do anything until you ask, either. This refusing anything but what you've earned is what hell is all about."

Sasha finished her chain and joined the two ends. She stood to place the crooked crown of flowers on Agatha's impeccable coiffure. "I don't think she wants to talk now."

"I guess she doesn't. Think about it, Agatha. It's up to you."

■ ■ ■

That evening, Matt sat alone in his office, feet propped up on one corner of the desk, scraps of paper spread out over the flat surface. It was his way of brainstorming. Each piece contained one or two words, names, occupations, objects, or concepts that seemed to have a connection to the case.

First, he'd arranged them in alphabetical order. Aconite, affair, Agatha, Alden, alternative medicine, book, boutique, businessman, Caroline, cup, Dennis, Diane, doctor, drug dealer, farm, farm manager, garden designer, Gina, herbalist, housewife, inheritance, journal, Luke, mercy, Regan, Reid, Rosemary, surprise, tea, teacher, ten years.

In this random order, they seemed like pieces from several different puzzles that coexisted as uneasily as these suspects did.

He began to divide the papers into separate piles. Alden, Regan, Caroline, and Dennis with their shared interest in plants and alternative medicine went into one. Agatha and Diane with their shared genteel poverty into another. The more prosperous Gina and Reid into a third. Luke was alone. Aconite, the tea, and the journal seemed to fit most appropriately into the garden category. Inheritance, though, would seem to be of more importance to Agatha and Diane. But what about Alden's enigmatic references to mercy, surprise, and ten years?

There was a strange dearth of any real clues in this case. The only fingerprints on the cup had been Regan's and Alden's. Fingerprints or hairs elsewhere in the room wouldn't prove anything. All of them had been in that room on the morning after.

The locked door couldn't have been finagled in the usual way; Luke had demonstrated that. And the french doors had also been bolted on the inside. Mathilda would probably assert that the latter could have been done by sleight of hand. That might implicate Diane, the only other suspect besides Regan whose room opened onto the balcony.

But if Regan was right about her father having finished his tea before she left the room, there would have been no point in Diane's poisoning the dregs.

Irrevocably, it all kept going back to Regan. But if she wanted to kill her father, why would she do it in so straightforward—and stupid—a manner? She wasn't a stupid person. Was it a bluff? Did she think a jury would never convict her on such obvious evidence?

It would help if there were more little pointers. Bricks to build a wall with. Now he had only the cup and the locked doors. They looked unshakable enough, but the motive had already collapsed.

What if it was suicide after all? Alden had seemed dispirited that evening. And Regan could be lying to save his reputation. But would she risk imprisonment?

It was an idyllic summer evening. He was alone in the building. People were going by on the sidewalk outside, couples and family groups on their way out to dinner or a movie, laughing and talking. Saturday night. Just now the lawns were striped with golden light. As the shadows grew deeper, his phone would begin to ring. Not all family groups were happy.

At least the Culvers didn't go in for drunken shouting matches and physical violence. Poison was a detached sort of weapon. Like Regan? If that was evidence, he would make a good suspect himself. His sympathy for another solitary type might be the reason he was hunting so doggedly for an alternative. He hoped so, anyway. He began to reshuffle the slips of paper as if they were a deck of cards.

■ ■ ■

Regan was in her studio working with a new computer landscaping program that had been sent to her in hopes that she'd write a recommendation for it. It was impressive. One could materialize whole beds of plants with a click of the mouse. Too bad it wasn't that easy in real life.

Not that this garden was going to be very satisfactory. It was for a client who believed that bigger was always better. Who wanted dahlias the size of dinner plates, cannas, glads . . . It was going to be loud. *Perhaps I could talk her into the perennial glads; they at least look a little more natural.*

Regan stopped to lecture herself. *This is not about what you like, but what she likes. At least she called to offer encouragement, not to cancel like the others. If you're any kind of designer, you can make this look good.* Regan began to reshuffle flowers as Matt was reshuffling clues.

Daylight faded; eventually only the computer screen glowed in the dark room.

She heard somebody come in the front door, more than one somebody. Their voices floated in from the dark hall. "And this is the kind of thanks I get," Reid was saying. "For that expensive education I gave you, the sports cars—"

"How like a serpent's tooth is an ungrateful child," Luke quoted in a bored tone. "Give it up, Dad. The answer is still no. Unfortunately for you, I'm not the feel-guilty type."

Reid persisted. "But why?" he demanded. "That's what I want to know. *Why?*"

"Why should I justify my actions to you?" Luke countered.

"You have no family feeling at all?" Reid sounded more baffled than angry.

"No. I don't feel responsible for what I didn't choose. Now, I suggest we suspend this conversation. You don't know who might be listening."

Regan hunched guiltily in her chair. She didn't think they could see the computer screen from out there. She heard the sound of their feet on the stairs, then the closing of doors above. Glancing at her watch, she was surprised to see that it was past midnight.

■　■　■

The next morning was Sunday. Regan got Sasha dressed for church first and let her run downstairs. When Regan came into the kitchen fifteen minutes later, Agatha was standing at the stove, stirring something. Sasha was primly seated at the table, eating scrambled eggs and orange juice.

Agatha demanded, without turning, "Is this parsley and chives?"

Only then noticing the minced greenery on the chopping

board, Regan crept forward to look at the crisp curly heads and oniony spears. "Yes."

Agatha picked up the board and whisked the herbs into her skillet with a flick of the knife blade. "Sit down. This will be ready in a minute."

Regan retreated to the far side of a table that was already set with plates and silverware. She pulled out a chair. The legs squeaked across the tile in the beginning of a silence that shortly seemed deafening.

Regan cast a furtive look around at the neat place settings. Straw mats, rolled cloth napkins contained by straw-flowered rings, juice that was no doubt freshly squeezed, a small bouquet of roses in a crystal vase. *Look!* it all seemed to intone. *This is how a summer breakfast is supposed to be done!*

Regan felt that old, tight, helpless feeling of inadequacy in the pit of her stomach.

The buzzer rang. Agatha whisked a pan of muffins out of the oven and crossed to the table to rank them neatly in a linen-lined basket. They would look better in an artistic tumble, Regan thought. "What's this?" Agatha asked.

Regan's mind went blank as she stared at the sprig of lacy blue foliage Agatha was indicating. It was tucked in with the roses and quite familiar. "Rue," she said finally. "That's rue."

"It stinks," Agatha said disapprovingly. She went back to the stove for her skillet and returned to spoon scrambled eggs onto Regan's plate. They were tossed with diced cheese and ham and smelled delectable.

"Well, yes," Regan agreed. "Rue is bitter. That's why they call it the herb of grace, I guess."

Agatha scraped the rest of the eggs into a glass casserole

dish, covered it, and stood, arms crossed, at the opposite side of the table. "Grace is bitter?"

Sitting under her half sister's overpowering stare, picking at the scrambled eggs, Regan could not think of a logical reason why rue should have earned that nickname, although it had always seemed strikingly apposite before.

"I suppose," she stumbled finally, "because it's both bad tasting and beautiful. Kind of like repentance." She stopped and shrugged, then took a bite of the eggs.

Agatha seemed to be waiting for something.

"Oh," Regan said. "This is very good."

Agatha relaxed a little, pulled out a chair, and sat down. "You needn't sound so unhappy about it," she said. "You really can't stand having to pay me a compliment, can you? I don't know how you're going to put up with us full-time when you've always been so eager for us to leave before."

Regan stopped chewing. She hadn't thought that her distaste for the weekend visits was so obvious. *I've always resented her criticizing me, but that's the first compliment I can recall paying her. Ever.*

Sasha slid out of her seat and made for the open doorway to the kitchen garden where the cat was sitting, washing himself. "I fed that animal," Agatha said. "He seemed hungry."

A few days ago Regan would have taken that as an accusation that she was starving her pet. But it could, she realized now, be a simple statement of fact.

She hurriedly swallowed her unchewed mouthful. "I'm sorry, Agatha," she blurted. "I have a hard time complimenting you, because, next to you and Diane, I always feel so inadequate. You are always so perfect about everything. Your clothes, your posture, all this . . ." Her gesture encompassed the table. She reached for a bowl of sugared strawberries. "I used to think that it was what they called breeding, that you were either born with it or you weren't. You were my nemesis; you represented everything that I couldn't hope to live up to."

Agatha looked taken aback at this sudden rush of words. She said dryly, but without malice, "You always did have too much imagination, Regan. My mother was a nurse before she married, not a socialite. I doubt that breeding comes into it. She was also what nowadays they would call obsessive-compulsive. Nothing was ever quite good enough. Father stayed away. Gina and I didn't have that option. I always thought that I would get it right someday. Gina just quit trying. Perhaps she was smarter. Are you finished with that?" She reached for Regan's empty plate.

Regan held on to it. "Actually I'm not. I'd like some more, if you don't mind. Aren't you going to eat?"

Their eyes met. A trace of a wintry smile touched Agatha's lips. "I'm still doing it, aren't I? Very well. We might as well finish these. Everybody else is late. It will serve them right."

"I got up early so I could go to church," Regan said. "Do you want to come?"

Agatha raised her eyebrows. "Is that wise? I know that church is supposed to be a refuge, but—"

"The pastor will not be happy to see me, and the others will simply be curious," Regan finished cheerfully. "Fortunately, the one I'm going to talk to isn't so easily embarrassed."

"You can talk to him just as well here," Agatha said with a trace of acerbity. "Assuming, of course, that we are discussing God, and not Matt Olin. Although, as often as the latter has been underfoot lately, it could apply to him as well."

Regan decided to ignore that. "I can't hide forever." She had broken up her muffin in the strawberries and was eating the resultant mess with every sign of enjoyment. Agatha was regarding this process with the stifled air of one who is with heroic difficulty refraining from comment.

"It would be easy for me to become a recluse," Regan explained, drawing a vague pattern in the air with her spoon and inadvertently dripping strawberry juice on the cloth. Agatha winced. "I have to face them and get it over with. That will be much easier in the home of the only one who knows the truth." Her overly bright gaze rose to Agatha's again. "And that *isn't* Matt Olin. There is something I'd like to ask you. You're the only one around here who's had a child. Except for Reid, and somehow I doubt he was much involved with raising his. Do you think I should send Sasha away?"

Agatha raised her brows. "Why?"

"Won't she become frightened of me? If she hears people say that I might have killed Daddy?"

Agatha looked across to where the child sat in the sun, playing with the cat. "She's probably heard all of that by now. Children believe with their hearts, not their heads. Do you know what she said when I gave her those eggs? 'This isn't what Aunt Regan gives me.'" Agatha went falsetto in a very good imitation of the child's haughty tone.

Regan's lips twitched. "And you said?"

"I said, 'You, young lady, will sit down and eat that without any back talk. And you will like it much better than those nuts and twigs your Aunt Regan gives you.'"

"She probably did too," Regan said, "but she will never admit it. Why were you in the herb cabinet the night of the party?"

Agatha stiffened. "You knew that? Why didn't you tell Matt Olin?"

Regan's reply was matter-of-fact. "Because I knew that you loved Daddy. You wouldn't have killed him."

Agatha turned her head away to look at Sasha and Gato again. "My headaches," she muttered. "Aspirin doesn't seem to help them. The only thing that does is your mother's formula. Did you think that I would admit that? I'd run out of what you gave me for Christmas, and I thought that cabinet would be easy enough to jimmy."

"Remind me to give you Daddy's key," Regan said cheerfully. "A lot of the cooking herbs are in there too. They lose their zing if they're kept on the stove too long."

Agatha looked at her again—resolutely. "I'll take the money. I can't pay you back."

"I don't expect you to. It's a gift, not a loan."

Diane rushed into the kitchen at that point, her worried gaze shuttling from face to face. "Sorry. I guess I overslept. I was going to make some waffles. Where is everybody? Aren't they coming down?"

"Thank you," her mother remarked acidly, "for the implication that Regan and I do not qualify as anybody. We ate all the eggs, so you'll have to make do with muffins and juice. I am going to go rouse that lazy Gina. I suggest that you change into something more appropriate than that sundress. We are going to church."

■ ■ ■

There was an excited rustle and then an embarrassed silence when the women and child walked into the vestibule. Regan and her father had always sat near the front of the sanctuary. Now, holding Sasha's hand, Regan sailed up the aisle to take her accustomed place. The other three women trailed in her wake.

The pastor was noticeably flustered. It could not be easy, Regan supposed, having a former Sunday school teacher arrested for murder, especially when the man who had done the arresting was sitting in *his* accustomed place on the far right.

The sermon, disjointed and rambling, was about forgiveness, though it was never made clear who was to forgive whom. Regan eventually stopped trying to follow and fixed her gaze and her thoughts on the cross behind the pastor. *Let my father and mother know that I am going to be all right.*

Sasha did not like church, but she knew better than to wriggle. Under her sulky glare, Gina's puzzled frown and Agatha's skeptically arched brows, the reverend sank further and further into his notes and incoherence.

Afterward, as the women moved toward the vestibule, conversations around them seemed a little too high-pitched and inconsequential. A few people said hello, nervously, to Regan, but none of them mentioned her father.

At a sudden hush, Regan looked up to realize that the police chief, coming from the side, was going to meet her in the doorway to the vestibule. *What do they think I'm going to do?* she wondered with amused exasperation. *Make a scene?*

"Hello, Matt," she said. "How's your jaw?"

"Much better." His quirky grin relayed that he, too, had noticed the constraint around them. "Are you sure that wasn't magic?"

"Science, pure science," she replied. "Good morning, Reverend. That was a *deep* sermon."

"Universal," Matt agreed from behind her. "All things to all people."

Regan carefully refrained from looking at him. She mustn't giggle. It wasn't funny, really. Reverend Morris looked so miserable.

"I am sorry about everything, Regan," the pastor said. He started to pat Sasha's head, but she ducked. He patted Regan's hand instead. His own was cold. "Would you like me to come and see you?"

"Oh, no," she said. "I don't think that will be necessary. I hope you didn't mind my asking Reverend Potts to do Father's funeral."

"Not at all, not at all." The reverend babbled out his profound gratitude at not being asked to do the funeral. "Known him much longer and all that. I perfectly understand."

Outside, Regan walked beside Matt toward the street. On her other side, Sasha still clung and cast distrustful glances across at the policeman. Regan was thinking about Reverend Potts, who had been a little too pungent for most of his flock and had been voted out a couple of years before. At the funeral he had said, "I don't intend to talk much about Alden Culver. He was a Christian man. No one can question that. I do have doubts about some of the rest of you, though. This is a namby-pamby, wishy-washy generation, and you know what God says about that. I would prefer that you were either hot or cold, but, because you are nothing, I am going to vomit you out of my mouth." A strange funeral sermon, but she thought her father would have enjoyed it.

"I hope you realize that Potts would have addressed you from the pulpit this morning," Matt said. "Me too, no doubt."

"No doubt," Regan agreed. "It would have been something of a relief."

"At least he wasn't one for beating around the bush." Matt leaned against the fender of his pickup, which was parked at the curb. The warm air smelled of cut grass and juniper. Up on the lawn, most of the chatting groups were looking his way.

Noticing those stares, Regan said, "Sorry. I do seem to get you in hot water, one way or another."

Matt shrugged his big shoulders. "It doesn't matter. If they're determined not to like you, they'll find some reason for it. I never did fit in here."

"If *you're* determined not to fit in," Regan suggested softly, "*you'll* find some reason for it."

She was wearing a cream-colored chiffon dress that floated around her like a nimbus of sunlight and a straw hat piled with filmy fabric roses a shade darker.

Matt tore his gaze away from those eyes that looked like inconstant water and crossed his arms. "Did Potts ask you if you killed your father?"

"Yes. I told him no. *He* believed me."

"I have to go with the evidence, Regan. You know that." He pushed away from the truck with what he hoped was an air of finality and went around to the driver's door. But he could not resist another look at her across the roof.

She was standing, watching him, with a smile on her lips. The sun was high, and from this distance, it was hard to read her expression under the hat's shadow. But her smile seemed almost tender.

Suddenly angry, he yanked at the door. She thought she was going to get off. Between her fancy lawyer and expending a little charm on the bumbling police chief . . . The most unnerving part about it was that she was probably right. He slammed into his seat and gunned the truck away from the curb. Somebody was stepping down into the street almost in front of him. He slammed his fist down on the horn so hard that it hurt. The offender jumped back.

It was his day off. He decided that he would drive up into the mountains and fish one of the remote streams he used to visit with his brother.

The other three women were waiting for Regan a little way down the sidewalk. "You'd better stay away from him," Diane said. "People are starting to talk."

Agatha raised her eyebrows. "*Starting?* Come now, my dear. That's a bit naive, even for you. Perhaps Regan has the right idea. Better be talked about out of prison than forgotten in it."

"People always talk," Gina said. "If we weren't us, we would be talking about us too."

Upon reaching the house, they all went upstairs to change. Regan hustled Sasha into jeans and a short-sleeve shirt and sent her down to play. Tossing her hat at the bed, Regan regarded her own reflection in the dresser mirror. She wondered why nobody had ever tried to set her up on a date with Matt Olin. There were not that many single men her age around, and helpful matchmakers had attempted to link her up with almost all of them. She had never gone out with anyone more than once or twice, though. *Perhaps people thought Matt and I would have nothing in common. And we don't.*

The shriveled pansies on the dresser reminded her that she hadn't taken any of the coneflower extract since the night of the party. To call these last few days stressful would be something of an understatement. Her father would be displeased with her.

Starting into the bathroom, she heard the phone shrill out in the hall. She paused until she felt somebody's hasty footsteps move in that direction and heard the pealing cut off. She was reaching for the bottle in the medicine cabinet when Diane called, "Regan, it's for you!"

Taking the extract with her, she went out into the hall. Diane held out the receiver. Both of Regan's hands were full. She had automatically unscrewed the lid and was holding the dropper in her right hand. Putting the dropper down on the phone table, she carefully released the rubber bulb so as not to squirt the liquid and accepted the phone. "Hello?"

"How is it going?" Caroline asked. "Did you get around to reading those entries yet? Was there anything there?"

"Not really," Regan said, eyeing the closed doors around her. The cat jumped up on the stand beside her and she stroked its insistent arching back.

"I suppose you can't say—there. Let's try just yes or no. Did she mention any of them?"

"Yes."

"Was there anything important enough to kill for?"

"No."

"Drat!" Caroline sounded annoyed. "What did he want to go hiding the things for if they weren't important? Are you sure—"

The cat was batting something around. Regan looked down to find a dribble of extract all over the table, and the animal crouching to lap at it with a small pink tongue. Annoyed, she shoved Gato off the table.

Caroline was still talking. "—might not seem important to you," she was saying. "But it could have importance in

177

context, say, if your father had more knowledge about the situation. Was there anything like that?"

"I don't think so." Regan frowned, trying to remember. "I *was* reminded of something, but couldn't think what I was reminded of, if you understand what I mean." She noticed that the cat was down on its side, playing again, batting at something with all its paws.

"But it was mostly about her plants. There wasn't really anything—" Regan was hazily watching the cat as she spoke. *"There isn't anything there!"*

She wasn't aware of raising her voice as she spoke, but she must have because Caroline said, *"What is it, Regan? What's wrong?"* And the others were there, crowding around . . .

Gato's paws were flailing, but there was nothing between them. Even as they watched, he went suddenly limp.

Regan dropped the bottle and receiver onto the table. The bottle rocked and would have gone over had Agatha not grabbed and steadied it. "It was in there," Regan whispered. "He got some of that." She knelt and scooped the cat into her arms.

Cradling him protectively, she looked up at the circle of closed, seemingly hostile faces. *"Why?"* she asked, her voice breaking. "What did we ever do to you?"

Clutching the limp animal close to her chest, she whirled and ran down the stairs. Diane started after her. "Where is she going?"

Gina grabbed Diane's arm. "That old veterinarian down the street. Better stay here. I don't think she's in a mood to see any of us right now."

Sasha had come into the hallway below only in time to catch the last of the scene. Now she stared with frightened eyes up at those on the landing, turned with a scream, and ran headlong after Regan.

Agatha picked up the fallen receiver and spoke into it, "Regan is all right, Caroline. Get off the phone. I need to use it." She stabbed the button with her finger, released it, and began to dial.

Diane sat down weakly on the top step. "If the cat hadn't . . . Regan would have . . ." She didn't finish.

"Got it instead," Agatha agreed. "That was quite fortuitous. It could mean that she did it herself to deflect suspicion, or . . ."

She did not sound convinced. Diane turned to look at her. "Or what? Luck? Coincidence?"

"No," Agatha said, listening to the phone ring. "I think they call that grace."

CHAPTER 10
· · ·

O, you must wear your rue with a difference.

Dr. Pauli was waiting on the sidewalk when Regan rushed up to him. He was holding a syringe. "Agatha called and said you were coming." He took the cat from her arms and briefly examined its bulging eyes and flaccid limbs. "She also said it was probably aconite, and I think she's right." He laid the animal on the grass and jabbed the needle into the skin at the scruff of its neck.

Regan squinted at him. The sunlight seemed overbright, the grass too intense a green. Dr Pauli's face swam in the glare. "Is he—" Sasha caught up then, half-panting, half-sobbing, and Regan put a hand on the child's shoulder.

"He's not dead," the veterinarian said. "I think he has a chance. He's young and healthy and, fortunately, we use aconite as a muscle relaxant during surgery. So we keep the antidote on hand in case of mistakes. *Digitalis.*"

Regan's lips mouthed a single word. "Foxglove."

"Yes," he agreed. "*Foxglove* to you. We might as well sit.

Here is as good as anywhere to wait. And I think Gato would prefer it. He never did like my clinic."

Sasha squeezed between Regan and Gato, lay down on her stomach beside the cat, and stroked its gleaming fur. Eventually her eyelids began to droop.

Dr. Pauli took out his pipe and began to pack tobacco into the bowl.

"Alden always tried to wean me of this," he said reflectively. "Until he decided that it was part of my content, as he put it. To Alden, content was more important medically than any so-called wonder drug."

"Yes," Regan said in a pinched tone, her hand resting lightly on Gato's neck. As always, the black fur soaked up the sun. "People would ask him for advice and he would say straight-out, 'Are you happy?' Most of them had a hard time answering that." A smile quivered on her lips. "Most of them didn't ask again, either."

After a while Regan said, "It was in my coneflower extract. Gato got at the dropper. If he hadn't—"

"Your father took that extract too, didn't he?" the old man inquired.

"Yes." She turned her head. "But the poison was in the tea."

"There was poison in the *cup*," he said. "It might not be the same thing. Do you suspect them—your family?"

She watched a man across the street mow his yard. "I don't know. I used to think of them as the enemy. But then it was like when you turn around in a dream to confront the ones who frighten you. And they're not nearly so . . ." She fumbled for the right word.

"Implacable?" he suggested.

"Yes. Not nearly so implacable as I thought. It never occurred to me that they might be afraid and unhappy and—"

"Human," he finished for her.

She smiled tremulously at him. "And human. I realize now that I never tried—never *wanted*—to communicate with them. I had begun to think that we could start over. But then this happened. Maybe it's too late. I told Agatha and Diane that they could stay. Do you think that is wise? I would take the chance myself, but"—her gaze settled on the sleeping child—"if there should be another *accident* . . ." Regan squeezed her eyes shut and shook her head.

Dr. Pauli's gaze was on Sasha too as he said, "You are more like your mother than you know, Regan. You have an empathy for the obviously helpless and hurting. But you get from your father your unwillingness to be helped in return—your determination to go it alone. He knew it as a weakness; he hoped for better for you. His dearest wish was that you would reconcile somehow with your sisters and your niece. He didn't realize that it would take his death to make it happen. They were in church this morning to back you up, you know. I thought then how happy Alden would have been to see you all together like that. But if you feel you can't trust them—"

Regan was shaking her head. "I may have disliked them, but I never doubted their integrity. Or their love for Father. But I do doubt my own judgment now. I have been so wrong—"

Dr. Pauli was smiling. "You have *always* doubted your own judgment, Regan. It's why you quote your parents so much. You've always attributed your success to their famous names, not to your own talent. Don't you think it's time to have a little faith in your own opinions?"

A couple of hours later when Regan returned to the house, she found Agatha sitting alone, ramrod straight, on the couch in the living room, reading a magazine. "Well?" Agatha inquired.

"Dr. Pauli thinks he's going to be okay," Regan said. "Gato had started to try to lift his head by the time I left. The doctor wants to keep him overnight. Sasha is going to stay with the Paulis for a couple of days. They've kept her before when both Daddy and I had to be away."

Agatha nodded briskly. "Good. I called your lawyer. She couldn't reach Matt Olin, so she got hold of the state police and insisted they send somebody out. A man picked up the bottle. He took one from Father's medicine chest too. You don't look too good. You didn't take any of that, did you?"

Regan shook her head and kept shaking it because it was too much trouble to stop. "I'm just tired."

Agatha stood. "Lie down then."

Regan tried to stifle a yawn. "Did everybody get lunch? What time is it?"

"I sent them out to eat. Lie down and I'll get you something."

When Agatha returned with a tray, Regan was barely awake enough to prop herself up on one elbow and accept the cold beef sandwich and glass of milk that was offered. She hoped fleetingly that Agatha was not the poisoner. The food tasted very good. Everything felt good, from the soft chiffon against her skin to the velvety cushion she sank back against. The cat had lived. Perhaps that meant it was over. The worst is past. . . . There was some kind of quote like that, but her sluggish mind could not dredge it up.

She smiled up at Agatha. "Thank you. You'll look after Sasha, won't you? If anything happens to me? See that she gets home to her parents?"

Agatha pulled a cotton throw from the back of the couch and tucked it around her half sister's legs. "Nothing's going to happen to you," she said. "Get some rest." Regan was asleep before the sound of Agatha's footsteps died away in the quiet house.

■ ■ ■

Mathilda Baker was on the phone, harassing private detectives. Harry had his chair tipped back on its hind legs and was whistling softly to himself.

"What do you mean, 'It's the weekend'?" Mathilda bawled. Am I or am I not paying your outrageously inflated wages? No, you listen to me. Drug dealers are no respecters of Sunday. Now you go out there and find some of your smarmy little coke-sniffing pals and find out what they know about Luke Hayden!"

Even from across the room, Harry could hear some squeaky imprecations from the other end.

"You walk a fine line? I know you walk a fine line, Bernie. Between sloth and idiocy. None of them are going to bother snuffing you; they find you too amusing. So what if they're scared of Luke! All the better. That means they don't like him, and they'll be happy to get him in trouble if they know their weaselly little names will be kept out of it. Tell them we will be discreet. We will not reveal our sources. What do you mean? I, Mathilda Baker, am the soul of discretion." She banged down the receiver.

"It's going to be kind of hard to be discreet," Harry pointed out. "If you're planning to bring all this out on the witness stand."

Mathilda turned a shriveling glare on him. "You're not here to think, Mr. Jarvis. Simply to take notes." She began punching out another number.

This time she did more listening than talking. "Well, I told you to dig up a scandal, and you've found one all right," she said finally, almost pettishly. "I told the stupid girl not to hire me. I don't know why nobody ever listens. Keep this under your hat, Jane. I'm not going to use it unless I have to." She looked subdued as she hung up this time.

"A scandal?" Harry poised his pen encouragingly above his notepad.

"In your dreams!" Mathilda said. "We would never be able to work it in unless we could find some indication that she's had a relapse."

"And she would be?"

"Nice try." Mathilda glowered at her desk pad, then brightened a little. "Not our client, anyway. Our client has no motive. Nada. Zilch. This is going to be so easy. Even you could do it."

Harry looked dubious. "That woman I saw yesterday would be capable of anything. Are we really sure that she didn't do it?"

Mathilda fixed him with a long stare. "Do you know horses, Mr. Jarvis?"

At the other's blank look and shake of the head, Mathilda went on. "I used to have a filly who would see more than was really there, and she always picked her way around imaginary obstacles. It was best to leave her to it, though, because if you tried to stop her, she would get scared, throw up her head, and lash out. I think that horse's problem was that she was entirely too intelligent—for a horse—and got bored if things weren't difficult."

Harry smiled amiably. "And the point is?"

Mathilda looked blank. "There was a comparison there when I started out. You're right. Regan is different. I like her. I'm going to get her off."

■ ■ ■

Luke phoned that evening to say that he would be staying in town. Regan relaxed after that call, only realizing then how convinced she was that he was the culprit. Because of the strained relationship she'd had with the others in the past, none of them could expect to benefit financially from her death. Her will left everything to her father or, since he had predeceased her, to various charities. It had been written several years ago. Now that she was in possession of the house, she would have to change it.

But Luke had already threatened her once. Probably he thought that she knew much more than she did, as much, perhaps, as her father had known.

That evening Regan sat alone in the living room and tried to read. The others had either gone out or to bed early. She missed Gato and Sasha, one of which would usually be curled up in her lap about now.

Finally she tossed her book aside and got up. Without any conscious thought, she found herself at the front window, holding the curtains aside, trying to peer through her own reflection to the driveway and the street below.

She made a wry face and leaned her forehead against the

glass. "Get a grip, girl," she could almost hear Mathilda saying. "The cop's the enemy, remember?"

Her brain was tired, but her body, refreshed from her nap, remained alert, tense. She knew that if she went to bed, she wouldn't sleep. She went into the bathroom instead to wash her hair in the basin. She tuned out all thought in favor of feel: the silky slide of soapwort through her hair, the scent of roses that crept up from the garden to the open window like the cautious whisper of a forbidden lover. She splashed rosewater into the rinse to make herself feel a part of the air, a part of the night—then poured it lavishly into the tub; she plucked petals from a bouquet on the counter and tossed them in too.

Luxuriating in the warm water, she remembered that it was June 23—Midsummer's Eve. There was a full moon too. In the Middle Ages, that would probably have been considered a dangerous combination.

When she was done, she was still not drowsy. She slipped into a white cotton nightgown and, drawing the matching robe over it, went out to the balcony. Leaning against the railing, she tried to remember how the old saying went. *Just before the clock strikes midnight on Midsummer's Eve, go into your garden and pick twelve sage leaves, one at each stroke—*

With a glance at the clock on her bedside stand and a gamine smile, she padded back across the room, let herself out into the dim hallway, and felt her way down the stairs. In the living room, long rectangles of moonlight from the french doors pointed the way.

She heard the slight clicking, like a clearing of the throat, that the clock always made just before it bonged, and hurried. Leaving the doors open behind her, she flew barefoot across the cool, smooth terrace stones and down the steps to the grass, crouched, breathless, beside one of the sage bushes there just as the chiming commenced, faint and sweet with distance. When it was done, she triumphantly clutched a dozen leaves.

She stood and padded on down the grass path toward the walled garden, trying to remember how the rest of the saying went. The warm, sweet scent of roses came to meet her, faint at first, then intensifying, intoxicating, until the aura was at once everywhere and nowhere, as soft as the petals themselves against the face, drawn in to become a lightheadedness, a tingling.

Inside the walls, her bare feet bruised the creeping thyme growing between the flagstones.

For the moment she felt free and giddy, as in one of those effortless dreams where one glides free of gravity and obstacles. She paused beside the bed that contained the oldest varieties. The Apothecary Rose, also called the Red Rose of Lancaster, beside its strangely striped mutation, 'Rosa Mundi.' Behind it the ancient Persian 'Quatre Saisons.' And clambering up the wall at the back, Alba semi-plena, the White Rose of York. The one used in Kazanlik for attar. Its pristine blooms were half-folded for the night, like a spattering of denser moonlight down the wall.

She didn't know afterward how long she'd heard the footsteps. They were barely audible, little more than a stealthy shushing in the grass outside. She might not have noticed them at all had she not been standing so still. A sudden twinge of alarm between her shoulder blades alerted her. She turned toward the sound and backed into the sweet alyssum bordering the path.

She wanted to call out, demand to know who was there, but her throat closed up. She backed farther, seeking the shadow of the wall. Not that it would do any good. Her white robe would stand out as clearly as the white roses did.

A grab at her shoulder from behind. Her breath caught in a convulsive hiss. She writhed against that grasp until she felt barbs stinging her back and realized that she had come up against the rose canes. She arched awkwardly, trying to reach behind and up. Like animal claws, the thorns caught and yanked her hair.

The footsteps were closer now, approaching the nearest door in the wall. She tried to quiet her heavy breathing and fight down a rising hysteria. She had neatly snared herself for her killer's convenience. Like Absalom, caught by his hair in a tree. She tried not to think of what had happened to Absalom as, throat parched, she fought to reach higher with her twisted arm.

Another cane slapped against her sleeve and dug into her wrist. A shower of petals tumbled over her hair and caressed her cheek with mocking softness. The smell of roses surged again on each panting breath, filling her flaring nostrils, her throat.

She forced herself to stillness. The garden was clear now. Black and white. Harsh and beautiful and cruel. York. Lancaster. Blood, brutality, treachery.

Trembling, she turned her head as far as the thorns allowed. At the far corner of her vision she saw a dark silhouette in the doorway. A large muscular shape clad in jeans and a dark T-shirt. The bill collector? Then he said "Regan?" and stepped forward into the moonlight.

Relief caused her to sink backward against her bonds. "Matt, are you trying to scare me to death?"

"What are you doing out here?" He sounded harsh.

"I'm stuck on these things. Come and help me get out."

He regarded her with perplexity. "Just yank. They'll come loose."

"It's not that easy."

He picked his way impatiently over and around the flowers at the front of the bed, put a hand on her shoulder and pulled. The canes came along, but one of them sprang free to slap him in the face. He muttered something unintelligible.

"All right," he said. "Lean forward. This might take a while." He sounded inexplicably angry again.

He started on the ones in her hair, trying, in a clumsy way, not to yank. She bit her lip and kept quiet. He was growling something under his breath that she could not make out, which she thought was probably just as well. One of his forearms rested on her shoulder, and his muscles were taut with suppressed tension. She had not been prepared for how his closeness, his fingers in her hair, would make her feel. With her own arms stiffly at her sides, she breathed shallowly, and kept her gaze turned downward. *I'm having an irrational emotional reaction to the stress of the last week. Shock, grief, loneliness. I'm—what's that word they call it—vulnerable right now.*

As her hair came free, Matt pushed her head forward against his shoulder so he could reach the canes on her back. She squeezed her eyes shut against the dark warmth of his shirt. *It's the old forbidden fruit. The only reason I'm attracted to this particular man is because he's verboten. There had better not be any of those reporters still hanging around. One front-page photo of the police chief with his negligeed main suspect more or less clasped in his arms*—There was the sound of something tearing, and Matt's fingers brushed bare skin on her back. She started, as if at a shock, and her head came up. Their eyes met for one brief, tingling instant, then she hid her face again.

"Sorry," he muttered thickly. "I was away all day," he said, as if talk was safer than silence. "I didn't get the message until I came back. Want to tell me about it?"

"What's the use?" she replied in a muffled voice. "Naturally, you think I poisoned the cat myself to make my case look better. After all, if I didn't hesitate to kill my father, I'm certainly not going to develop qualms over a cat. Too bad I didn't actually die. Then you could have called it suicide and spared yourself a lot of grief."

"Spared myself—" He pulled her against him and held her there, one big hand cupping the nape of her neck. With a small sigh, she let her arms creep around his waist and her hands come up against his back.

"Did your father take that stuff too?" he asked.

"Yes."

"Would he have taken some that night?"

"Probably. But"—she had to turn her head to make herself heard—"there was poison in the teacup."

"That could have been added later. You were all in there in the morning. What does that extract taste like?"

"It has a numbing effect on the tongue, and it's bitter. I usually hold my nose." She shuddered again, and his hand tightened as his voice relented.

"You people were just asking to be poisoned, weren't you? I think you're in the clear now. Keep your head down and your arms in. If we go very quietly, maybe it won't realize that you're escaping. Ready? Follow your partner." As he plucked the last of the thorns from her hair, he slid his free arm about her waist.

She laughed softly, with only the faintest hint of hysteria, as they moved in a dancelike shuffle away from the wall and around the other bushes that loomed darkly between them and the path.

A final far-reaching branch tugged at her hem, fell away, and they were in the open, scuffing through the honey-sweet alyssum.

"In the clear," she repeated. "I suppose that doesn't apply otherwise."

He was silent for too long. Finally he said, "I knew I should have kept that room sealed up. But we had the poisoned tea. And since everybody had been in there, any other forensic evidence wasn't going to tell us anything. There's been plenty of time for that bottle to be taken away. Or replaced. Most likely simply switched with the one in your room."

"By someone wearing gloves," she said, "so there wouldn't be any prints except mine on the one the police took from Daddy's room."

"But there should be some of your father's on the poisoned bottle too."

"That won't prove anything. Daddy bought that extract. So his prints would naturally be on both bottles."

Throughout this terse, low-voiced conversation, they had contrived to ignore the fact that their tight embrace continued even though they were standing on the path with the nearest rose bush a good six feet away.

They were both silent for a time; he combed rose petals from her hair, his callused fingers snagging occasionally on the silky strands.

"Mathilda is almost certain she can get me acquitted," Regan said finally. "There's reasonable doubt strewn about on all sides."

"If I resign—" he began.

She broke away from him. "No! Why would you do something like that?" Now that she was free, she thought it safe to look up.

"Why?" He stretched out a hand and traced the line of her jaw with one finger. A tingle followed that touch, suffused her face and neck with warmth. Lips parted, she met the turbulent emotion in his eyes and could not look away.

"When I think that you could have died today while I was out fishing . . ." He managed to wrench his gaze aside. His hands worked. "Well, let's just say that conflict of interest doesn't begin to describe how I'm messing up this case. I don't think I would feel any differently even if I knew you were guilty."

A strong, musky smell almost overpowered the roses, and she looked down to see that she was still clutching the sage leaves.

"Regan?" He was waiting for a response.

She started. She had just remembered how that saying ended. *And your future husband will come quietly up behind you.* She deliberately flung the leaves away. "It's moonlight and roses, Matt. That's all it is. And maybe loneliness. You'll thank me later for not taking you seriously. Come to think of it, Mathilda said that I was only to entice you as a last resort."

She laughed and caught one of his hands briefly before she turned away.

"Regan." There was just a hint of huskiness, of entreaty, in his voice. Already halfway up the terrace steps, she made only a fractional pause and did not look back.

■ ■ ■

She was in the living room, curled up in a corner of the couch in the dark, clutching a pillow to her chest, when someone opened the door from the hall and switched on the light. Diane, also clad in gown and robe, crossed the room to stand looking down at her aunt and said, "What's wrong with you?"

Regan was too startled to respond.

"I could see both of you quite clearly from my room," Diane said. "I couldn't hear what you were saying because, out of sheer courtesy, I didn't go out onto the balcony. Not everybody would have been that polite, you know. It's just your good luck that nobody else is on that side of the house right now. Didn't I warn you to stay away from him?"

Regan compressed her lips and turned her head away.

"All right," Diane said, sinking down onto the couch. "I'm not being very comforting. I was never good at that. It's probably why I don't have many close friends. Maybe I take after my mother more than I realize. But, honestly, what were you thinking?"

"That's easy." Regan's voice was quiet, controlled. "I know there can't be any future in it. If I were acquitted and we got together afterward, it would be impossible for him to keep his job. And it's more than just a job to him. It's respect and respectability."

She paused. "He needs that job, and this town needs him. You know, I heard that the Denton girl wrote him a letter and said that he'd restored her faith in men. And all of those old people he looks after . . ."

She leaned forward and proceeded with difficulty. "I can't

destroy all that over his infatuation with a woman he can't have. Over"—she laughed harshly—"a little midsummer madness. That's all it is. He never looked at me twice before I was a murder suspect. I at least deserve something to remem—" Her voice caught there. "I didn't even kiss him, did I?"

Diane sighed. "If it's any consolation," she said, "none of the Culver women have ever had any sense about men. Look at my mother. My father deserts her, then she and Gina both fall for the same pompous bore."

"Not to mention somebody else falling for the pompous bore's son," Regan said.

Diane looked startled. "Luke?"

"You were in love with him once," Regan insisted. "Everybody knew it. And you haven't trusted any guy since."

"I was?" Diane seemed genuinely taken aback, to search her memory for verification. Finally she shrugged, "Perhaps. It would explain a lot. I'm hardly one to preach, huh? At least yours is one of the good guys." Dubiously eyeing the rips and red smears on the back of Regan's robe, she added *"I think."*

Regan smiled with difficulty. "The villain there was a rose-bush. And that's mostly Matt's blood." The smile quivered. She stood and walked to the door, still clutching the pillow. She turned to look back. "Thanks, Diane. For caring."

Diane sat for a few moments longer. When she finally went out into the dark hall, someone moved in the shadows. Luke. "What," he inquired, "was that all about?" And, at her cold stare, "I just came in."

"I bet. Don't bother asking. It isn't something you would understand. The whole concept of sacrifice, that is."

"No?" His face was suddenly somber.

Her hair had fallen forward around her face and he reached to push it back, to hold it bunched at the nape of her neck for an instant, to let it go. It was not really the kind of touch she could object to. His fingers had only grazed her skin. With the other hand, he touched her lightly on the nose in an almost brotherly fashion.

"Midsummer madness, eh?" he said. "It has a nice ring to it."

CHAPTER 11

■ ■ ■

There's a daisy.

She was just having a little fun, Matt told himself. She was leading him on. She didn't even try to hide it.

All of which, of course, did not prove that she had killed her father. Driving into town the next morning, he noticed the wild daisies in bloom along the highway. Consulting one of those—she did it, she didn't, she did it—would probably get him about as far as his investigation had.

He planned to reinterview everybody in the more daunting atmosphere of the police station. He would have to start over, in effect. Try to forget that whether he loved her or hated her, he was way beyond neutral now.

At his desk he put away all the little scraps of paper in a paper-clip box.

He sharpened pencils, replaced the batteries in his tape recorder, and took a telephone call from the prosecutor. "We need more, Matt," he was told. "That woman is going to make buffoons of us in court."

"Which woman?" Matt asked. Feet up on the desk, he had

a scratch pad balanced on his thigh and was drawing finely crosshatched lines on it with his left hand.

"Mathilda Baker, of course! Who did you think I was talking about?"

"The other one," Matt said. He replaced the receiver gently in its cradle, then lifted it at once and dialed again.

He was both dreading—and hoping—that Regan might answer the phone herself. She didn't; it was Diane.

After he explained what he wanted, she left him on hold while she talked with the others. She returned to say, "I can come right away if you like. Mother says that one o'clock will be okay for her. Gina is moving her stuff into their house today and asks if she can wait until tomorrow morning—tenish. Luke just got back from somewhere, and he's on his way out again. He says he'll try to make it sometime tomorrow afternoon. Reid has already left for Boston. Is this all okay?"

"Yes." There was a significant pause.

"Did you want Regan too?" Diane asked finally.

"Everybody." Matt was curt.

"She says she had better bring her lawyer. She has to call Mathilda, but she'll try for three this afternoon."

"All right." Matt hung up, feeling sick. If Regan told her lawyer about that scene last night, Mathilda could make a very good argument for getting Matt thrown off the case. Perhaps that had been the whole purpose of it.

Diane was prompt, appearing within fifteen minutes. She seemed more than usually closed in and guarded, the lines in her face more pronounced. She was still a beautiful woman, but the rigid set of her lips dragged her beauty slightly askew.

She was, he realized with surprise, growing to look more like her mother.

"Regan says you know about my being fired." She got that out at once, in a rush, even before she was properly seated. She fumbled with her purse and finally set it down beside her chair.

"That's not relevant to this case," he said. "Unless it made you desperate for money."

She tried to smile. "Well, it did. Mother and I are living on Regan's charity now. Of course, we'll each get some money from Grandfather's will, but that's not—"

"Not enough," Matt finished. He was leaning forward, head down, seemingly preoccupied with his doodling. He had long ago learned to watch people without appearing to do so.

"It's enough for now. Regan is going to get me a job on the herb farm."

"And will that keep you," he asked, "in the manner to which you're accustomed?"

She laughed shakily. "The manner to which I've been accustomed for the past ten years is rank poverty with a very thin icing of bluff. I expect I'll manage."

"Did you expect to get more from your grandfather?"

She hesitated. "I hadn't really thought about it."

"You're lying," he commented mildly, shading in his squares in an alternating pattern. Like a game board—or a brick wall.

"All right." Her voice was high. "So I lied. Of course I thought about it. When you live on a constant edge of desperation, you consider all the ways out. Over and over and over—ad nauseam. But I—we didn't kill him. Mother was going to ask him for help, but she never quite managed it. She had too much pride."

"Why did you think it necessary to continue subsidizing your mother's failing business?"

"I don't think that's relevant." As if frightened by her own audacity, she hurried on. "Mother has never had much. My father left her. Her own father never paid her much attention. The business was the only success she had. That is, until her partner ran out on her. The partner was the one who was good with people. Sales began to fall off. We always thought they would come back. I mean, there are always hopeful little signs. You keep saying to yourself, next month or next year."

Diane had picked up her purse and put it back down again, as if not quite aware what she was doing. "Maybe I should have quit my job and helped her, but I'm not really a people person, either. I thought it would be best to have some kind of steady income—"

"Is that why she was dating Reid Hayden before he married Gina? Money?"

Diane's face went white. "That's insulting. That was before things got really bad. Believe it or not, Reid could be quite charming. Still can, when he puts his mind to it."

"Like his son?"

She didn't respond.

"Is Luke a drug dealer?"

"I don't know."

"I talked to the dean at your alma mater. He seemed to imply that you would know if anybody does."

"I've seen very little of Luke over the past ten years."

"He lives quite well. Don't you, in your circumstances, find that rather unfair?"

"His father has money."

"I understand that he and his father don't get along."

She was defiantly silent again.

"Did Luke deal drugs in college?"

"I don't know."

"Would Rosemary have been in a position to know if he did?"

"Possibly. I doubt it."

"Did anyone go near the cup that morning?"

She stared, blinked, swallowed, as if in relief over the change in subject. "I passed by it when I was taking Regan out. I don't think anybody else was over there before then."

"Did you notice it—particularly?"

"Yes. I thought it made a pretty still life. Prettiness seemed inappropriate just then."

"It was empty?"

"Yes."

"Except," he qualified "for a tablespoon or so of tea at the bottom."

She stared again. "No, it was completely empty. A few tiny flecks of green on the sides. There might possibly have been a trace of liquid, not enough to show. Nowhere near a table-spoon."

His pencil point snapped. "You're sure of that?"

Her bewilderment was palpable. "Yes. Is it important?"

He ground the stub of lead blackly against the paper then stood up. "All right. That's it."

Confused by this sudden deliverance, she groped for her purse again and jumped up, bumping the chair away from her. She paused as if at a loss for something to say. "Thank you," she managed finally, turning.

He had to smile. "Diane."

She turned fearfully.

"If you've done nothing wrong, you have nothing to be apologetic about. When somebody browbeats you like I've just been doing, you have nothing to thank them for."

She smiled more naturally. "I guess so. That other thing . . . I'm really not crazy."

"I believe you. Why did you let them run you off? Running becomes a habit."

"I know that—now." She clutched her bag tighter. "I saw you and Regan last night. In the garden."

He hoped his wince didn't show on the outside.

"I won't tell anybody," she hurried on. "But I suspect that Luke might have been hanging around too. And it could be useful to him. Please, Matt, be careful."

It was, he thought, a little late for that.

■ ■ ■

He returned from lunch to find Agatha sitting, bolt upright, on a bench in the corridor outside his door. He glanced guiltily at his watch. It still lacked a few minutes of one.

"Good afternoon," he said, unlocking the door, and standing aside to let her go in first.

She answered his polite greeting with a brief, impatient nod, centered the visitor's chair in front of his desk, and sat, hands folded neatly over her purse.

"I really don't think this is necessary," she said. "I told you all I knew the first time. But nevertheless . . ." She nodded again, as if in permission for him to begin. She seemed in an unusually mild mood—for Agatha.

Standing behind the desk, he said, "Do you still think that Regan killed your father?"

"I am not going to be intimidated by having to crane my neck at you," she retorted, "so you might as well sit down. The answer to your question is no. I don't."

Taken aback, he pulled out his chair and sat, without shifting his gaze from her face. She met that stare unwaveringly.

"Why not?"

"She wouldn't have poisoned the cat."

He began a grin, but stopped when she did not smile. "So," he said. "You were willing to accept that she might have poisoned her father but not the cat?" His voice rose incredulously.

"You do not understand me. I never knew Regan that well. She seldom shows emotion. But animals and children, I understand, can tell when someone cares about them. Which is why," she inserted tartly, "they tend to avoid me. But they like her. I suspect that she is, after all, the typical artistic type. Oversensitive, overemotional, and overromantic. She just hides it better."

Matt still didn't understand Agatha's reasoning, but didn't think it wise to admit that ignorance. She was not the type to suffer fools gladly—if at all.

He felt, in a sense, betrayed. He had expected support from her at least for the arrest.

The prosecutor had called him again just before lunch, nervously suggesting that perhaps they should drop the charges until they came up with some more evidence.

Matt had been curt with him. *I'm overcompensating,* he had thought. *Because I want desperately to drop this case, I can't.*

He had hoped that the prosecutor might go ahead and override him. But Clymer had conceded instead. "I suppose you're right, Matt. If we quit now, we look like we're intimidated." He had sounded intimidated as he said it.

"So," Matt snapped, "do you have any other suspect in mind?"

"You would have done much better," Agatha suggested coolly, as if she had never accused Regan, "to have arrested Luke. Drug dealers are notoriously violent."

"Do you have proof that Luke Hayden is a drug dealer?"

"His lifestyle is proof enough. Anne left him enough money so that he could live fairly well, but not at the exalted level of society he moves in now."

"Speaking of money," Matt said, "you needed some pretty badly didn't you?"

Agatha raised her brows. "Yes."

"And you expected to get quite a bit upon your father's death."

"No."

"No?"

"I knew that Regan would get most of it. He told us so."

"He said, if I am not mistaken, that he *was going* to leave most of his money to Regan. You might have assumed that he had not yet done so."

"I did not assume any such thing. I never assume. It's sloppy thinking."

"Why didn't you tell me about your financial difficulties?"

"It is not something," Agatha responded, "that I am eager to have spread around." Her tone implied that anyone of intelligence might have been able to deduce that.

"I," Matt ground out, "do not make a habit of spreading confidential information around. With the exception," he added conscientiously, "of your daughter's resignation from her job, which I mentioned to Regan because I thought she already knew about it."

Agatha's eyelids flickered. She said, "That has nothing to do with this."

"Perhaps not. Did anyone go near that cup on the morning the body was discovered?"

Agatha did not hesitate. "Not that I noticed."

"Your daughter tells me that she went out that way."

Agatha's eyelids flickered again. "Perhaps she did. Regan would have been with her at the time."

So much for not noticing.

"Could you have distilled poison from those plants?"

"If I want to find out how to do something," Agatha said, "I read a book. I am very good at following directions, which cannot be said for the majority of the population. But I would not have pulled up the whole clump of monkshood in that silly, wasteful way. It was as if somebody wanted to call attention to somebody in the house. I would suggest that you look more closely at that woman who runs the herb farm—or her manager. They, no doubt, have plenty of monkshood out there."

Agatha rose. "A silly name. The hood is not brown after all."

Matt stood too. "You're assuming that all monks wore brown because that's how they're usually depicted. Isn't that sloppy thinking?"

Agatha gave him a tolerant half-smile.

"I would suggest that you be a little more circumspect in your attentions to Regan."

He glared wearily. "Were *all* of you at your windows last night?"

She raised her brows. "Last night? I was speaking of the fact that you've been hanging around her more than seems necessary. I didn't see you last night. A policeman," she concluded with triumph, "should not be so hasty to jump to conclusions. Good day, Chief Olin."

■ ■ ■

Matt glanced at the clock. It would be at least an hour and a half before Regan showed up. Too long.

He sat at the desk and resharpened his pencil. He told himself that he was behaving like a teenager. Perhaps if he'd allowed himself to act like a teenager when he was one . . .

He called Thyme Will Tell and talked to Caroline Stanton. She agreed to come around four and promised to send Dennis in the following morning. He hung up and dialed Reid Hayden's office. Reid consented to stop in on his way to work on Tuesday.

Matt looked at the clock again. Not yet two. On a Monday. He got up and went out.

Old John was shambling furtively out of the grocery store, his black coat lumpy. Seeing Matt, he stopped with his usual resigned, sheepish air. Without comment, Matt reached under the coat to extricate a can of salmon and one of oysters. He handed them to Bob Fisher, who had followed the old man out. "Developing expensive tastes, John?" Matt inquired.

John shuffled his feet and produced the usual gap-toothed grin. "Got 'em for the old lady," he confided. "Connie is a great 'un for seafood, you know."

Matt exchanged a glance with Bob. Connie had been dead for years. "What did you say your daughter's name was, John?" Matt inquired, casually producing a notebook.

The old man beamed. "Carla. She's blind, you know. But always cheerful. Like sunshine, Carla is."

Matt regarded the blank page of the notebook to avoid that ingenuous gaze. "Carla was your sister, John," he reminded gently.

He forced himself to look up then.

"My sister? Yes, she was, wasn't she? And she's dead too?" The milky, beseeching eyes filled with tears. "Everybody's dead." Old John shuffled away.

Bob shook his head. "The daughter's name is Sanders," he said. "Grace. She lives in Chicago, I think." He looked down at the cans. "Why don't I just let him have the stuff?" Still shaking his head, he turned back into the store.

Matt had been vaguely aware of two teenagers watching the scene. One was Chris Colby, who worked as a stock boy, and was gathering grocery carts. The other, a red bandanna knotted over his head, was Gabe Johnson.

As Matt started toward them, Gabe deliberately turned his back and walked away.

"Sorry about that, Chief," Chris said. "He's got a real attitude, Gabe has. Mr. Fisher offered him a job here, but he wasn't having any of it. Wanted to go to a movie tonight. I told him a bunch of us guys were getting together to go over tapes from last season's games. Work out some new plays, you know." Chris sounded self-consciously virtuous, as if expecting approval.

"That's good." Matt watched Gabe's defiant back as he spoke. "But you should go to the movies sometimes too, Chris. You're only young once."

Chris looked surprised. "Yes sir," he said uncertainly.

Gabe had disappeared.

Matt strolled on down the sidewalk, nodding to those who addressed him. Their greetings were constrained today, gazes avidly speculative.

Down where the buildings were more widely spaced was an old feed mill, long boarded up. Matt caught a flash of red in the dusty yard at the back and turned in.

Gabe, sitting on the high loading dock, regarded his approach with a sneer. "So, Chief," he said, making the title an epithet. "Afraid I might break in here? What do you expect me to get—a little moldy corn?"

"Just wanted to talk to you," Matt said.

"The same way you just talked to poor old John?" Gabe asked. "I suppose you're going to have him put away now, aren't you? The old coot isn't hurting anybody."

Matt felt unutterably weary. "Somebody has to do it."

"And somebody is always you, isn't it? The guy they call to tidy up their messes. And Aunt Lily has the nerve to hold you up as the great white hope. The hero who crawled out of our slimy little world to make something of himself. Myself, I think you're just a glorified mucker."

The kid jumped down from the dock to stand spraddle-legged in front of Matt. "I got news for you, Chief. Your image ain't quite so shiny anymore. It's all over town that you're getting it on with the that Culver dame—"

Matt hit him. Even in mid-swing, Matt knew that he was dealing a deathblow to his own career, but he could not stop. He took a certain dull satisfaction in the solidity of the impact. Gabe went down but bounced back up like one of those spring-back clowns. The kid was grinning feverishly, despite the trickle of blood from lip to chin.

The contest was short and brutal. Both were too angry to employ any kind of martial science. They simply waded in, slugging, making no effort at defense. The kid went down first.

Matt dropped to one knee in the dirt, breathing hard. The old gray building seemed to rotate around him. After a moment he regained his feet, staggered across to the steps of the loading dock, and collapsed, leaning forward and glaring at the ground until it gradually came into focus again. "You okay?" he gasped.

Gabe pushed up a little, winced, and lay tenderly back again. "Hardly." Grinning up at the sky, the kid added, "So you're human after all, Chief. I was beginning to doubt it."

"You can get me into serious trouble over this, you know," Matt said.

"Fat chance." Gabe was wiggling Nike-clad toes in an experimental fashion. "You only have to say that I hit you first. I know who they'll believe."

Matt squinted at him across what seemed a glaring space. "I wouldn't do that."

"No, I don't suppose you would. Well, you didn't break my neck, anyway." Gabe sat up, looked from his own bloody knuckles to Matt's face, and grinned again. "I marked up that clean-cut look some, anyhow. I feel better. How about you?"

"Why do you hate me so much, Gabe?" Matt asked.

The kid's expression darkened. "You and Aunt Lily," he said, "both look at me the same way. Kind of sad and resigned. Like you think I'm a disaster waiting to happen."

"It makes the temptation to act the part almost irresistible?" Matt suggested.

Gabe gave him a startled look, and Matt said, "Somebody else told me that."

"Somebody else is right on the money. Do you know how it feels to have people watching you all your life, waiting for you to screw up, just so they can have the satisfaction of saying 'I told you so'?"

"Yes, I do." Matt spoke so quietly that the kid stopped in mid-spate. "And do you know what the funny thing is, Gabe?" Matt continued in that mild, half-amused tone. "They were right. They said that heredity would tell, that I was weak at the core and would crack under pressure. And I did. At least I know when to quit." He stood.

"Hey!" Gabe scrambled up, looking alarmed. "I'm no snitch, man! Do you hear me complaining? I insult the lady; I get whacked. I know the rules."

Matt grinned. "I wasn't defending the lady's name, Gabe. I always thought that was a bit presumptuous on the guy's part anyway—to assume that a woman's honor depended on him. I hit you because I was angry—and not just at you. Police brutality is police brutality. A good cop has no business losing his cool. It's time for me to get out. I should have left this town years ago."

Gabe did not respond to that grin. His expression was tight, closed in. "And what about Chris and all those other guys, Chief?" he asked. "And their precious championship? You gonna drop out on them too—just like their daddies did?"

Staring across at the burly six-footer, Matt imagined for an instant that he was looking into the hating, hurting eyes of all the little boys who had been left behind. Jerking free of that accusation, he said, "They'll still have Bob and Tom."

"They ain't going to be the same." Gabe was implacable. "They didn't come from where you came from."

"Be reasonable, Gabe," Matt insisted. "You should know now, if anybody does, that I'm not cut out to be a role model."

Gabe crossed his arms. "You're better than anything else they got."

Matt shook his head. "I was thinking of resigning anyway. I'm in an impossible situation. This just clinches it. I wouldn't be any sort of example if I didn't know when to do the honorable thing."

The teen's closed expression did not change.

"You don't understand, Gabe—"

"Oh, I understand well enough. You found out that you aren't Super Cop after all, so you've got to crawl off and lick your bruised ego. And everybody else can go hang. Your girlfriend might, at that. I'm just sorry I didn't hit you a little harder when I had the chance." Arms still crossed, Gabe turned and shambled away toward the Flats.

■ ■ ■

Mathilda was expostulating volubly to Regan when they came in at three. "There isn't much point in hiring detectives if you aren't going to let me use any of what they find out!"

Mathilda was dressed in shocking pink. Regan, by contrast, looked cool in turquoise with a spray of daisies tucked into her belt. She raised her eyebrows upon seeing Matt. "Maybe I should have brought some more *arnica*."

Mathilda regarded him with interest. "Somebody finally biffed you one, huh?" she asked unsympathetically. "It's about time. I hope you called us in here to tell us that you're dropping the charges because you haven't a leg to stand on. Even if

I don't bring up all these people's sorry little secrets. You know about Diane, I hear.

"I talked to that old harridan at the school myself this morning. But she was singing a different tune from when my detective interviewed her. Seems somebody instilled the fear of God in the old lady. I got the suspicion that this somebody knew a few unpleasant things about her, other teachers she's railroaded out and so on." Mathilda's tone approved of this anonymous somebody.

"She was whining about how she'd already said that Diane could have her job back if she wanted and that it was Diane's own choice to resign, et cetera. Somehow she must have got the idea that I was Diane's lawyer. I don't know how," Mathilda added virtuously at Matt's sardonic look. "Anyhow, she made me so mad that I said we hadn't decided yet rather we were going to sue or not. She went almost hysterical. I'd like to congratulate whoever reduced her to this state. You?"

"Not me." Feeling like the interview was getting away from him, Matt clicked on his tape recorder and said to Regan, "Did you notice the cup the morning you found your father's body?"

"No." Her hands lay still in her lap. Although she was meeting his gaze, she was a long way off. "I wasn't noticing much that morning."

"So you wouldn't know how much liquid was left in it?"

"Very little, I suspect. Father deplored waste."

"A couple of tablespoons?"

"Considerably less than that, I would think."

"Could Diane have put anything in the cup when she was leading you out?"

"I wasn't looking at her, but I doubt it. I seem to recall her pulling at me with both hands. She seemed afraid that I might make a scene. Diane and I both abhor scenes."

"I adore a good fit myself," Mathilda said. "It clears the air." She had been wandering around the office, poking curiously at things and tugging at the doors of the filing cabinet, which were fortunately locked.

Ignoring Matt's quelling look, she added, "If you people would have things out as they come up, you'd be a lot healthier. Like throwing up. Get it over with; you'll feel better."

A momentary gleam of suppressed laughter lit Regan's expression for a moment and invited Matt to share in her amusement.

He was in a reckless mood. "What were you doing in the garden last night?"

Her face animated with alarm. She cast a quick glance at Mathilda, who was standing with her back to them, reading a wanted poster. "Talking to you, part of the time," Regan said in a stifled tone.

He was impersonal. He could play at that game too.

Mathilda turned and watched them with frowning interest. "I've told you not to tell him anything when I'm not around."

"I'm afraid," Regan said, "that I was playing the flirt. Without much success apparently." She returned a cool challenge to his stare.

Mathilda moved to stand behind Regan's chair and grasped its back. "Let's put our cards on the table, Matt. I happen to like you better than I like most cops. I don't want to have to show you up in court. Cautious Clymer will back down if you tell him to. We both know that. We've got plenty of evidence now that the poison probably wasn't in that tea, that it was planted there afterward. And we've got the even more convincing fact that somebody tried to kill Regan."

"Are you telling me," Matt asked, "that she isn't smart enough to know that planting evidence on herself could ultimately clear her?"

Regan smiled.

Mathilda laughed. "Oh, she's clever. I grant you that. But can you believe that, in real life, anybody would try a double bluff like that?"

"He would believe it," Regan said. "He has a suspicious mind—where I'm concerned anyway."

"Be quiet!" her lawyer ordered her. "The more you provoke him, the more stubborn he's going to be. If this is some warped kind of flirtation, I don't want to know about it. You won't think it's so funny, Regan, if he ends up losing his job over this. At least I hope you won't."

Regan bit her lip.

"It will be better," the lawyer resumed, "for you to admit that you made a mistake now. It doesn't even have to look like a mistake. Just the result of new evidence."

Matt felt only an unyielding heaviness. Whatever he did wasn't going to be right.

It wouldn't be as easy as Mathilda was implying. He could almost hear the whispering voices now. They might not put it as crudely as Gabe had—"because you've been getting it on"—but the implication would be there.

He turned his head to the side to avoid their expectant gazes.

How could he know that his peculiar inability to resist Regan Culver hadn't blinded him to the real facts in the case? That she and Mathilda Baker hadn't planned all of this?

When he turned back, Regan was watching him. Sympathy was there—and perhaps something warmer.

He shook his head and lunged to his feet. "That's all."

Mathilda opened her mouth to say something, but Regan, her gaze still steady on Matt's, reached back to touch the other woman's hand in a silencing gesture.

As Regan stood, one of the daisies from her belt tumbled to the floor. She looked down at it, then back up at him again. "For innocence," she said. Then she turned and led Mathilda Baker toward the door, despite the lawyer's indignant mutters.

Once there, Regan looked back to say. "I *am* sorry, Matt."

When the door closed behind them, he was left to stare at the limp flower on the floor.

■　■　■

Caroline did not comment on his injuries beyond a lifting of eyebrows as she sat down; she did not seem, in fact, to find them particularly surprising. Perhaps she thought that the police regularly indulged in fisticuffs. A square, practical figure garbed in spare, practical clothes, she looked anything but the introspective dreamer who had written *Rosemary for Remembrance*. She set her bag beside her chair and left it alone throughout the interview.

It occurred to him that he was not going to get objective memories from these people if they consulted one another in the meantime. "Have you talked to anyone at the Culver house lately?" he asked.

"Not since yesterday afternoon. As Regan probably told you, I was speaking to her on the phone when her cat got poisoned." Caroline grimaced at the memory. "I am not particularly fond of cats, but I may make an exception for this one since it inadvertently saved her life."

"And you haven't talked to Regan since?"

"I tried, believe me. Agatha cut me off right after it happened. I called back a short time later, demanding to know what was going on. Agatha simply said, 'It was the *cat* who got poisoned, Caroline. If you think we're stashing Regan's body somewhere, you're welcome to come and look. I'm sure she'll tell you anything you want to know later.' And she hung up again."

Making another face, Caroline said, "If you wanted to be kind, you might excuse Agatha on the grounds that she was still shook up. But Agatha doesn't shake. She just doesn't like me—never has. But she made me feel silly; she's good at that. I mean, you really couldn't imagine them all being involved in some collective plot to get rid of the resented younger daughter, on a sunny Sunday afternoon no less. But I must admit that I worried all the way into town. I had an appointment for supper with my editor. Sundays are the only time I can really get away."

"Your editor? You're going to write another book?"

She moved her shoulders gracelessly. "Maybe." As if embarrassed, she reverted to her account. "Regan and I have a meeting scheduled tomorrow—about one of the gardens she's doing. I decided to wait until I could talk to her away from that house and those people, where she doesn't have to be careful what she says. What *did* happen?"

"The cat got at some herbal extract that she had in a dropper." Matt made it short because he did not care to think about that scene. If it were not for the curiosity of cats, he might have another death tacked on to the first. And his world would be considerably bleaker. Not that it was exactly sunshine and roses at the moment. Which might be just as well.

If sunshine and roses were anywhere near as potent as moonlight and roses—

"Did you notice the cup that morning?" he asked. "When you all found Culver's body?"

"Not par-tic-u-lar-ly." Caroline drew out the answer, watching his face, trying to determine what he was getting at. I mean," she added, "I saw it there, of course, but I didn't think much of it. I saw her taking it up to him."

She was, he thought, leaving all alternatives open.

"Do you remember how much liquid was in it?"

She didn't respond for a moment, still eyeing him narrowly, trying to determine what answer would be most in Regan's favor. Apparently she received little help from his expression because she opted for neutral. "No, I don't recall—at the moment."

Implying that she might later.

"Were you anywhere near it?" he pressed.

"I may have been. We were all milling around rather aimlessly, the way people do around a crisis situation when there's nothing that can be done. I'll try to remember."

Caroline would, he suspected, remember whatever was most convenient.

"I assume," she continued, "that you are going over all this again because you're going to drop the charges against Regan. If somebody tried to kill her, she obviously can't be the murderer, unless—" Caroline stopped.

"Unless she put the poison in the extract herself," Matt finished. "The charges stand—for the moment."

Caroline raised her eyebrows again. "Do you think that's likely?"

"According to the state police lab, her prints and Agatha's

were the only ones on the bottle. Agatha handled it after the cat got poisoned."

"I see." Caroline's tone was dry. "So there's no way to tell whether she handled it *before* the poisoning—Agatha, I mean. That is convenient for her. Quick on her feet, Agatha is. I'll give her that. Mentally, I mean."

"There were no prints at all," Matt said, "on the other bottle. That's suspicious, isn't it?"

A crease appeared between her brows. "Other?"

"From Alden Culver's medicine chest. He took the stuff too. Do you think an alcohol-based extract would be a better medium for poisoning someone than tea? More bitter perhaps?"

Caroline was watching his eyes again, like a wary animal. "Bitterness is all a matter of taste," she said finally. "Some people learn to like it. There were hops, chamomile, catnip, raspberry, and mint in that mix. We sell it at the farm too. It tastes rather good, I think. As for the extract, *echinacea* does have a slight temporary numbing effect. They say that drawing a stem of monkshood across your gums will do the same. I have never been rash enough to try it."

"You say you sell the exact same mix at the farm?"

Caroline shrugged. "Certainly. All of our mixes were devised by either Regan or her mother. So what?"

"So anyone wanting to plant a small amount of that aconite-laced tea wouldn't have had to have the keys to that cabinet. Have any of the people involved in this case been out to your farm recently? Besides Dennis and Regan, that is?"

Caroline shrugged again. "I'm not out front that much. You'd have to ask the girls who lead the tours and do the selling. Anyway, Regan's always handing out teas and sweet bags and stuff as gifts. They've probably all got some of that mix from her at one time or another."

"All the same," Matt persisted, "I would like to know who has been out to the farm recently. After all, it isn't the sort of thing anyone would naturally bring along on a brief visit—especially if they knew that Regan had a more than adequate supply on hand."

Snapping, "All right, I'll ask them!" Caroline reached for her bag and stood, indicating that her time—and temper—were exhausted.

"I'll ask them myself, if you don't mind." Matt politely stood too. "Good luck on your second book. I enjoyed the first one."

She stopped and looked back at him suspiciously. "I wouldn't have thought it the sort of thing to interest you."

"A cop has to know a little bit of everything." Caroline was, he thought, a bit ashamed of her own writing, as if it were a weakness rather than a talent.

"By the way," he added. "What kind of salary do you pay Dennis Hailey?"

■ ■ ■

When Reid Hayden came in the following morning, Matt was sitting with feet up on the desk, blearily downing lukewarm coffee from a plastic foam cup. "Have a seat," Matt said without moving.

Reid paused, regarding the police chief's battered visage with a certain dubiety. *As if,* Matt thought, *he questions the wisdom of wasting time on me.*

Reid put his briefcase beside the visitor's chair and sat. "I can't stay long," he said. "There's not much I can tell you. I didn't really know Alden Culver that well."

"You two didn't like each other?"

Reid smiled with no resultant crinkling around the eyes. "Nothing so drastic. We just didn't see that much of each other. My fault, I suppose. I'm a busy man."

"Me too. Who do you think killed him?"

Reid raised his palms and shoulders. "I was under the impression that you had already arrested Regan for that."

"You're right. Do you think she did it?"

Reid looked faintly irritated. "I really have no idea. I wouldn't have thought she was the type. Quiet little thing. But sometimes the quiet ones—"

"What about your son? Is he the type?"

Reid paused again. "I suppose this brusque style of questioning is necessary in your line of work," he said finally, his tone implying that it was work to which he himself would not stoop. "I have disassociated myself from my son. We rarely speak. I have no idea what he is or isn't capable of."

"You dated Agatha once. Did her father approve of that?"

Reid stood and picked up his briefcase. "I have endured as much as I care to. My social life is no concern of yours."

A knock sounded on the door as he approached it. He held it open to allow Dennis Hailey to enter. "Ah," Reid said. "Another victim for the third degree. I would advise you that you are not compelled to answer any of Mr. Olin's questions. He is in a surly mood this morning."

"Don't like you, does he?" Dennis said, dropping into the chair Reid had vacated. "And," he added, taking in Matt's face, "it seems like he isn't the only one. I'd be careful if I were you. Hayden could probably get you the old heave-ho if he wanted to."

Matt put his feet down on the floor and leaned forward. "Why were you at Alden Culver's party?"

Dennis lounged back and smiled. "I am a, shall we say, *friend* of Regan Culver's."

"If you're implying that there is a romantic connection," Matt said, "rumor has it that you went out with her once. And only once. That hardly makes a relationship, does it?"

Dennis looked sulky. "That's once more than you have," he said, "but rumor has a lot to say about the two of you."

"We'll leave me out of it. Did Alden Culver discourage your attentions to her?"

Dennis laughed. "Now *you're* sounding like a melodrama. Culver didn't play the heavy parent; Regan could do whatever she wanted. She isn't a teenager, after all."

"Did you know that she was going to inherit?"

Dennis shrugged lightly. "I didn't *know* it. I could have guessed. Anybody could."

"You have expensive tastes, I hear. It would have been convenient for you to marry a rich woman."

Dennis grinned. "A little more money is always convenient. But I'm not desperate for it."

"Your job must pay very well then."

"I get by." He was becoming uneasy.

"I asked your boss yesterday. She didn't mind telling me. You make about thirty-five thousand a year."

"So?"

"So your car cost more than that. How do you manage?"

"Caroline Stanton lets me raise and sell some of the more exotic plants that she doesn't want to bother with. I happen to be good at it. And they bring nice prices."

"Do you think Regan killed her father?"

Dennis relaxed. "Of course not. You made a real blunder there."

"She wouldn't hurt a fly?"

"Not if it was the trich type." Dennis grinned at Matt's bewilderment and added with elaborate patience. "One of the beneficial insects that parasitize the bad guys. Regan murders aphids and Japanese beetles by the thousands. All in the most environmentally friendly way, of course. But she didn't kill her father."

"Of course she didn't." Gina Hayden had wandered into the office and now stood regarding Dennis with a certain puzzlement, as if wondering what he was doing there. "I don't know why everybody was so convinced that she did," Gina continued. "It's so out of character."

Dennis stood, and with a sweeping bow, offered her his seat.

"Regan is the good girl in the plot," Gina went on, accepting the seat with equanimity and dropping her purse on her lap, from which it promptly slid off. "Not good enough to be a bore, fortunately. Diane rather verges on that. She's become something of a doormat. But she's too good-looking. That would generally make her one of the femme fatales, but I suspect that Regan has more SA. Regan is really a tad too exotic for the good-girl bit too. It's all rather confusing."

The two men looked confused.

"Though really," Gina plunged on, "Dennis is a much more likely suspect. He's the dark horse, you know. The mysterious stranger. It would be very convenient if it turned out to be him because nobody really cares about him. He could be eliminated from the story line quite easily."

Taken aback, Dennis said, "On that happy note, I'll make my exit."

Gina looked after him uncertainly. "Did I offend him? I didn't mean to. Though it doesn't matter. I suspect he'll turn out to be a bad one."

"The mysterious strangers usually do?" Matt asked, trying to keep a straight face.

"At the moment. The hometown boy as hero is coming back into style. I suppose that's you."

"Must everybody play a role?"

"They usually do—if you think about it." Spying her purse on the floor, Gina picked it up, looked at it, and put it back down again. "Everybody's always afraid to change, you know, once they've got it down pat."

"Wasn't the hometown boy usually something of a bore too?" Matt inquired, rocking back in his chair and propping his feet on the desk again.

"I expect that Regan thought *you* were a bore to begin with," Gina said with devastating candor. "That pose, for example. Very down-home country cop. Almost aggressively so. Regan's an artistic type, and, if there's one thing artistic types can't stand, it's predictability. They're predictable themselves in that way. But then you weren't, after all."

"I wasn't?"

"No, actually you're really more like the mysterious stranger type. A man made a little dangerous emotionally by his shaky past. Exactly the type an imaginative sort would go for." Gina frowned. "Nothing is what it's supposed to be. Real life can be fuddling."

Intrigued, Matt said, "And what are you?"

"The parasite, I expect," Gina answered serenely, "who's of

no earthly use to anybody. It's what my mother used to say, anyway. But there's the advantage that nobody dislikes me quite like they disliked her."

Hands clasped behind his head in the aggressively predictable pose, he said, "Sorry. I didn't know your mother. Does she have anything to do with all this?"

"I expect so." Gina had been surveying the office curiously. "You need to liven this place up some. It's kind of a vacuum. Though I suppose that might work for you, since people feel compelled to fill up a vacuum—with talk if nothing else. Anyway, I imagine that Agatha hated Regan so much because Regan got the nice mother and Father's attention and most of the money."

"You think Agatha killed your father?"

"Oh, no." Gina turned her bewildered stare on him. "She would have kept trying—Agatha would have. Kept competing, I mean. Agatha never gives up."

"Well, then, who"—Matt tried to hold her roving gaze without success—"do you cast in the killer's role?"

"It would be nice," Gina said, regarding one of the wanted posters as if speaking to it, "if it turned out to be Dennis. Or that woman he works for. Regan thinks Caroline is a sensitive type under the crust. I think it's all crust myself. Some people *are* just what they seem to be." She stood. "I'm talking too much. I do that sometimes. I expect I had better go."

Matt stood too. He suspected that Gina possessed a sharp intelligence under the softness of that plump body and unfocused gaze, but he didn't know how to get at it. He was not a psychologist.

"Did you notice the cup that morning?"

"No, I was looking at Father." Her fingers tightened on

the purse. "I loved him. We all did, I think. He didn't realize how important he was to us. Just like he was embarrassed by how some of his readers idolized him. He still saw himself as a small-town doctor. He never quite realized the impact he had. Regan is like him in that way. She doesn't see herself as being significant enough to hurt anyone. Do you understand?" Gina's gaze had finally stopped roving to settle with earnest sympathy on Matt.

"She doesn't mean any harm?" he suggested with forced lightness.

"I put that wrong," Gina said in a vexed tone. "I'd better go. I'm just making things worse." And she went, with surprising decision and speed.

CHAPTER 12

*I would give you some violets, but they withered all
when my father died; they say 'a made a good end.*

"So that's the list of what we'll need." Regan flung a paper
down on Caroline's desk and dropped into a chair.

"The hops vine was kind of iffy. The museum director is
afraid his chief sponsor for the project won't like it. She's a tee-
totaler."

Regan kicked off her shoes and wiggled her toes. "'So am
I,' I told him. 'But if you're running a colonial museum, you
can't get around the fact that beer was the beverage of choice.
Besides, it's a pretty plant. You don't have to tell her what it is.'
Seems that they're going to be putting up those metal tags
though. And you know how I feel about gardens that are la-
beled."

Caroline cracked a smile. "Well, you can't expect everybody to be able to identify herbs on sight. Besides, it's good
for business. If they see a plant they like, they can write it
down and trot on out here to buy it."

"I suppose so. But I try to design these gardens to look
natural, and plants in the wild are not neatly tagged."

"Might help if they were," Caroline said, going down the list and checking names off against a catalog. "It would keep anybody from chowing down on water hemlock in mistake for parsley. Oh, sorry—"

"Never mind." Regan waved it off. "We've all got poison on the brain right now."

"We're out of costmary." Caroline made a circle instead of a check mark. "There was a run on that this year for some reason. People are asking for more of the old roses too. But I suspect that it would take too much manpower to grow many of them."

"Yes," Regan agreed. "We'd better stick to the most ancient ones—or those that have some historical significance. I was just thinking about something else on the way over here. Natural root beer extract. Most of the ones you get in the grocery stores these days are artificially flavored. What did they use for that originally? Sarsaparilla?"

"Maybe." Caroline jotted the name on a notepad. "It's an idea—a good item for the tearoom. Though I suspect that it might have been sassafras, and some people claim that causes cancer. If we could think of some other sodas flavored by plants . . . Some customers bring their kids along, and kids aren't big on tea. Ginger ale maybe?"

"There's nothing wrong with sassafras in moderation," Regan said. "If people understand that too much of anything can be bad for you. How about cordials, as in Anne of Green Gables? Could we make those nonalcoholic?"

"Funny you should mention that," Caroline said, as the intercom on her desk buzzed. "Diane was saying yesterday that maybe we should do a line of drinks and snacks based on literary allusions. Mad Hatter tea, for example. The kids might go for that. Yes?"

"Mrs. Gillard on the phone," the secretary said. "Shall I put her through?"

Caroline grimaced. "All right." And to Regan, "She's into gentians now."

"Those things are devilish to grow."

"Let her find out for herself. She's making Dennis very happy anyhow. Good morning, Mrs. Gillard." Caroline sounded as genial as she could. "What can we do for you today? Gentian *septemfida lagodechiana*?" Caroline raised an eyebrow at Regan.

"That's the only fragrant one, I think," Regan said. "Fringed."

"Fringed and fragrant?" Caroline queried the phone. "Good. Frankly, I don't know if we have any on hand just now. Let me ask my manager."

Caroline reached into a drawer for a portable phone, punched out a number on it, and sat with a receiver to either ear.

Finally, she shook her head, putting the portable phone down and tapping it. She mouthed to Regan, "See if you can find him. Have him call me back on this."

Regan nodded, scuffed back into her shoes, and went out. It had been one of those days. The museum director seemed like the type who would wait until everything was in place before, under a screen of effusive flattery, suggesting that it all be shifted around. At least he was not put off by her recent notoriety. Or perhaps he didn't keep up with the news. The rich female sponsor would probably be a different story. And now, she had to go looking for Dennis, who was better avoided.

The day was dull and overcast; even the greens of trees and grass looked drab and sullen. Regan didn't locate the manager in the main greenhouses or the display gardens. She met a hassled tour guide leading a group in which one stout woman was complaining loudly and bitterly about the prices. Under cover of that monologue, Regan asked the guide, "Seen Mr. Hailey anywhere?"

"I think he went up to those greenhouses where he keeps the rare stuff," the girl answered. "He doesn't let us up there even though he keeps everything locked up, but"—she winked—"he won't mind you."

Regan followed the path that wound between fields of perennials toward the tree line. The old greenhouses up there had been in bad shape when Caroline bought the place. Recently she had let Dennis start using them after he volunteered to pay for the repairs. He raised many rare tropical and alpine types that weren't in high demand but could fetch a good price from connoisseurs.

Regan climbed a small rise and rounded a gently wooded curve to come out in the clearing where the two greenhouses stood. They were attached to each other at the narrow ends and sided with the cheaper Plexiglas, through which the plants were only a blur. Regan tried the near door, which opened readily. Apparently, he didn't keep them locked all the time.

With the sky cloudy, she wasn't met by the usual wall of heat. Overhead, fans spun lazily.

Strolling down the graveled aisle, she entertained herself by trying to identify some of the plants before reading the tags. Meconopsis in blue, white, and yellow, some of the more obscure hardy geraniums, columbines, cyclamens, and hellebores. Cinnamon tree, cardamom, the deadly daturas, Parma violets. Violets for faithfulness. Meek, loyal, sweet. People used to think her the violets type. Recent events would have disabused them of that notion. She had a sense that she was disintegrating. Eroding.

She found the gentian and carried it with her as she tried the door to the other greenhouse. "Dennis?" she called, peering around the jamb and, when there was no answer, slipping inside.

His portable phone was lying on the edge of one of the benches. Apparently he had gone out for a moment. This greenhouse contained very large plants—most of them three to four feet tall—and all of the same variety.

A bit coarse for ornamentals or houseplants. She reached out to touch. A hollow stem with grooves, leaves like five-fingered hands. One of the new fiber plants? But hardly worth space in a greenhouse, surely.

Or maybe not one of the *new* fiber plants. One of the old ones. A chill traversed her spine. Hemp. *Cannabis.*

She turned quickly. Nobody was there. Yet.

She picked up the phone in her right hand, still clutching the potted gentian with her left, and clumsily punched out numbers. She backed up hard against a bench, so she would be out of direct line with the door.

The phone was busy. Apparently Caroline had grown tired of waiting for her and was summoning someone else to the search.

As she listened to the beep-beep, Dennis appeared at the far end of the other greenhouse. He seemed to have come not from the direction of the farm but from the woods higher up. He hadn't seen her yet. He turned to look back, as if waiting for someone.

She clicked the phone off, dropped awkwardly to her

knees, and edged under one of the slatted benches, support-
ing her weight with one hand, still clutching the gentian to
her chest with the other. The plants were so thickly massed
overhead that she didn't think she would be visible to anyone
standing.

Lying full-length on her stomach on the unrelenting
stones and staring at the phone up close, she tried to think
whom she could call. The county didn't have a 911 system yet,
and she had never bothered to memorize Matt's number—or
that of the state police. And should she call them if she could?
The resulting publicity would surely hurt the farm and Caroline.

Dennis paced impatiently in the other greenhouse. She
tried to keep track of him by sound, but the breathy whir of
the fans was confusing.

■ ■ ■

Gina approached Regan's house on horseback at about four
o'clock. After moving back into the Hayden mansion, she had
retrieved her horses from the stable that had been boarding
them. She was leading the second one, saddled, in the hope
that one of the other women would go riding with her.

She came up to the house from the rear by the field path
and saw Luke's car vanishing down the drive toward the road.
To her disappointment, there were no other vehicles parked in
the space beside the garage.

Not easily deterred, Gina dismounted, tied the horses to a
rail near the back door, and went in through the kitchen.
"Anybody home?" she called, pushing through into the hall.
The question echoed, unanswered, from corner to corner of
the high ceiling.

Gina puffed up the stairs to rap on bedroom doors. Again,

no response. She shrugged and went into the room that had been her own to see if she had overlooked anything. The stomp of her booted heels and the opening and closing of drawers reverberated loudly.

She found a silk scarf fallen in a corner of the closet and a piece of hard candy behind the lamp on the bedside table. Putting the candy in her mouth and the scarf loosely around her neck, she strolled, humming, out to the upstairs hall. She heard the sound of movement below, followed by the closing of the front door, and ran to the railing to peer over. Whoever it was had vanished into the living room. She leaned there, frowning, for a moment, lips parted as if to call. Then the phone shrilled, almost at her elbow.

Starting convulsively and nearly choking on her candy, she scooped up the receiver. She pushed the sweet to a safe pocket in her cheek and said, "Huwwo?"

"Is that you, Gina?" It was Regan's voice, strained and low—a virtual whisper.

At Gina's "Uh-huh," Regan went on. "Listen carefully. I haven't much time. I've just discovered that Dennis is growing marijuana in his greenhouse up here at the farm. But I'm trapped. He's near the door, and I can't get out without him seeing me. I'm hiding under one of the benches. Call Matt. If you can't get him, you'll have to try to explain it to the state police. Do you understand?"

Gina spat out the candy and said clearly, "Yes. Okay."

"I have to go. He's coming this way. Hurry."

Holding the sticky sweet in one hand, Gina hung up with the other, pulled the phone book out of the drawer of the telephone stand, and consulted the inside front cover. She was so intent on what she was doing that she did not hear hurried steps on the stairs behind her. She started to turn as the scarf was yanked from around her neck. Then blackness, as the soft cloth was jerked tight over her eyes and a hard hand pushed at her from behind. Not able to see where she was going, she staggered like a drunkard. She had time only for a gasped, "Don't be ridic—" before the hand shoved her. She pitched forward against a wall, and a door clicked behind her.

The scarf slid off. She popped the candy in her mouth, that being the quickest way to dispose of it, and turned, licking the stickiness off her palm, to survey her situation.

She was in a closet, an empty closet, so it must be her own. Trying the handle, she ascertained that the door was locked from the outside. Turning toward the east end of the closet, she got down on her knees, felt for a certain knothole in the wood, and yanked. The entire panel came away. She and Agatha had devised this method of getting from one room to another when they were children. Of course it was a tight fit now. She wriggled determinedly through, dislodging several neatly hung garments of Agatha's in the process.

Once free of Agatha's room, she barreled down the stairs and out through the kitchen to where the horses waited. The herb farm was much closer cross-country than it was by road, and those greenhouses were way at the back. She thought she might be able to get there before a car could.

She untied both horses, threw the reins of her own mount up over the pommel, and struggled, panting, to get her left foot up while holding the lead rope of the second horse. At home she had a mounting block. Once her boot was precariously stirruped, she entwined her fingers in the bay's mane and dragged herself up. As she straightened her knee so that she was standing on the left stirrup, her toe jabbed into the horse's side and it began to move out. "No, no!" she gasped, throwing herself forward against its neck, her face buried in the coarseness of its mane while she strove to swing her right leg over its back. The chestnut jerked to the side just in time to avoid being kicked in the face by a booted foot.

At the full stretch of the lead rope, it nudged its way around to the bay's other side. The bay continued its obstinate trudge down the path toward the fields without looking back.

After much wriggling, Gina sat up and succeeded in hooking the right stirrup with her toe.

"Giddap!" she said, reining the bay off the path and kicking at its sides. It broke into a rib-jarring trot. "Faster!" she said impatiently, kicking it again. It graduated to a gentle lope. When she booted the horse the third time, it rolled an eye at her as if to say, "It's your funeral," stretched out its neck, and began a series of lunges.

They ate up the field. She looked between the horse's ears to avoid seeing the ground rushing past below.

She knew vaguely that the rider was supposed to make some effort to adapt herself to the horse's movements. Regan had tried to explain it all to her before. Head up, heels down, weight on the balls of the feet—and lean forward over the animal's center of balance. Gina found all of this confusing to accomplish at once, so she preferred simply to sit. Many of her acquaintances seemed surprised that she seldom fell off. Still, she usually didn't go this fast.

Now she thought that maybe she should take up western riding instead. It provided a much more convenient handhold.

■ ■ ■

In her cramped position on the gravel under the bench, Regan was beginning to question her fear. It was only Dennis, after all. He wouldn't hurt her. And it was only marijuana, the plant people made jokes about smoking in college. They didn' give long jail terms for that, did they?

They did yank up the crop, though. And she seemed to recall hearing on the news recently that marijuana brought very high prices these days.

She could pretend that she hadn't recognized it, ask brightly what was the new exotic he was growing so much of. Allow him to lie to her. But she didn't think that he would believe that ignorance.

Had her father found out too? Was that why he was killed? She dismissed that almost immediately. This wasn't the sort of thing Alden Culver had been talking about. He would have had no qualms about turning Dennis in. And Dennis hadn't even been around ten years ago. Of course, the subject uppermost on her father's mind may not, after all, have been the motive behind his murder . . .

There was a scuffing of feet on the gravel walk.

Regan huddled against the Plexiglas wall, holding her breath.

She could see only his lower legs and feet. He was wearing jeans and tennis shoes, like a teenager.

The telephone buzzed at her ear. Regan's heart jolted. She shut her eyes. Caroline had gotten tired of waiting.

Dennis was still for a moment. She could almost see his puzzled gaze scanning the rows of plants, searching for his phone.

Her pulse and breathing resumed again, but uncomfortably fast.

She stabbed at the answer button and held both hands tightly over the earpiece.

She could hear only the faintest thread of sound—Caroline's puzzled voice. "Dennis, are you there?"

"Dennis!" The call came from outside like a distorted echo. "Dennis, are you there?"

He swore. Regan heard him sprint out, slamming the door between the two greenhouses.

As soon as he was gone, Regan switched the phone off and scrambled out from under the bench. She didn't have time to explain things to Caroline now. That had been Gina's voice outside. Regan tiptoed to the door and tried it gingerly. He hadn't locked it; the latch turned under her fingers. She eased the door open a crack, looking down the length of the other greenhouse. She could hear Gina's voice, but for the moment couldn't see either of them.

Crouching to the level of the benches, Regan shuffled down the aisle. She had progressed almost halfway and her back and knees were beginning to throb when she heard Gina say, "But I insist, Dennis! I really do! I must have one of those poppies Regan showed me. The big blue ones. From the Andes or somewhere."

"Himalayas," Dennis corrected, trying to block her determined progress toward the greenhouse door. "Meconopsis. But those flowers are very difficult to grow, Mrs. Hayden. I can show you something easier down at the shop. Besides, you can't carry a plant while you're riding."

"I don't want anything easier," Gina insisted. "I want one of the blue ones. Or maybe two or three. Regan told me that you grow them up here. I'll just pick them out and you can have them delivered."

Regan was still carrying the phone and plant. She set them hastily on the edge of one of the benches and rolled under it just as Gina appeared in the doorway with Dennis, still protesting, right behind her. The plants were not nearly so thickly massed here.

Gina scurried down the aisle, her constant chatter matching her roaming gaze. "I brought both horses because I thought Regan might be down at the farm with Caroline, and she could ride back with me. Of course that was stupid because if she is here, she probably has her car with her and wouldn't want to leave it. My husband tells me that I never think things through. I'm too impulsive, he claims. Like my stopping here to pick out a flower. I really hadn't intended to do that. But, as I was passing I remembered that I wanted some of those Andes poppies, and, since I'm here anyway, what better time . . ." As she passed the spot where Regan was hiding, Gina's wandering gaze settled ever so briefly on the phone, and she kicked out. Regan was too far back for that pointed toe to connect with her flesh, but a large piece of gravel caromed off her thigh.

". . . to pick them out," Gina continued without pause. "Ooh, there they are!" And she headed at a determined canter for the far end of the greenhouse.

The Himalayan blue poppies were actually, Regan knew, under a bench near the door where the two had come in. Dennis plunged after Gina, expostulating. Regan writhed out into the aisle again, scrambling clumsily to a standing position, and began to back away. She was prepared, should Dennis turn, to pretend that she had just come in.

Not, she suspected, that that pretense would hold up very well, since her face seemed set in a rigid cast of apprehension.

The distance was interminable. Her feet dragged and stumbled on the gravel underfoot. Because she didn't dare avert her gaze from the two at the far end, she kept bumping up against the benches. Finally, she stretched out her arms. The leaves sliding past under her rigidly outstretched fingers kept her in the center of the aisle.

Then she was outside with grass under her feet. She turned and fled down the path toward the farm. Beyond the first bend, she had to stop and lean against a tree because her knees had gone weak. She could hear, as from a great distance, Gina's compulsive chatter emerging into the open again with an occasional reply from Dennis. At the moment Regan was not capable of concentrating enough to make out the words.

She heard the thud of horses' hooves behind her. "Come on," Gina ordered. "You don't want to be here for what's going down next." Regan had ridden all during her teen years and swung up automatically. She let her mount follow Gina's off the trail and through the trees toward the fields beyond.

"Going down?" she inquired.

Gina didn't reply. Regan heard a car snarl up the path to the greenhouses, but they were well into the trees by then, and she didn't turn her head. When they reached the open ground, the horses broke into a lope. The fresh air fanning her face gradually revived Regan. The old rhythm was reassuring. She had always felt more powerful on horseback.

Gina did not pull up until they reached the highest point in the fields where they could look back at the farm and see Dennis's greenhouses in miniature in their circle of trees. A car was there now, and Dennis was talking to another man. Their attitude appeared tense and angry. They finally turned and went inside.

"Isn't that . . ." Regan began, but after a glance at Gina's intent face, did not finish the question. She felt pleasantly weak, like someone recovering from a serious illness. Between her knees the horse's heavy breathing gradually slowed. When the animal pulled at the bit, she let it put its head down and crop the clover.

Gina gestured, and Regan turned to see in the distance a big truck picking its way up the rough track on the far edge of the field behind the greenhouses. The truck had the name of a local nursery on the side—a nursery that often made deliveries to the farm.

The truck was lost to view for a couple of minutes among the trees. Then it emerged beside the greenhouses and came to a stop facing the car. The driver ran around to the back to open the truck's big doors. He and a passenger went into the greenhouse and began carrying out plants. Big plants. The marijuana. Dennis and the man from the car were helping them. They all seemed in a tremendous hurry.

Regan moved restlessly. "Shouldn't we—?"

Gina shook her head without looking around, gesturing again. Now Regan saw three Jeeps creeping up the track. One of the men by the truck dropped the plant he was carrying and pointed frantically. He and his friend slammed the doors and scrambled into the cab, Dennis and the other man into the car. The car made a U-turn, and both vehicles plunged toward the path that led down to the farm. Then Jeeps appeared from that direction also, surging in around the truck and car. Men spilled out of the Jeeps, surrounding, enveloping, overrunning. They all wore jackets with large letters on the back.

Regan's horse moved. She grabbed at the pommel to steady herself as the scene she was watching whirled away from her. Gina had turned her mount and started for home, and the other horse was following.

Urging it into a trot to catch up, Regan said, "Wasn't that man in the car—"

"Reid?" Gina said, fixed gaze not veering from a spot between her horse's ears. "Yes, it was. He overheard your phone call to me, put a scarf over my eyes, and chucked me into a closet. As if that were enough to keep me from recognizing my own husband! I don't think he really would have hurt you, but I couldn't take a chance on it. I should have seen all of this long ago when his business improved so suddenly after it nearly went under. I suppose I didn't want to see it."

"He was in it with Dennis?" Regan ventured, still trying to catch up. "Of course. He got Dennis his job at the farm by recommending him to Caroline. She didn't know about it, did she? I'm sure she wouldn't—"

"No," Gina agreed. "She would never jeopardize her business that way. I don't think they can do anything to her if she didn't know. But they will seize our house and cars, I expect. They can do that now."

"But if it's just marijuana—" Regan began.

Gina shot her an impatient look. "Of course it won't be just marijuana! My husband is an importer, remember. You don't have to import marijuana. This will give them an excuse to look for other stuff—and I don't doubt they'll find some. It serves me right. I should have known better. On TV, women who marry for money always suffer for it in the end."

"But what about Luke?" Regan asked, reining in her mount. "Wasn't he in it too? Shouldn't they—"

Gina pulled up to fix her with a glare of pure exasperation. "Don't you realize yet what Luke is?"

■ ■ ■

"You're DEA, aren't you?" Matt said to Luke Hayden.

Luke had just arrived for his interview and made himself comfortable in the seat in front of the desk. Slouched down on his tailbone, one ankle hooked over the opposite knee, he made it look like an easy chair.

There was no perceptible stiffening of that relaxed position. Only his mouth moved, stretching into an incredulous grin. "Me, a narc? Whatever made you think . . ."

As if realizing that that wasn't going to work, he dropped the protestation suddenly, though the grin took longer to fade. "Who told you?"

"Nobody. It suddenly occurred to me that I might be seeing you backward, so to speak. Your friend's death might have been caused by you, granted. Or it could have sparked you into a personal crusade."

Luke moved his shoulders impatiently. "It wasn't revenge," he said. "Revenge doesn't accomplish anything. Regan is right. It doesn't bring them back." He jerked to his feet and paced around the room, opening the door to the borough office on his way past, briefly scanning the empty chair and the blank computer screen.

"I'm into prevention. Just as Regan's father was. I think he realized that. I rather think my stepmother has an idea too; she's a little cagier than people give her credit for."

He had moved on to open the door to the hall. Matt said to his back, "And your father?"

The door clicked shut again. When Luke turned, the mocking grin was back on his face. "Does my father suspect?

No, I doubt that he does. Otherwise, he wouldn't have tried to sell me the stuff. He thinks I have connections, you see? Oddly enough, I never guessed his little sideline before that. I would have thought him a little too careful of the Hayden name. But then I realized that it was the prosperous façade that was most important to him. He'd got himself in financial trouble and couldn't maintain his lifestyle any other way. Or so he claims now."

Luke dropped into the chair again, leaning forward, rubbing the heel of one hand against the other. "Me, I'm a little luckier. The government pays for my car and clothes. I have appearances to keep up too."

Glancing at the clock behind Matt's head, he added, "Speaking of which, I hope you'll remember to mention to everyone where I was at this hour. Right about now, some agents are raiding Dennis Hailey's greenhouses out at the herb farm. Sorry we didn't tell you about that. We knew that someone bigger was in on it, but we suspected for a while that it might be Caroline or Regan or both. Some herbalists have lenient views on plant stimulants, you know. And your getting invited to a family dinner implied to me that you were on pretty friendly terms with Regan."

Ignoring that, Matt said, "Your own father?"

"I kept trying to discourage him, but he kept telling me more. Like somebody said, we don't choose our relatives. I used to feel guilty about disliking my pater. Not anymore."

"Did he kill Alden Culver?'

Luke raised his eyebrows. "Don't ask me. I don't pretend to understand anybody anymore. I did like Alden; I would have let Regan go for his sake. I even gave her a warning. Poor girl probably didn't have the foggiest idea what I was talking about. And I'd been picturing her as a crime boss."

"I arrested her for murder," Matt said with an abstracted gaze.

■　■　■

"He was super smart, and he'd been studying law," Gina was explaining to Regan as their horses jogged on. "Just the type that the DEA and the FBI like to recruit. If you watched TV, you would know that. Anyway, as soon as it hit me this afternoon what Reid was up to, I realized what he and Luke must have been arguing about all week. And I knew that it was only a matter of time until those greenhouses got raided."

"What are you going to do now?" Regan asked.

"I don't know." Gina rubbed her mount's sweaty neck. "Do you think I'll lose the horses too? I don't think that would be fair. They're mine. I mean, I know I'm not the greatest rider in the world, but they're used to me. And I'm not like you. I don't have to be good at something to like it."

Regan furrowed her brow. "Are you saying that I'm a perfectionist?"

"You're a control freak," Gina said tolerantly. "Just like Agatha, though you're more subtle about it. And you know that you can't control Matt Olin, so you're freezing him out. Like me, you prefer your comfort. I can tell you from experience that gets dull mighty fast."

Regan's face wore a thoughtful but unoffended frown. She was thinking of the severity of the blow that had been dealt to Gina that afternoon and her matter-of-fact acceptance of it.

"You might come home," Regan offered tentatively. "We can take the horses back to my barn now, if you like. It's empty. Then we'll call Mathilda. They won't seize anything from me easily; she'll see to that."

Gina smiled. "You're getting a rather full house, aren't you? Are you sure you're prepared to put up with that?"

"I used to think I understood you all pretty well," Regan said. "The last few days have showed me that I don't know anything. But we Culver women have at least one thing in common; we're all in trouble. Not to mention that, as Diane pointed out, none of us has an ounce of sense about men. I think we need to pull together now—for Daddy's sake, if not our own."

Gina considered. "A female family dynasty? Arms linked against the world and all that? It might be fun. Would make a good scene for the opening credits, anyhow."

"Speaking of TV," Regan said, "we're going to be lucky if we aren't the lead story on the local news. The public is going to have a hard time believing that Caroline and I didn't know what Dennis was doing. Especially with my brother-in-law involved. And heaven forbid that they discover that story about Diane . . ." Regan paused.

"Amen," Gina agreed without surprise. "Agatha told me about it. She does tell me things, you know. As for you, I'd keep in mind that publicity is a good thing when you're running a business."

Regan looked dubious. "Even bad publicity?"

"As long as it doesn't reflect on the quality of your product. People will come flocking out to the farm to gape. Consider. Would you rather buy a plant from any boring, old nursery, or one associated with a stunning woman who may or may not have knocked off her father to cover up her drug trade—and perhaps vamped the chief of police on the side? If I were you, I'd stop hiding out up here and do a few interviews, preferably dressed in black and looking suitably mysterious. Half of your audience will immediately decide that you didn't do it, and the other half will be just as convinced that you did. Either way, they'll be fascinated. Not to mention that newspeople love puns. Can't you just hear them now. 'As to the guilt or innocence of Regan Culver, only Thyme Will Tell . . .'"

■ ■ ■

Regan appeared on Boston TV the following evening. The interview had been conducted in her garden that afternoon. She sat on a pergola seat with a tumble of roses as a backdrop, flanked by her half sisters and niece.

She was calm and collected, taking her time to answer the reporters' often impertinent questions. The women looked coolly elegant in the dappled light from the latticed roof. United, they made quite an impression. "A class act," raved Jean Harris in her editorial. "The Culver women show remarkable poise in the midst of devastation—their patriarch dead, Gina's husband arrested, along with a family friend, for drug trafficking, the family business suspect, Regan, shortly to go on trial for murder . . . Some will call this composure on the eve of battle arrogance, but most of us can still recognize courage when we see it. It is too bad that the men in this drama don't measure up. There have always been rumors about Luke Hayden, but this town has been stunned by the arrest of his father, Reid, one of our most eminent businessmen and philanthropists."

She couldn't resist a shot at Matt Olin before she finished.

"The raid was conducted by DEA agents assisted by the state police. Where was our chief, the man who was reportedly Regan Culver's guest at her father's birthday party? Once again, like it or not, Hayden's controversial chief of police is back in the spotlight."

CHAPTER 13

■ ■ ■

Thought and affliction, passion, hell itself,
She turns to favor and to prettiness.

Matt stopped at the diner on Thursday evening for pie and coffee. He had not seen Regan on the local news the evening before, but he had certainly heard about it. As he came in the door to the restaurant, a group of guys—most of them bachelors and widowers with nobody to go home to—were clustered at the counter, looking up at the TV. "You really can't blame him," one of them was saying. "She's not bad, not bad at a—"

The speaker stopped abruptly when a companion elbowed him in the ribs. They all turned to stare at Matt, and an awkward silence fell.

He looked up at the TV screen to see Regan's face. She had been made up by professionals and looked sleeker than usual, her dark hair and eyes showed off to advantage by a bittersweet red dress and a black brooch at her throat. For someone being interviewed on a national news magazine show, she seemed amazingly cool and composed.

"I'll have cherry pie and coffee." Matt wrenched his gaze away to speak to the counterman.

"Sure, Chief. Coming right up." The man rattled the china and silverware. It was the only sound in the place besides the interviewer's voice.

"We are coming to you live from the home of Regan Culver, daughter of well-known naturopath Alden Culver, who was poisoned one week ago," she was saying. "Regan has been charged with his murder and is currently out on bail. Miss Culver, your father wrote the bestsellers *Never Say Die* and *Life More Abundant,* didn't he?"

"Those were two of his books," Regan agreed, indicating several volumes on the table in front of her. She was seated against a backdrop of leaves and flowers in her conservatory. "Father brought hope—and often healing—to the terminally ill and their families."

"And one of the patients he healed was your mother?"

"That's right." Regan chose a volume titled *Roses for Rosemary,* and turned it over to reveal a picture of a slender, dark-haired woman laughing up at the photographer from the shelter of Alden Culver's arm. "This was my mother." The camera zoomed in on that vital face.

"Rosemary was much younger than your father, was she not?"

"Yes, about twenty years."

"And that caused some antagonism from his family? There were jealousies, perhaps?"

"Yes," Regan agreed, setting the book gently back on the table.

"Especially since Rosemary became quite well known herself as a garden columnist. They might have thought that she traded on your father's name?"

Regan's brow furrowed. "I never heard any of them suggest such a thing. My mother was an exceptional writer. No one argued with that."

"Of course not," the interviewer agreed smoothly. "But she had no books?"

"She would have. It wasn't long after she became well known that she died."

"At the peak of her popularity, so to speak. Do you think that her name fueled your own career?"

"Undoubtedly."

"You look very much like her."

"Thank you."

"And you have attained your own fame. If I may?" The interviewer held up a glossy magazine, *Garrets and Gardens,* and opened it to a full-page spread of Regan seated in her own lushly blooming landscape with a lapful of flowers. "Horti-Culver" ran the two-inch title above her head. "In this article, you are called the queen of the heirloom craze."

Regan said tolerantly, "They always exaggerate."

"But the readers of this magazine don't exactly live in garrets, do they?"

Regan smiled. "No."

"It seems strangely ironic," the interviewer suggested, "considering your family background, that your father should have been poisoned with a cup of herbal tea. You *did* make that cup of tea, did you not, Miss Culver?"

"Yes."

"You carried it up to his room?"

"Yes."

"And by your own admission, nobody else had access to that cup at any time?"

"Not that evening. They did the next morning."

The interviewer paused for effect. "And why is the next morning so important?"

"It is our belief that poison was planted in the teacup then, that the actual poison that killed my father was in a bottle of *echinacea* extract in his medicine cabinet."

"And you think you can prove that that bottle was replaced?"

"Either replaced or switched with the one in my cabinet. So that I was almost poisoned too."

"Ah," the interviewer agreed. "And your cat saved you. Is that right?"

"Yes, Gato lapped up some of the extract that was accidentally spilled. He went into convulsions and nearly died."

The interviewer's eyebrows were raised high. "Don't you think that's just a bit too convenient to be believable, Miss Culver?"

"I don't call it convenient. I call it divine deliverance."

The eyebrows climbed, if possible, higher. "I see. When you say 'our belief,' to whom are you referring?"

Regan lifted her own brows. "Me and my lawyer. And my family."

"I see. You have resolved your differences with your father's first family?"

"Yes."

"And which of them," the interviewer asked sweetly, "do you think killed him?"

"I believe—I hope—that none of them did."

"And that would leave whom? Your partner, Caroline Stanton? Your farm manager, Dennis Hailey, who has just been arrested on drug charges?" The interviewer ran on without waiting for an answer. "Do you honestly expect us to believe, Miss Culver, that you and Ms. Stanton had no idea what Dennis Hailey was growing in your greenhouses?"

"I don't expect anything from you," Regan said with a certain asperity. One of the men in the diner laughed. "Caroline and I did *not* know what Dennis was growing. He was allowed those particular greenhouses for his private use."

The interviewer appeared to consult a notepad. "How well do you know Dennis Hailey?"

"I went out with him once. I did not choose to pursue the relationship."

"I see. And did you choose to pursue a relationship with Police Chief Matthew Olin?"

Regan's expression did not change. "I have no relationship with Matt, beyond that of a casual acquaintance. We went to high school together." The men in the diner kept their gazes glued to the screen and were careful not to look at Matt. He had his head down, eating his pie.

"I see." It seemed a favorite phrase of the interviewer. "Why, then, did your half sister say that Mr. Olin was your guest at your father's birthday party, at what was clearly a private family affair?"

"Because she thought that he was. My father wanted to consult Matt about something but didn't want anyone to know about it. So he let her think that I invited Matt."

"Hmm. What did your father wish to talk to Mr. Olin about?"

"I don't know. He never told me."

"By he, you mean—"

"My father never told me. Matt didn't either because he never found out. My father changed his mind, apparently deciding that it was not a police matter."

"And you have had no kind of romantic relationship with Chief Olin?"

"No."

"If someone said they saw his truck parked in front of your house after midnight—"

Regan smiled. "That was the day I almost got poisoned. Chief Olin was away and didn't hear about it till he got back. So naturally he came around to question me about it."

"I can't believe the nerve of that reporter," muttered one of the old men at the counter. "Asking a lady like her stuff like that."

"Yeah, but she's cool," one of the younger ones said. "She isn't letting it get to her."

She is cool all right, Matt thought. She didn't lie. He hadn't caught her in a lie yet. She simply left a lot out. She sat demurely through implications of murder, drug abuse, and suspect relationships without any of it touching her.

The interviewer looked frustrated. This obviously wasn't going the way she had planned it. She abandoned the subject of Matt Olin with reluctance. "This cat that saved your life. Is it your contention that he knew?"

It was the first time that Regan looked taken aback. "Knew?"

"That you were in danger," the interviewer insisted, leaning forward. "Do you think he *sensed* it?"

Regan smiled. "No, I don't. Gato will try anything."

"And there were no fingerprints on the bottle—except yours?"

"Except mine," Regan agreed, "and my sister's. She saved the bottle for the police."

"Is it true that your father made most of his fortune over to you before he died?"

"Yes."

"He was an old man. Is it possible that you coerced him into taking that action, then killed him so he couldn't change his mind?"

"No. No one who knew my father would believe for a minute that he was coercible."

"And you two were on good terms?"

"The best."

"Then how do you explain this?"

The interviewer reached to the side, and a manila envelope was handed to her. She tilted it, and a small tape recorder slid into her hand. "Do you recognize it?"

Regan leaned forward. "It looks like the recorder my father carried in the car to tape ideas that occurred to him while he was driving. Where did you get it?"

"It was mailed to us. Anonymously. Perhaps someone didn't trust your police chief." The interviewer clicked the button. The voice of a dead man filled the diner. "Regretfully, I have to conclude that she was always mercenary. That even Rosemary's death touched her only because it would affect her financial situation."

The interviewer clicked the tape off. "Was your father talking about you, Miss Culver? After all, who else would be financially affected by your mother's death?"

"I wasn't affected at all," Regan said, settling back in her chair again. "My mother only made one will, when I was quite small. She left everything to my father."

The interviewer looked disappointed. "But *now* it all goes to you?"

"Most of it, yes. But if I were that greedy, would I have waited ten years? I know how some TV programs love to ferret out dysfunctional families. We weren't one of them." She flipped over another one of the books to show a photo of Alden and Rosemary Culver looking adoringly down at a four-year-old Regan walking between them and holding both their hands. "*This* is the way we were," she said.

The interviewer tried to interrupt; time was running out. "But Miss Culver, if your father wasn't talking about you, then who?"

Regan ignored her and looked at the camera. "I want everyone out there who adored my mother and father to know that they were the best parents a little girl could have had. Thyme Will Tell has always been about what my father and mother believed, that the slower, time-tested ways to health and happiness are the truest ones and that life is a gift to be respected and protected. Thyme Will Tell is not going to fold because of one man's dishonesty. We will continue as we began. Thank you for letting me tell you my side of the story. Good night."

She elicited a rattle of applause from the men in the diner.

A commercial flashed on the screen. Matt's beeper went off. The others stiffened to attention without actually looking at him. The counterman helpfully pushed the phone across, and Matt dialed.

"Hello, Cal," Matt said, raising his eyes to the television where a couple of models were chatting comfortably about antacids. "There isn't much point in telling *me* that she can't do that. You'd better tell *her*. No, I can't stop her. The judge didn't impose a gag order on the case. Yes, I know that this is not L.A. Certainly, Mathilda knows better, but I doubt very much if Regan asked her. Look on the bright side. Now you have her story on tape, and if she tries to change—Yes, I *plan* to get it. Good-bye, Cal."

Just as he was rising from his stool and dropping some coins on the counter, the beeper sounded again. After a disgusted glance at it, he dialed again. "Hello, Mathilda. Watching TV? No, I'm not trying to be cute. No, I didn't know anything about it. How could I? At least she seems to have made a good impression. Yes, I *plan* to get it. Good-bye, Mathilda."

The door of the diner had only half-swung shut behind him, when he heard a rush of talk. He smiled grimly.

As he climbed into his car, the cellular phone was ringing. He was a good deal more cautious this time. "Good evening, Judge Parker. No, I agree with you. I don't think anything will be gained by clapping her back in jail. She has a lot of prominent clients, and I have a feeling that most of them are going to come down heavily on her side. In all fairness, I doubt if anyone told her that she couldn't do something like this.

"Yes, I agree. She's intelligent enough to *know* that she shouldn't. But she's also smart enough to point out that if no one *told* her differently . . . Yes, she *is* a clever one. Yes, I *will* get it."

■ ■ ■

He guessed that the reporters would have to make quick work of their breakdown if they wanted to catch a plane back to New York that evening. Sure enough, as he drove up the tree-lined avenue toward the Culver house, he saw a rental van pulling out.

He made a U-turn, switched on the revolving light, and touched the siren briefly. The van drifted to the berm and stopped. Still in his reckless mood, he got out and walked up to the driver's window with that slight swagger that bad cops assumed in bad movies. *Makes the temptation to act the part almost irresistible*, he thought.

The female reporter was in the passenger seat, twisting to order one of the photographers behind her, "Film him!" She glared at Matt. "Chief Olin, I presume."

"The same," Matt agreed, then said in the same mild tone to the photographer, "I wouldn't, unless you want it broken." He extended a hand toward the female reporter. "Gimme. Unless *you* want to be charged with obstructing justice or interfering with an investigation. I have special orders from the judge to get that tape recorder."

She looked sullen. "I don't have it. Your girlfriend does."

"Girlfriend?"

"Regan Culver," she ground out. "It was either her or one of those other women that live there. They all disappeared. Fun and games. What kind of Podunk is this, anyway? A cross between Mayberry and old Salem?"

"You wouldn't believe it if I told you," he said, shaking his head solemnly. "You city people have absolutely no idea the things that go on in small towns like this. Innocents, that's what you are." Glancing furtively over his shoulder at the shadowy street, he lowered his voice. "In the future, I would be *very* careful not to annoy women like Regan Culver. Her cat drank poison and lived. Think about it."

The cameraman was smirking. The makeup woman was staring at Matt with mute fascination. The interviewer was doing her best to look skeptical, but she started violently when Matt stepped back and slapped the side of the van.

"Okay. Get along."

He was grinning as he swaggered back to his car, reversed to the Culver driveway, and pulled up only partway so that they wouldn't see him coming. No one answered the bell, but the door wasn't locked. He walked into the lighted hall just in time to hear the women coming across the terrace from the garden, giggling like schoolgirls. He advanced into the living room to meet them as they came through the french doors.

They didn't seem surprised to see him. "Here you go," Agatha said, handing him Alden's tape recorder. "Of all the vapid vixens in this world, she took the cake."

"Gina asked for her autograph," Diane explained, "and we all crowded around her while Regan casually picked up the envelope and walked off with it. Regan's very good at blending into the background when she wants to."

"Then we all sneaked out and hid in the arbor until they were gone," Gina concluded. "You should have heard her when she couldn't find anybody. They wouldn't allow *that* kind of language on TV. But she was afraid to come out in the garden in the dark."

"Probably thought there were bears in them thar hills," Agatha said scornfully. "The cat rubbed across her ankles and she almost wet herself."

They all giggled again. They had had, Matt realized, little

enough to laugh about in recent days, and were on the fine edge of hysteria.

And he had been taking himself much too seriously. Hayden would survive without him. He could take a job where he actually got weekends off—and vacations. He had been fortunate, actually. Fortunate that Gabe Johnson hadn't wanted to press charges, fortunate that Regan Culver hadn't used her opportunity to get even.

"We were saying," Regan contributed breathlessly, "that we hoped nobody found out about those heirloom opium poppies in the garden. You have been quite remiss, Chief Olin. I do believe that those plants are illegal."

"Considering all the seed that your mother passed out, I would have had to arrest most of the gardeners in town. That might have got a bit sticky, politically speaking."

"Speaking of sticky," Agatha gestured toward the tape player, "we all knew at once who Father was talking about there. Regan did too, though she wouldn't admit it to that reporter. Caroline. Father never liked her. We listened to the rest of it, by the way. It sounds like he was working on the introduction to the book he was going to make out of Rosemary's diaries. I doubt if he would have used that part; it was too libelous. I think he just stuck it in to let off steam, never expecting anybody else to hear it. Even if he was right, there's nothing illegal about being money-minded."

Regan looked rebellious. "Never mind," Agatha said to her. "You know that I never liked Caroline either. But she's clean. Mathilda has investigated her up and down, and all Daddy's money is well accounted for. She *is* a good businesswoman. I have to admit that. Much better than I am, actually. This was all about Thyme Will Tell, of course," Agatha informed Matt. "It's the only reason Regan agreed to do the interview. She was hoping to convince people that the business was still ethical, even if its manager wasn't."

"She did a good job," Gina said. "She didn't let that woman shake her once."

"Mathilda will say I should have cried." Regan made a wry face. "Or at least welled up a little at appropriate points. Actually, I almost did at the end when I was looking at that picture, but I'm too used to . . ." She stopped.

"Hiding your emotions," Gina finished, patting Regan on the shoulder. "But we're not going to do that anymore. We've agreed. Mathilda is right. We have to get it all out, even if it means a few shouting matches. We won't be able to live together otherwise."

"Good luck," Matt said, and meant it. He slid the recorder into a plastic bag and tucked it in an inner pocket of his jacket.

There was something a bit final about his tone. They all looked at him. "You're not going somewhere, are you?" Agatha asked.

"Home," he said, "I hope to get at least a few hours of sleep tonight. I would advise you not to do this again, Regan. The judge was *not* pleased, to put it mildly."

"I won't," she said. "This was a one-shot thing. But I had to try. I couldn't let the family name and family business be smeared like this without making some effort—"

"I understand," he said, "but I don't know if Mathilda will. It's your *skin* she's interested in saving. Good night."

It was a fine evening, warm and still, as he walked down the drive to his car. He stopped beside it to look back at the big house, and Regan was standing in the lighted doorway, small in proportion. He could tell it was Regan from the red dress, though the distance was too great to see her clearly. It wasn't her fault. The distance was just too great.

They stood that way for an instant, then she raised her hand. He waved back before sliding into the seat of his patrol car and backing away.

CHAPTER 14

■ ■ ■

And will 'a not come again?
And will 'a not come again?

Tim called on Friday morning. "Hello, big brother," he said. "I wasn't expecting to hear your name on a major network last night." He was trying to make his tone light, but he sounded worried. "You okay?"

"Sure." Matt looked down at the rough draft of his resignation letter. "I'm fine. Thought you didn't watch TV, kid."

"Well, we usually don't. But Kate saw something in the newspaper about this case in Hayden and thought that we'd better. On that show, they were kind of implying . . ." He stopped.

"That I was indulging in behavior unbecoming an officer?" Matt too kept his tone light.

"Something like that." There was a waiting silence at the other end.

Matt laughed edgily. "Thought you had a little more faith in me than that, kid. I am *not* having an affair with a murder suspect. Okay?"

"Okay." Tim sounded relieved. "I didn't think you would,

but Kate has always said that you were the overdisciplined type who would fall violently for the wrong kind of woman. Not that this Culver woman *seemed* the wrong kind. I liked her, but I knew from what they were implying that my judgment was a little off."

Matt laughed again with genuine amusement. "You're still naive, aren't you, kid? Reporters get away with implying anything they please, true or not, as long as they don't say it straight out."

"So you're going to be all right?"

"Depending," Matt said, almost cheerfully, doodling in the margins of his letter, "on whom the good citizens of Hayden believe. You know, Timmy, I've been thinking that I might get out of this business."

"Get out?" Tim sounded incredulous. "You want to stop being a cop?"

"It's getting kind of wearisome. No vacations. Too little sleep. And public relations. I was never good at public relations. I've been thinking maybe I should try something else."

"It's this case, isn't it? You're not telling me all the truth."

"Hey," Matt said sharply. "Can't I just want a change sometimes? Like everybody else?"

"I guess." Tim still sounded stunned. "If you're serious, they're looking for a head of security at the company. I'm sure an ex-cop would be ideal. I could put in a good word for you." He began to sound more enthusiastic. "You could get an apartment near us here. We don't see enough of you. Do you want me to ask?"

Matt looked around his office. It seemed small and lonely and bleak. "Yeah, kid," he said finally. "You do that. You ask. Say hi to Kate for me." He set the receiver down gently.

Matt had not got much farther with the letter when the phone rang again. It was Kate this time. She was a psychologist and ten years older than her husband.

"All right, Matt," she said briskly. "Tim called me here at work, and he never does that. He's really worried. I know what it is. You've set yourself up some impossibly high standard that you can't hope to measure up to. And so you think you've failed. Tim does it all the time. It's one of the reasons I love him, but it makes me yearn for a blunt instrument sometimes too. I would be quite happy to have you move closer to us. After what you did for Timmy, I think you should be on a pedestal and draped in bunting and gold stars. But you would hate it here. So what's the hang-up? You're in love with that woman, aren't you?"

Matt didn't answer.

"I thought so. Because you're feeling a natural human emotion, you think you should quit."

"I can't be objective about this case, Kate."

"So? Then pass it on to someone else. Just this case. Not your job. It is not an either-or thing, Matt. The state cops would love to have a high-profile crime like this, so let them have it. Did she do it?"

"No." Matt hadn't realized how positive he was of that until just now.

"Then why did you arrest her?"

"I had no choice. She was the only one with access to that tea. If I hadn't, people would have thought that I was showing favoritism."

"That you were intimidated by her class, you mean. And if I know you, you were. In your mind, you're still that little kid from the wrong side of the tracks, trying to pretend that you don't care. It figures that you would fall for a woman you think is unreachable. But is she really? This isn't feudal England, pal; this is twentieth-century America. What does she think of you?"

Matt stabbed at the paper with his pencil. "She finds me amusing," he said gloomily.

"Hey, that's a good sign. I thought Timmy was a riot when I met him. With that long cowlick always falling down over his glasses. He was so cute. Me, I think you're giving up too easily. Stick with the case. Nobody is completely objective, after all. If she didn't do it, she needs somebody like you on her side."

"That isn't all of it," he said, and found himself telling her about Gabe Johnson.

When he was finished, she gave a sigh of pure exasperation. "Men are so dense!" she said. "You have to have everything explained to you. How big is this kid, Matt?"

"About my size."

"And he wasn't handcuffed or bound in any way? You might call that brutality. I call it a fair fight. Obviously he wanted you to hit him, and he got what he wanted."

"Why?"

"That would be a little difficult to explain, and I doubt if he could verbalize it himself. It's probably all mixed up with authority and father figures. He may be angry at his real father. Since you are another guy who's exercised authority over him, he's made you a substitute target for that rage. On one level, he wants to prove that you are as bad as his real father was. On another level, he wants you to be better.

"Probably his father hit him. So, by getting you to do the same, he could justify his anger at you. Only after it happened, he wasn't as happy about it as he thought he was going to be. You might not be the perfect standard, but you're the only one he's got. So instead of tearing you down, he tries to prop you back up again. Does all of this make any sense to you?"

"No."

"I admit it's all pretty tangled, but in his mind, it's probably tangled too. Listen, Matt. Let him do this favor for you. Take it from me. He needs to do this. I know you cops have this thing about justice and responsibility and taking your punishment like a man, but just this once have a little mercy on yourself and let somebody else help you. As for this woman, there's no reason that she shouldn't go for you. You're better educated than most of the intellectuals I know, you're something of a softie under all that machismo, and if a lady can't have an outlaw, she'll go for a cop every time. We will *not* go into the Freudian implications of that. If she *did* off her father for a few hundred grand, I'm really going to regret saying all this. Is any of my chatter doing you any good, or am I just talking to myself here?"

Matt grinned suddenly, shoving back from his desk and dumping the letter in a drawer. "I get it. In other words, 'Stop whining and get back to work.'"

"I didn't want to put it that crudely."

"Thanks, Kate. I can see why my brother married you."

"Save your sweet talk for the lady," she said. "I'm not giving you any guarantees. She might be out of reach emotionally. And this kid might hate you, at least on the conscious level, all his life. But if you always demand a return on your investments, you've missed the point. Speaking of getting back to work, my ten o'clock has been waiting for fifteen minutes. Hope I *don't* see you soon."

■ ■ ■

"This Stanton woman has got to have a scandal," Mathilda Baker said. She had her feet up on her desk and her hands behind her head and was glaring at the ceiling. "Everybody has a scandal."

"Miss Culver doesn't," Harry pointed out. "According to you."

Mathilda shifted the glare to him. "Miss Culver is a client. We don't *want* scandals for clients. Besides, Miss Culver did not have much of an actual life, if you think about it. To have a scandal, you have to do things."

"She made a lot of gardens."

"Right!" Mathilda said more enthusiastically. "And she's going to make one for me after I get her off. That's why we need some more scandals."

Leafing back through his notebook, Harry said, "Not all of these people had their own *personal* scandals. I mean, you can hardly blame Gina because her husband smuggled drugs or Agatha because her business partner took off with all the money."

"Sure I can," Mathilda thumped her feet to the floor and leaned forward. "People should be more careful about whom they hook up with. Some women give more thought to the wedding gown than they do to the groom. Gina thinks too little, and Regan thinks too much. *She* would have talked herself out of the whole thing two weeks into the engagement. You ever notice, though, that it's the nervy sorts like her who live to be a hundred and four? You'd think they'd burn up by then. But I've got a theory about nerves. The more you use 'em, the tougher they get. You know, like muscles. It's the down-to-earth types who claim not to have any who crack up big-time. One day they break a fingernail, and it's 'Oh, I can't take anymore!' Then look at Regan. Lost two parents, got arrested for murder, business going down the tubes. Hardly blinks an eyelash. Get what I mean?"

Harry was staring vacantly again. "You, Mathilda," he said, "are a true original."

Mathilda beamed smugly. "Don't I know it. Got more ideas than a slew of shrinks. It's how I get people off. Back to Caroline Stanton. I *don't* like her. Her brother died, didn't he? Maybe she poisoned him."

Harry consulted the notes he'd taken over the phone from the private detective and shook his head. "Malignant melanoma. I don't think you can induce that."

"She left him out in the sun when he was a baby!" Mathilda snapped. "Anyway, I bet she was why the animals he treated never got well; word has it she doesn't like animals. What else have we got?"

"Maybe she just cleaned up after too many of them." Harry tapped the notebook with his pen. "She wrote a book. And here"—he reached triumphantly into the bag beside him—"it is. I stopped at the library and got everybody's."

"Who's everybody?" Mathilda asked, miffed because it hadn't been her idea.

"Just Dr. Culver and Miss Stanton. Rosemary Culver probably would have had some too, eventually—if she'd lived. Poor woman. First, she didn't have one because she died, then she didn't have one because he died."

Mathilda was chewing on a pencil eraser and regarding him shrewdly. "You know, you might have something. Rosemary Culver should have had a book, and Caroline Stanton shouldn't."

"Why not?"

"Everybody says so. That Caroline isn't really the writer type. Hand over her book. I suppose I'll have to read it. In garden books, you should only have to look at the pictures."

"Maybe if you actually read them, you'd know how to make your own," Harry suggested. "How about if I do one of Dr. Culver's?"

"Anything," Mathilda growled, "as long as you shut up."

Harry was slouched on his tailbone in an easy chair, three chapters into *Life More Abundant,* when Mathilda said, "Where does the moon come in?"

He looked up, blinking. "What?"

"When we asked Regan where her father had been on the day before he was murdered, she said she thought he'd gone to see his publisher. Who is it?"

Harry paged back to the front of the book. "Sun."

"Okay. According to the kid, they went to the farm first, then to a building with a sun, then to one with a moon. Where does the moon come in?"

"I have no idea." He gestured toward *Rosemary for Remembrance.* "Yours?"

"No, this was published by a place called Langston Press."

"It didn't necessarily have to be a publisher. Maybe it was a toy store. Maybe he was going to buy the kid another ugly hare."

Mathilda gestured toward the bookshelves. "There's a *Writer's Market* over there somewhere. Find me a publisher who would use a moon as a symbol."

Harry hefted the thick volume onto the edge of her desk and paged through the M's. "Nothing with *moon.*"

She pushed a thesaurus across to him.

"How many words can you have for *moon*?" he grumbled. "Okay, here we are. *Satellite, Sputnik, crescent. Crescent* maybe; the other two don't sound likely."

But Mathilda had already dragged the book around and turned to the Cs. She shook her head.

"Okay," he said. "*World* in parenthesis. We'll look up *world*." He didn't sound optimistic. "Hey, there's a much longer listing for *moon* here. This is more like it. How about *demilune*? I like that." He continued to sing "demilune, demilune" softly to himself while she searched. She shook her head again.

"Well, *plenilune* seems even more unlikely. We come to moon goddesses. *Hecate, Selene—*"

Mathilda slapped the table with the palm of her hand. It made a noise like a pistol shot, and Harry jumped. "I've heard that recently!" she said. "Where have I heard that? Oh." She looked downcast. "It was the company that was going to publish Rosemary's journals. It figures that he would visit them too. I thought we had something there for a minute."

She turned the pages of *Writer's Market* dispiritedly. "That's funny. It's not here."

CHAPTER 15

No, no, he is dead:
Go to thy deathbed:
He never will come again.

On Friday afternoon, Gabe arrived home from his job at a horse farm to find two men in suit coats waiting beside their car. Aunt Lily ran from the porch to meet him and whispered, "Oh, Gabe, what have you done?"

The men flashed badges and muttered some names that he didn't catch. They were state police detectives. "You're out of your jurisdiction, aren't you?" Gabe demanded warily. "Does Matt Olin know that you're here?"

The heavy balding one said something about special circumstances. "We've been having some complaints about Olin, actually," he said. "There's the suspicion that he's rather close with the Culvers. You've heard about them, I suppose. Then," he added, looking significantly at Gabe's face, "someone has mentioned police brutality. Who beat you up, kid?"

Lily's hand clamped around Gabe's arm. Her outraged gasp, he knew, would precede a furious spiel. He said quickly, to head her off, "The chief and I had a friendly little disagreement. I'm not going to file a complaint."

"We understand." That was the thin, constantly smiling one. "But we will protect you, you know, if—"

"You heard me." Gabe crossed his arms, laying one hand reassuringly over his aunt's. She was trembling.

"If you'll answer one more question for us," the thin one said. "Who started the fight?"

Gabe didn't hesitate. "I did."

Lily gave a long shuddering sigh, but whether of relief or dismay, he wasn't sure.

"In that case"—the heavy one was beginning to look hostile—"why didn't Olin charge you with assault?"

"Why don't you ask him?" Gabe walked toward the porch, pulling his aunt along. "Come on. These bozos don't have any authority here."

The thin one called after him, "You know where to find us if you change your mind." Gabe ignored him.

Inside the house, his aunt cried, "Why would you fight with Matt? What did you do?"

"Nothing," he said. "Listen. I don't like this. I can't talk now. I've got to take a shower, and then I've got to go see somebody."

■   ■   ■

Late Wednesday afternoon, Regan took *Rosemary for Remembrance* down from the shelf again. She was determined to finish the journal entries this time.

She shaped each word silently with her lips as she read, forcing herself to concentrate.

She had been virtually barricaded inside the house all morning, with the gates at the end of the drive locked. The phone had rung and rung. She had been asked to appear on one of the TV morning shows. She had told them that she would call them back. Regan was now alone in the house. Agatha and Diane had gone to help Gina fetch some things from her house.

Heaven forbid that anyone but Diane had seen that little tableau with Regan and Matt on Sunday night, She had a feeling that that particular moment of self-indulgence was going to come back to haunt her—and him. Her eyes brimmed. She blinked fiercely to clear them and read on.

Gardening is a microcosm of what it means to be human . . . Déjà vu. The book fell from her lap again. Clutching the handwritten papers with trembling fingers, she watched its pages riffle and glanced blindly toward the french doors, half-expecting the cat and the pungent odor of rue. She forced herself to pick up *Rosemary for Remembrance*, to turn to a certain page in the book, to run her fingers under the words, looking to the journal entry and back again.

■ ■ ■

Matt bent over his scraps of paper, making one last concentrated effort to make the words on them fit some sort of pattern. But his brain was so tired, the words were just sounds with no meaning. And there were a lot more of them: marijuana, cat, extract. An obvious solution was that Alden had found out about Dennis and Reid's drug trade and had been poisoned by one of them. But *how* had he found out?

According to the girls at the farm, Alden had been there on Friday morning with Sasha, but only briefly. They were pretty sure he hadn't gone near Dennis's greenhouses. They were careful to keep people away from there because Dennis was so touchy.

At least they no longer had to wonder *why* Dennis was so touchy. Caroline was keeping the farm open and had already issued statements to the press disclaiming any knowledge of her manager's illegal sideline.

Still, her phone continued to ring constantly, and she had little time or attention to give to Matt's questions.

Yes, Alden had been there for a few moments on Friday morning to talk to her about some business matters. She supposed that he might have gone looking for Dennis afterward.

"But he didn't, Ms. Stanton," her secretary said, coming in at just that moment—looking hassled. "Somebody from NBC is on the line and wants to talk to Regan, but I imagine she's taken her phone off the hook by now." As Caroline turned to her extension, the secretary turned to Matt.

"Alden Culver went directly to his car after he left Ms. Stanton's office that day. I was getting some coffee from the machine out front and saw him. He turned left, like he was going to the city, not back into Hayden."

So that was that. It hadn't really fit in with Culver's equivocal attitude on the night of the murder. He would have had no reason to shield Dennis. His son-in-law, Reid, however, might be another story. To spare Gina, would her father . . . ?"

There were too many maybes. That was the problem. Nobody could definitely be eliminated. And that was why it was going to be so hard convicting one of them.

Rosemary, book, Caroline. He stopped in an effort to remember what book he'd been talking about there. Rosemary's journal or *Rosemary for Remembrance?* Either of them could be called a book. That thought caught like a struck match. He stared fixedly at the far wall, urging this spark to smolder into something more illuminating. . . .

■ ■ ■

"The book," Regan said to Caroline. "It was the book, wasn't it? You didn't write it—except the first chapter. My mother did. It was all taken from her journals. That was why Daddy hid the journal pages in *Rosemary for Remembrance*. He was comparing them to passages from the book. When did you have her journals?"

The older woman had just approached with "I thought I might find you out here." Regan was standing a couple of steps up from the lily pond. The cat was sitting on a stone by the edge of the water, trying to pat at the flashing glints of koi without getting its paws wet. Regan turned, arms crossed, and made her accusation without preamble.

Caroline didn't flinch. "I knew you would remember eventually. I didn't have the journals until recently. Your mother made them into a book herself. She had an editor interested, and it was supposed to be a surprise for you and your father. She wanted me to read the manuscript before she sent it in to make sure that it was good enough. It was, of course."

"Did you kill *her*?"

Caroline finally showed shock. "Of course not! I would never have hurt Rosemary. Her death shook me as much as anybody. I knew that without her, your father might abandon interest in the farm. He never liked me. I had to be prepared to make it on my own. And the book was right there. It would make money, but even more important, it would get people interested in Thyme Will Tell. I went to a different editor, of course."

She paused. "Rosemary didn't need the book after she was dead. But I did. She would have wanted me to have it."

"That was the letter I found in the wastebasket," Regan

said. "Asking for a manuscript before September. I thought the paper was a bit yellowed. Daddy must have found it with the journals. And he threw it out. Do you understand that, Caroline? *He had thrown it out.* He must have decided not to do anything about what he'd discovered."

"Well, I didn't know that, did I?" Caroline sounded exasperated. "When I spoke to him on Friday morning, he just told me what he had discovered, not what he was going to do about it. I suppose he thought keeping me in suspense would somehow punish me. And he had to find out now, just when we were starting to be successful. The scandal would have ruined everything. That book made the farm; it could break it too."

"I gave you the perfect excuse to be up in his room," Regan said bitterly, "when I asked you to smuggle that plant in. That wasn't the only thing you smuggled in. I suppose you had the aconite left over from the days when your brother was a veterinarian. And you made sure to be there in the morning so you could poison the dregs of the tea and make it look like I was the guilty one. Do you hate me that much?"

Caroline shook her head. "I don't hate you at all. I hadn't planned on that until I saw you making the tea. And I didn't know if I would be successful in planting the poison the next morning. I didn't even know that you were going to stay there while he drank it, or have the door locked behind you. There were a lot of people in the house that night; the suspicion could have been spread out. I don't think they would have convicted you."

Unheeding, Regan plunged ahead, not realizing that Caroline had dropped her into past tense. "You came back on the night of the storm and switched the bottles. Were you actually in the house when Matt was there?"

"I went in after I saw you down by the creek. I had to wait until Olin left to get out again. I hid in your father's bathroom since I knew nobody would be using it. I was in there when you came into his room to shut the balcony windows."

"As easy as that. Might as well make use of a little leftover poison. You always were the practical one."

"I begged you to leave it alone," Caroline said. "I didn't want to do it. You're the only reason your father stuck with the farm all these years. If he had decided against telling, that would be because of you too, because whatever hurt the farm would hurt you. I held off as long as I could. But after you found those pages he'd taken out and hidden, I knew that it was only a matter of time until you realized. You might have let it go before your father's death; you wouldn't now. If only you weren't so obstinate. If only you weren't like him—"

"What did you do with the rest of the journal?" Regan interrupted. "Did you burn it?"

"No. I probably should have, but people have been bugging me lately about writing another book. There's plenty of material left in there. I wrapped it in plastic and put it under the soil in that kettle of geraniums on my porch. It'll be safe enough there until . . ."

Regan frowned. "Until what?"

Caroline advanced and put her hands on the other woman's shoulders. "Until after you're dead," she said, then shoved.

Totally unprepared, Regan staggered backward off the step, tried, too late, to catch herself with a foot that twisted agonizingly . . . Then she was lying full-length on the flat stones beside the pool, squinting against sunlight and an arc of dazzling blue sky. *I should have seen that coming,* she was thinking. *But I've been slow on the uptake all around. I was so sure that it must be one of them, my family, my enemies. Nothing has been what it seemed. . . .*

The impact left Regan as limp as a rag doll. Perhaps she'd broken her back. No, she felt pain in her ankle, although it seemed distant, detached.

Caroline's face swam into view above her, upside down. "They'll think it was suicide," Caroline said, that face looming grotesquely large as she bent to get her hands under Regan's arms to drag her backward. "They'll think you couldn't take the guilt any longer. Drowning in a flower-filled pool is just the way you'd go about it too." She paused briefly, panting. "Like that woman in Shakespeare."

Regan's lips mouthed the name, "Ophelia."

"That's right. You always did know all that stuff, and what good did it do you? If you'd just been a little more practical—"

The cat screamed; Caroline jerked and dropped Regan's arms. With difficulty, Regan turned her head to see bloody scratches on the nyloned leg closest to her. Caroline had stepped on Gato's foot or tail, and now the animal was in the pool, paddling, wet fur slicked to a body that seemed pathetically thin, its head held as high as possible above the water, topaz eyes glaring.

Regan rolled over onto her stomach. The movement made her dizzy. The cat and Caroline's legs and the water lilies swam in an iridescent haze around her.

"Vicious beast," Caroline muttered. "I *hate* cats." Turning to see Regan's new position she said, "Good," briskly, as if approving one of her partner's ideas. "Facedown is much more likely."

Regan thought, *I should have grabbed her ankle and tried tipping her in.*

But she could not move at all. She could only lie, nauseated, with her cheek against warm stone, breathing in the hot green smell of the water, which surged ever more powerfully into her brain, obscuring thought. She could not see Caroline anymore. The other woman was behind her, straddling her body. Tugged forward by that invisible presence, Regan looked down at the koi that were swimming under her eyes like flashing lights before unconsciousness.

She felt a weight on her shoulders and pressure on the back of her head. Regan stiffened her neck. It was the last bit of resistance she could muster, but she concentrated all her will power on keeping her face out of the water. This close, its lapping seemed unnaturally loud, the faces of the gaping fish surrealistically close.

The pain at the back of her neck was intensifying, but it, like the pain in her ankle, seemed something observed, something that was happening to somebody else. Someone had told her once that she was such a stoic because she wasn't in touch with her own feelings, her own body. On the whole, she supposed, watching her own reflection approach, she had never really been in touch at all—not even with the face in the water.

Her hair had fallen forward, the ends already submerged, swirling gently, peacefully. *I'm sorry,* she said in her thoughts to everyone and no one. *Sorry also that one of you will have to find me like this—*

She made a sudden, wrenching movement, and grasped at the stones, trying to bring one knee up under her. She had automatically pulled up her right leg, the injured one. When it banged against stone, she gasped and subsided. Her resistance was momentarily broken and she had time only to draw in that breath and hold it before her face merged with her reflection in the warm, soft water.

■ ■ ■

Returning to the house by the back way, Agatha parked her car beside the garage. Approaching the house, she discovered a burly teenager loitering on the front porch. He was not a prepossessing figure; his dark-skinned face was bruised and puffy, his knuckles bandaged. "How did you get in here?" she asked.

"I climbed the fence."

Agatha regarded him with a certain respect. "That's more than any of the reporters managed to do. Who *are* you?"

"My name's Gabriel. I want to talk to Regan Culver."

The unexpectedness of it brought a smile to her lips. But from his pugnacious expression, she suspected that any reference to angelic messengers was not going to be appreciated.

"If she didn't answer the bell, she's probably in the garden. Many people want to talk to her. Is there any particular reason why you should succeed?"

"It's about Matt Olin."

"I see." Agatha fished in her purse for a key. "She'll probably want to hear it then. We might as well go through the house. It's shorter."

As he followed her across the living room, he said, "You're a trusting sort, aren't you, lady?"

"Not really. But I try not to jump to conclusions."

That silenced him. She went down the terrace steps, paused to glance toward the front of the garden, then went on through the door in the stone wall, across to the opposite one.

Emerging on the path above the lily pond, she paused so abruptly that he caromed into her.

∎ ∎ ∎

Far off and muffled, someone was shouting. The weight on Regan's head eased and she pulled up for an infinite distance, water gurgling in her ears, the curious fish bumping against her face, until she was out again in the overloudness of sunlight and Agatha's shrill voice.

"Get off!" Agatha was screeching. The rest of what she said was virtually unintelligible—and accompanied by blows. The weight on Regan's shoulders was tottering. "Get off my sister, you poisonous wretch!" A final decisive impact had Regan's body shrinking in sympathy. Then the weight was gone, and somebody was rolling Regan over onto her back. A black kid, a teenager, looked down at her as if debating the necessity for resuscitory measures. "Who are you?" she whispered.

The kid looked relieved. "Gabriel," he said.

She sat up and looked around. The pain was at once her own, raging up her leg to envelop her whole body in its heat, all except her wet face and hair, which, under the mild summer breeze, felt icy by contrast. The haze that had shrouded her thinking was gone.

"Oh. When you said . . . I thought for a moment there that I must have ended up somewhere else."

Agatha and Caroline seemed abnormally clear and sharp-edged. Agatha stood, triumphant, holding one high-heeled shoe in her hand. Caroline was half-sitting, half-lying at the other woman's feet, dazed, one hand up, as if in defense.

Diane and Gina rushed onto the scene like extras in a play, chattering, incredulous. Regan turned back to the stranger.

"You're not really an angel, are you?" she asked quite seriously. For the first time, she noticed the bruises on his face. "Oh," she said. "You must be the one Matt—"

"Beat up on," he finished, sitting down beside her. "Yeah. I've been trying to provoke him into hitting me ever since I met him."

She wiped at her wet face with her sleeve. "Why?"

"I don't know. He just always seemed so controlled that you couldn't help wanting to—"

"Shake him?" Regan spoke through teeth clenched to keep them from chattering. "I can relate."

"You're not going into shock, are you?" he asked. "Maybe you should lie down again."

Regan opened her mouth enough to reply. "No, I'll be okay. Keep talking. So you cracked his cool. Did it make you feel better?"

"Yeah," he said defiantly. "It did. But then he got too serious. He'd been thinking of quitting anyway because of you, I guess. That made his mind up. He said he couldn't be a cop and lose his temper." The kid turned toward her, looking plaintive. "I knew he would tell those state cops the truth if they asked—that he hit me first. But that was only because I made a crack about you. I thought maybe you could change his mind, make him see that he has to go along with my story. It isn't a lie, after all. They only asked who started the fight, not who threw the first punch. And I *did* start it. I didn't mean for it all to be such a big deal."

"Neither did I." She winced as she straightened the injured leg. "When *I* started provoking him, I mean."

"Those kids on the team . . ." Gabriel looked absently at the other women. "They kind of depend on him, you know." Gina was in the process of tying Caroline's hands with a silk scarf. "He's the only guy a lot of them have around who expects things." The kid paused, as if at a loss how to articulate what he meant. "They almost wag their tails when he says, 'Good job.' That always disgusted me. This guy got rid of all my friends from the city. Deliberately. He hassled and hassled them till they quit coming. Where does he get off?" Gabe choked, turned toward Regan again, and clenched his fists. "I swore that when I got big enough . . . I could have taken him too, if he hadn't caught me off guard. But if he goes away . . ."

The teenager looked so bewildered that Regan had to smile. Fishy-smelling water trickled down her face and neck from her sopping hair. "Can I borrow this?" she asked, reaching for the bandanna on his head and pulling it off without waiting for an answer.

Tugging at the knot, she said, "You guys are too much alike. That's the problem." And, at his disbelieving glower, "I mean it." She leaned forward to wrap the cloth around the dripping ends of her hair and squeezed. "The defensive attitude's basically the same," she continued in a muffled tone. "That's a polite way of saying that you're both paranoid."

She shook out the already saturated handkerchief and rubbed the back of her neck. "I suppose that Matt recognized the similarity and felt compelled to rescue you the same way that McNeil rescued him. McNeil was more subtle about it, though. Unfortunately, tact is not one of Matt's strong points."

A shadow fell across her feet. She looked up to see the police chief standing on the path above, looking somberly down at them. Regan wondered how she had ever seen him as pompous—or predictable.

He came down the steps and, ignoring a trussed Caroline,

strode straight across to Regan. Putting a hand under her chin, he turned her face to the light to scrutinize one cheek. "Just a scrape, I guess," he said impersonally. "Did you hit your head?"

And as she shook that head, or tried to shake it without success because of his grasp, he said, "It was the journal, wasn't it? No specific information was important, but the words were. Because they were the same as the ones in Caroline's book."

"Yes," she said. "How did you figure it out? I had the journal entries." Her gaze dropped guiltily. "A few of them, anyway, that Daddy had hidden."

"She hadn't written anything else." Matt released Regan and straightened. "In ten years. That seemed unusual, considering the success of the first. And writers—"

"Keep writing," she finished for him. "Yes. Daddy claimed that it becomes something of a compulsion."

"Once I went over the tape of her interview, I got to wondering how she knew what kind of extract the poison had been in. You hadn't mentioned it over the phone, and, according to her, Agatha hadn't been forthcoming either. You have more than one extract, I imagine."

"Oh, yes. Goldenseal, uva ursi, rosemary . . ."

Thus far, Matt had ignored Gabe. Now he said, "What are you doing here, Johnson?" in that same flat tone.

"He's our angel," Agatha interrupted. "If he hadn't come to talk to Regan, we wouldn't have found her in time."

"And what did he want to talk to her about?"

"None of your business," Gabe said resentfully. And then, "Hey!" He jumped up. "If that dame's the killer"—he gestured at Caroline—"there's no reason for you to resign. Nobody's going to care what you and her"—he tilted his head toward Regan— *"you know."*

Agatha smiled. Matt didn't.

"I hit you," he said. "This doesn't change that."

Gabe shrugged. "So? Like I told those state cops, I started it. I'm not complaining."

There was silence in the garden for a long moment as the two stared at each other. Regan found herself holding her breath again.

Then Matt turned, leaned down to lift Caroline Stanton to her feet. He clamped handcuffs over the scarf. "You have the right to remain silent . . ." he intoned as he urged her toward the steps.

Caroline looked back at Regan, "You'll have to look after the farm now."

"Yes," Regan responded. "Yes, of course."

The others began to move again, as if released from a spell. Diane was crying with relief. Gina was vigorously rubbing the cat dry with her skirt. Agatha said, "Somebody should call Mathilda, I suppose. And get supper started. Is that leg broken?"

They all turned to look at Regan. "No," she said. "Just a bad sprain, I think."

"Perhaps we can get that veterinarian of yours to look at it." Agatha stood on one foot to put her shoe back on. "A strained fetlock is a strained fetlock after all. He can bring Sasha home at the same time. I guess it's up to you, young man"—she nodded at Gabe—"to carry Regan back to the house."

"It'll get you started in weight training," Regan suggested, making an effort at cheeriness. "For football."

"Yeah," Gabe grunted as he lifted her, toiling up the steps. "I join that guy's team now, he is going to make my life miserable." He sounded strangely happy about it.

■ ■ ■

Mathilda and Harry turned up about an hour later, triumphant, then chagrined when they found out that they were too late for the denouement. Mathilda had called a publisher friend and found out that Selene Books had changed its name six years earlier to Luna. "So naturally that letter you fished out of your father's wastebasket had to be a pretty old one. We went to town and talked to the folks at Luna, asked them why Alden Culver had visited them. Alden had found a letter from Selene tucked into his wife's journal. He demanded to know if they had once considered publishing a book from her. A senior editor acknowledged that he had been waiting to see the final manuscript before offering her a contract. When he heard that she'd died, he simply let it go. He knew that her family wasn't aware of what she was up to, and the publisher wasn't interested in an author who couldn't produce more books down the line. The editor couldn't quite understand Alden's interest in the whole matter at this late date, and Alden didn't explain. He never mentioned Caroline Stanton."

Perched on the edge of the couch on which Regan was lying, Mathilda added crossly, "I don't know how anyone in his or her right mind could ever believe that Caroline Stanton wrote that book. The first chapter, granted; it was a pretty botchy job. But the rest of it was clearly by an entirely different writer."

Regan smiled weakly. "Daddy always did say that he thought Caroline imitated mother's style."

Sasha spent most of the afternoon perched on Regan's couch or on the floor beside it as people came and went. She sensed that Regan's mood did not match the jubilation of the others and went out once to return with a bouquet of tiny, velvety-black violas. She climbed up to tuck them behind Regan's ear, patted her face, and said gravely. "It will be all right." Discovering that Regan's damp hair was drying in tangles, she went upstairs for a comb and worked patiently through the snarls.

■ ■ ■

Regan called all of the women together that night to make a proposal. She wanted them to work with her at Thyme Will Tell. "Caroline was handling way too much. I suggest that we split it up." Diane would be in charge of the new tea and gift shop, Agatha the mail-order business, and Gina the tours. Regan herself would continue with garden design and oversee a new manager for the greenhouses.

"What about Caroline?" Agatha asked.

"I'm hoping she'll sell. But with that and the expansion plans, it's going to take a sizable chunk out of what Father left me. And it's risky. It all depends on how much the public has heard of what's been going on around here lately—and how they react to it. I certainly can't do it without you. What do you think?"

"Count me in," Diane said at once. She was curled up in an armchair, looking sleepy and more peaceful than she had in some time.

"Talking to people I can do," Gina agreed. Sitting cross-legged on the floor, she stretched luxuriously in imitation of the cat.

Agatha, bolt upright at the opposite end of the couch from Regan, hesitated. The others looked at her.

"I don't know much about plants," Agatha said, "and my track record in business isn't that good. But," she shrugged, "why not? I'll give it a go. When do we start?"

"Tomorrow. And"—Regan gestured wryly at her foot—"you'll have to start without me. Let me just fill you in on a few things."

Regan spent the night on the couch, and between the pain in her ankle, worry about the farm, and memory of Matt's distant attitude, slept very little.

Now the ankle twinged whenever she moved it, and she couldn't seem to get comfortable. She felt stiff and achy all over—probably a result of her fall.

What had she been thinking? She couldn't possibly run an herb farm assisted only by three amateurs.

It was raining and the other women had gone out to the herb farm, taking Sasha along. They had left her a cold lunch, but she only picked at it before pushing the TV tray away. It tipped on its teetery legs and fell, the thermos rolling and splashing milk on the wool throw rug in front of the couch. The cat jumped down and licked at the wool pile, gave up, and began to eat the remains of the sandwich.

Regan watched him apathetically. That rug was going to stink when the milk turned sour.

She began to cry silently, the tears seeping unchecked to sting her cheeks. And Matt was quite conspicuous by his absence again. Probably glad to be able to stay away. He had just been sorry for her; that's all it ever was.

Having cleaned up what it could, the cat climbed back up to sit on her stomach and lick itself. The smell of damp cat fur was suddenly repulsive, and she pushed the animal off. Gato left the room in a huff.

Leaning dangerously out from her position on the couch, Regan tried to sop up some of the moisture from the rug with a handful of facial tissues, but they only shredded, leaving a trail of white lint behind.

When the car pulled into the driveway around four, she was slumped down, almost full-length, on her back in a kind of self-pitying torpor. She had stopped crying, but her face felt tight, chapped.

When a knock sounded on the front door, she started and sat up, flinching as pain swept up her ankle. "Come in!" Through the lace curtains, she could vaguely make out the bubble light on top of the car. Too late, she tried an ineffectual pat at her rumpled hair.

He was already standing in the doorway, looking across at her, as unreadable as ever in the dark glasses and hat. What she could see of his face looked tired. His jaw was shadowed with stubble. *Who does he think he is fooling anyway?* she thought irritably. *Sunglasses? When his uniform is actually damp with rain?*

"She's decided to plead guilty," he said. "I thought you'd want to know."

"Thank you," she said. She could think of nothing else to say.

His gaze fell on the bandaged ankle. "What's wrong with your leg?"

"Just a sprain. It's fine."

"Good." He shrugged. "All's well that ends well, huh? See you ar—" He began to turn toward the hallway.

"Matt, come back here!" He cast a wary look over his shoulder.

"My ankle is *not* fine. It hurts dreadfully."

She lowered the injured member to the floor.

He was already crossing toward her. "Keep the foot up! What do you want?"

She stretched her leg out over the cushions again and gestured toward the rug. "Come over where I can see you."

Lips tight, he lowered himself awkwardly to his knees, gun belt creaking. He would get shredded Kleenex all over those dark pants.

She plucked off the sunglasses and met his fulminating glare with one of her own.

"I suppose this"—she tugged at the sleeve of his uniform—"means you changed your mind about resigning. What possessed you to even consider it when I specifically told you—"

"That you were kidding?" he finished bitterly for her. "Well, I wasn't. Is that all?"

"No, it isn't all! You know very well that I never said any such—"

"Not in so many words maybe." He put a hand on the cushions behind her to push himself up. "Was it revenge you were after because I arrested you?"

She shook her head in a silent but emphatic negative. On the verge of helpless tears again, she slumped against his arm and felt him go quite still.

Looking up into his face, she said, "I wasn't after anything.

I don't expect you to believe that. You never did trust me. And I think that was the attraction. I'm not a femme fatale. Look at me, Matt." She made a rueful gesture that encompassed her chapped cheeks, tired eyes, and tangled hair.

"There's nothing dangerous, nothing glamorous here. That was all in your mind. And it will fade pretty fast now that I'm no longer the villainess of this place."

Suddenly he was very close. He kissed her. She had time only to put a questioning hand against his chest before his arms were around and underneath, his bristles stinging her skin. Her body tingled with something like galvanic shock.

Eventually she managed to shove at him with that open palm, and he turned his face aside against her throat.

She was trembling—or one of them was anyway—and breathing hard. Her mouth burned.

He raised his head finally to look at her. "Sorry," he said, "but you don't have the faintest idea what you're talking about. Don't worry. I won't be bothering you. I do have a modicum of pride left." He pushed himself to his feet and turned away.

She laughed, but it was more like a sob. She tried to stand and listed to one side. Hobbling after him, she grabbed at the furniture she passed to keep herself upright. "You're not bothering me. Will you wait? Of all the thin-skinned, touchy, obstinate, headstrong—"

She had reached the center of the room, and there was nothing more to hang on to. Her ankle threatened to buckle under her, but he wasn't stopping. Swaying, vulnerable, she said, "Matt, *I love you.*"

He paused then, hesitating, unsure of what he had heard,

before turning to look at her across the shadowy space between them.

"Oh, darling," Regan said crossly. "Come here."

He scooped her up. She clung to him, as to life, crying with pain and relief, her arms around his waist and her face against his shirt as in the garden. Her injured foot rested on one of his boots.

"I suggest," he finally murmured against her ear, "that you take the gun and shoot me now. It will save you a lot of misery in the future, no doubt."

She wiped at her wet cheeks with one hand. "But could Mathilda get me off?"

"Extreme provocation."

"That might do it." She looked up at him and saw that his expression was very different from his light tone. "Oh, Matt, Matt." She cupped his chin between her palms. "I *want* you to be happy. I didn't think you would be without—"

He interrupted her. "You thought my job was more essential to me than you were?"

"I guess so," she faltered, dropping her gaze. "You don't really know me that well, and I—"

Glancing around, he located the nearest armchair and backed into it, disposing her in his lap. *"Regan."*

She peeked up at him under her lashes, almost frightened by the intensity of what she saw in his face. "In words of one syllable," he said, "I love you. *You.* An infuriating, exasperating, provoking—"

Regan was tracing the line of his jaw. "Those words have more than one syllable," she pointed out softly. "Aren't you supposed to be on duty?"

"This is it. The council president told me that I'd better be nice to you so you don't sue the town for false arrest."

That irrepressible mirth sprang up in her eyes. "Nice? Is *that* what this is? Well, I must say that you're one dedicated cop, Chief Olin, because with that cut lip and those bruises, kissing me has got to hurt."

"Pure agony," he agreed. "But, hey, nobody said this job was going to be easy."

When the women returned shortly after five, Matt's police car was still in front of the house. Gina, who was driving, dropped off the others before attempting to maneuver around it. Agatha, heading for the kitchen, cast over her shoulder at her daughter, "You'd better check to see if *he's* staying for supper."

Gina was getting out of the car when Luke veered his Lamborghini around the cruiser and pulled up behind her. He emerged and stood looking at her over the roofs. "Sorry about all this, stepmother o' mine," he said. "I've got to be going. Do you need anything?"

"It's no fault of yours," she said. "You did right. I'm proud of you."

"We do our little bit," he said lightly. "Have you told anybody else about me?"

"Only Regan. But I think Diane should kn—"

"No. It's much better for her if she goes on hating me. You understand?"

Gina nodded slowly. "Because there's no future for her with you."

"There may be no future for me at all. That's something I can live with, but I'm not going to ask any woman to. And the fewer people who know what I am, the lesser chance it will slip out. Warn Regan."

"Diane is inside, if you want to say good-bye."

He hesitated. Then, leaving his car door open, he moved toward the porch.

Sasha had clattered on ahead toward the living room. She froze disapprovingly in the doorway. Coming up behind her, Diane saw Matt sprawled comfortably in an armchair with Regan curled up against his chest. She was talking in a low sleepy tone, and his gaze never wavered from her face. Only the cat, crouching on the chair's high back, looked across at them with wide, bright eyes.

Diane smiled and gently pulled Sasha back with her, colliding with Luke, who had come up behind. He looked beyond her toward the living room and raised his brows.

Her smile vanished. "It's not something you would understand."

"You're probably right. I just popped in to say good-bye."

"And where are you off to this time? The Riviera?"

"Perhaps. Incidentally, if you ever get tired of the herb farm, your old employer is quite willing to give you a good reference. Or to take you back, but I wouldn't recommend that."

"Never. I hated that place. So you were the one who scared her to death. Sicked some of your criminal friends on her, I suppose?"

His gaze flickered. "Something like that. Look after Gina, will you?" He took Diane's hand, turned it over, and pressed a paper into her palm. "If any of you get in any kind of serious trouble again, you can leave a message for me at this number."

"We'll make it," Diane said, staring coldly back at him. "On our own."

"I hope so. But there's no shame in asking for help when you need it." He flicked at Sasha's temple. "So long."

Following him to the door, Sasha said, "So long."

Diane stayed where she was and said, "Good-bye" with an air of finality.

Outside, Gina was sitting in the driver's seat of the Lamborghini, admiring the console. She slid out as he approached and looked up at him. "Take care of yourself, Luke."

"I always do. Diane has a number where you can reach me if you need anything. Though maybe you'd better snare it before she throws it out."

"She won't." Gina stood on tiptoe to kiss him on the cheek. "Women are usually reluctant to toss anything, including guys."

"Call me if she gets in trouble again."

"I will."

She watched him drive away. It was cool and dark for a summer evening. She crossed her arms tightly over her chest and told herself that things would work out. "We'll be all right, now, Daddy, Rosemary," she said aloud. "Good-bye."

Some birds flew up from the trees behind her and wheeled away against a gray sky. She turned and went into the house.